All that matt...
and the quar...

It was only when the ... Jegrai realized just where that unseen herdsman was taking his horses.

He's heading right for the wizards' pass. If the wizards see us—oh, Wind Lords—what if those are the wizards' horses?

Jegrai knew he should give up the chase. But he also knew he dared not; he would lose face—and they would go on without him. Even if he could not lead them to safety, still he would lead. Jegrai whipped at his horse, and prayed to the Wind Lords that they would overtake the herd *before* it passed into the wizards' protection.

The Wind Lords were not listening.

An eerie whistling seemed to come from somewhere above—and Jegrai had a fleeting impression of something large and boulderlike thudding down the trail before them—

Then the wizards called lightning down upon them out of the clear and cloudless blue sky.

Thunder roared in their ears, flames and dirt sprang up before them—the very earth was torn open and flung into the air.

The horses screamed and would have fought their bits—but as one man the raiders let them turn tail and gallop for the shelter of the cliff-face. There, afraid to move lest the lightning find them, the Vredai cowered with their mounts and looked to Jegrai to get them safely out—

—Jegrai, who had no more notion of what to do than the rest of them did. . . .

THE SWORD OF KNOWLEDGE STRIKES BACK!

C. J. Cherryh
Mercedes Lackey

REAP THE WHIRLWIND

Book III of The Sword of Knowledge

REAP THE WHIRLWIND:
THE SWORD OF KNOWLEDGE, BOOK III

This is a work of fiction. All the characters and events portrayed in this book are fictional, and any resemblance to real people or incidents is purely coincidental.

Copyright © 1989 by Tau Ceti, Inc.

All rights reserved, including the right to reproduce this book or portions thereof in any form.

A Baen Books Original

Baen Publishing Enterprises
260 Fifth Avenue
New York, N.Y. 10001

ISBN: 0-671-69846-X

Cover art by Larry Elmore

First printing, November 1989

Distributed by
SIMON & SCHUSTER
1230 Avenue of the Americas
New York, N.Y. 10020

Printed in the United States of America

Dedication:

To my partners in crime
Nancy Asire
Leslie Fish
But most of all, to the lady
who made it *all* possible
for all three of us
C. J. Cherryh
with respect, admiration,
and a touch of impertinence

Chapter One

Felaras stood in the open window of her study and let the cold night wind whirl around her, tying her hair into knots and cutting through the thick red wool of her tunic. That wind was the herald of a storm crawling its way toward her; thunderheads blackening the already dark night sky, growling and rumbling. Lightning danced along the tops of the mountains to the east in blue-white arabesques; jagged streaks of fire that leapt from the clouds to lash the world's bones.

There was no real need for Felaras to endure the ice-fanged wind. The study traditionally belonging to the Head of the Order of the Sword of Knowledge had one of the few glazed windows in the Fortress. Felaras could have shut that window and still been able to see the storm. But the current Master of the Order preferred to feel the wild wind on her face this night. The wind was uncontrolled and cleansing, and she had a need to remind herself that such forces existed beyond the petty squabblings of humans. That they would continue no matter what happened here below. That they waited for some human to learn their whys and wherefores, and to tame them to human hands. And one

1

day—one day she knew it would happen. Some day, some man or woman would call the lightning, and it would answer.

For a moment it almost seemed to Felaras that if she called in her need, it would answer her.

But—no.

Hubris, old woman. Hubris and desperation. The gods aren't listening—if they ever did.

The storm wouldn't answer her, as the superstitious believed—but it was nice to imagine, for a few moments, that the foolish tales about the "Order of Sorcerers" were truth.

Ah, you winds—if only you would blow those damned horse-nomads right off the face of the earth—or at least back to their steppes.

She sighed, and lifted her face to the first scent of cold spring rain.

Gods above and below, I do not need this mess. An invading horde—and me expected to magic up an army. I don't suppose they'll take this storm as a sign from their gods to turn around and go home—

Someone pounded on the outer gate, set into the Fortress wall almost directly below her window.

I'm the only one going to hear you, sirrah. You'd best find the right way of getting our attention before you break your fist. Unless you really didn't intend to spoil the wizards' rest, just make a show of trying.

But after doubtless bruising his knuckles on the obdurate portal without getting a response, the pounder discovered the bell rope and set up a brazen clangor not even the thunder could drown.

That one of the valley-folk would dare the storm *and* the wizards' wrath could only mean one thing.

—my luck's out.

Felaras remained at the window savoring her last few moments of freedom, while Watcher novices scuttled about with torches and lanterns, and the gate below creaked open and shut again. Her hair might be mostly grey, and she might be moving a bit stiffly on winter mornings, but there was nothing wrong with her ears— she heard every stumble the messenger made on the stone staircase leading to her study, and heard how long it took him to recover and resume the climb.

Whoever he is, and judging by the weight and pacing it's either "he" or a damned big woman, he's fagged out. Must've come all the way from the other end of the Vale on his own two feet.

A light tap on her door; then the creak of the door itself. The wind streamed in as the newly opened door created a draft, plastering Felaras' clothing against her chest and legs.

"Master, a messenger from the Vale." Felaras knew *that* voice; a high, breathy soprano, female, and more often heard shaped into profanity than into such a studiously respectful phrase. That was Kasha, Felaras' own Second and strong right hand, and she was putting on the full show for the newcomer.

"Bring him in," Felaras replied, only now surrendering her last fragments of pretended peace; closing the window and turning to face the room.

It took a moment for her eyes to adjust to the lamplight; a moment while tiny Kasha opened the study door wide and the messenger shuffled uneasily into the soft yellow glow.

Farmer, and, like Kasha, almost pure Sabirn; his race was plain enough, he was smallish and dark, and Felaras read his trade in the tanned, weathered face with the oddly pale forehead where his hat-brim would shade him all through the long cycle of plant, tend, reap. Read it in the stoop of shoulder and the hard, clever hands; the wrinkles around the eyes that spoke of years watching the sky for the treacherous turning of the weather.

And also read the fear of something worse than the

wizard he was facing, for the farmers of the Vale were directly in the path of the oncoming horde.

Not a man that she knew personally. *Ah gods, one of the superstitious ones. Which means my people have their hands full. Worse and worse.*

He shivered; from nervousness, and from cold. He was soaked to the skin, and as he stood before her, twisting his hat into a shapeless mass, a puddle of rainwater was collecting on the polished wood at his feet.

Poor, frightened man. You may be Sabirn, but you're as legend-haunted as any of the Ancar.

"Kasha—hot wine for the Landsman—"

Kasha nodded, round face as unreadable as a brown pebble, and slipped out the door without making a sound.

High marks for the stone face, m'girl, and high for spook-silence, but a demerit for not thinking of the wine yourself.

Felaras ghosted around her desk and slid into her massive chair with no more noise than Kasha had made. She nodded and waved her hand at the heavy chair beside the farmer.

"Sit, man; a little water isn't going to harm the furnishings."

While he was gingerly seating himself she reached over to the fireplace and gave the inset crank of the hidden bellows a few turns. The flames roared up and the man jumped, and stared at her with eyes that looked to be all startled pupil.

Gods.

"Just a kind of bellows, Landsman. Built right into the chimney—like what your smith has in his forge."

Felaras cranked it again, sending the flames shooting higher.

"I thought that you needed some quick heat, from the look of you."

The farmer relaxed; a tiny, barely visible loosening of his shoulder muscles and his grip on his hat. "Aye that," he agreed slowly. "Storm in th' Vale; raced it here."

"So I see." She leaned back in her chair, rested her elbows on the carved wooden arms, and steepled her fingers just below her chin. "And raced it because of the barbarians, I presume?"

"Aye. They be just beyond th' Teeth." He leaned forward, hands once again white-knuckled from the grip on what remained of his hat. "Master, they be comin' straight for us—on'y way through's the Vale. We need yer help! We need yer wizard-fire!"

Felaras stifled a groan. "Landsman—excuse me, but what is your name, man?"

He gulped, then offered it, like a gift. "Jahvka."

"Your name is safe with me, Jahvka. I am Felaras, Master only of those who allow me to guide them; I am not *your* Master, and you need not call me so."

A bit of a lie, though not in spirit—

"Now hear me and believe me, Jahvka; the Order cannot stop these nomads."

He looked shaken and began to object in dismay. "But—the wizard-fire—the magic—"

She shook her head. "The truth, as others would doubtless have told you if they didn't have their hands full, is that we have no more magic than these barbarians. The wizard-fire isn't magic, Jahvka, it's just something like my bellows. We have twelve fire-throwers, of which six are built into the walls and can't be moved. That leaves six more. How many passes into the Vale besides the Teeth?"

His eyes went blank for a moment as he thought. "Dozen, easy. More 'f ye count goat-tracks."

"And those steppes ponies are as sure-footed as goats, let me tell you." She leaned forward, gripping the arms of the chair to channel her own anxiety into something that wouldn't show. "We can't cover all the passes with fire-throwers, and nothing less is going to stop them. They're trapped between us and the River Ardan, and there's no fording that now that the spring rains have started. I have no army, and getting one out of Ancas or Yazkirn is—not bloody likely. I've tried; they won't believe the nomads are a threat until they're trampling the borders. We are—expendable. Have you any suggestions? I am not being sarcastic, Jahvka, if you have any, I'd like to hear them, because I'm fresh out of ideas."

He swallowed, bit his lip, then looked her squarely in the eyes. "Nay. Nothin'. They been eatin' Azgun alive—"

"I know." She sighed, and sagged back into the chair. "All right—here's my only suggestion, Jahvka. You go home, and you tell your people to run; make for the hills. There's caves, you'll be sheltered and safe—" She raised her voice, though not her eyes. "Kasha, get me copies of the maps of the caves—"

Kasha had made another silent entrance; in her charred-grey tunic and breeches she was a lithe, dark-haired shadow. Jahvka started as she set the earthen-ware mug of hot wine on the desk in front of the farmer, made a tiny bow, then slid back out without speaking.

Now if I could only get her to give me that kind of respect when there aren't strangers about. . . .

"We'll give you complete maps of the caves; we've been stowing what we could in there against some time of need like this one for as long as we've been here. You people can take your choice; you can head either for there or come here to Fortress Pass and go through. We *can* hold this place against all comers, and it's the only way into Yazkirn for miles about. We'll keep this bunch off your tails if you want to go for sanctuary in Yazkirn or Ancas."

"But—" he gestured helplessly, hat still clutched in one hand. "The plantings—the stock—"

"What won't come willingly, easily, kill and *leave behind*. Seed can be replaced."

—I hope. Are you listening, gods?

"And stock can be bred back or bought. The land won't run away. The one thing we cannot replace is you, your families, your lives. Listen to me, man. It'll be a hungry winter, but if you take what you can and destroy what you have to, these nomads will have nowhere to go and nothing to raid. Then they'll try the pass—when we scare them off, they'll go home."

—oh you gods, I hope you're hearing me—

"Then you can come back; we'll work together to make your lands bloom again. But we cannot sow a seed that will bring forth your dead; and your wives, your children, and you yourselves will die if you don't run from these horse-warriors while you can!"

She closed her eyes for a moment and pinched the bridge of her nose, feeling a headache coming on.

Jahvka looked about ready to cry; she didn't much blame him. She was about at that point herself.

"Drink your wine," she said gruffly.

He looked at the mug as if he had forgotten it was there, then, as obediently as a child, picked it up and cautiously sipped it, his eyes never once leaving her face.

"It isn't the end of the world, Jahvka," she said quietly. "I know it seems like it is, but it's not. The Order ran farther, faster, and with less than you'll be able to save, and we survived."

He bobbed his head, but his eyes were doubtful in the lantern-glow.

"So tell me; what's your people's choice likely to be? Sanctuary or the caves?"

"What you got in them caves?" he asked bluntly. "What they like?"

"Well, let me think; fodder mostly, there's wild grass all over those hills and we set the novices out for a haying holiday every summer."

And fair bitching I used to hear about it, too. No novices to cook and clean and run errands for four whole weeks. Now maybe my lazy children will understand why I ordered it.

"The upper caves are dryer than this Fortress; there's hay up there ten years old that's still good. Some grain; not as much as I'd like, though, and no good for seed. And some things you folk have no use for, books and the like."

Oh precious blood of our Order, you books. Stay safe.

"If I were to put my people up there, I'd put the stock in the upper caves near the fodder and where they can smell the outside; they won't get so twitchy that way. The middle caves would be best for living; the lower are damp at best. There's a couple underground rivers and a lake, so you'll have good water."

Jahvka took all this in, and nodded. "The caves, then; be hard enough gettin' most of 'em out of sight of their land. Most of 'em likely to see goin' over Fortress Pass as givin' up. And my kind don't give up easy."

She inclined her head with real respect. "I take it, then, that you speak for the whole Vale?"

"Aye. I didn't want it, but I was the only Elder still in the Vale, able t' leave the people with someone else, and fit enough to run up here. Mera's on the Teeth with some of the wilder kids; she reckoned on giving them something to do that'd keep 'em out of bowshot. Other younger ones, they with their people, keepin' 'em calm. Old Thahd's with mine; he got wounded he don't want t' leave, so he's watchin' both our garths. Lenyah an' Beris are too damned old t' be runnin' about in a storm."

"No argument from me."

I trained Mera myself; she's no Watcher, but she's as canny as they come. Same for the other younger ones; and I'd bet on them getting their folks ready to march right now. They knew what my answer was going to be. Wounded—I don't like the sound of that; I'll send somebody on down to see if we can do anything. If only these farmers had horses instead of oxen—if only we had more of them trained.

"Will you have enough able-bodied folks in your two garths to run the alert through the Vale?"

He nodded emphatically. "Guess we got no choice, an' might as well go now. Most seed hasn't been put in yet; likely we can save it. 'F Mera an' the kids can hold the Teeth a bit, might even be able t' save the oxen."

Felaras sighed, and glanced out the window. The storm was almost on top of them; she could hear the low grumble of the thunder even through the thick stone walls. A moment later Kasha slipped back in the door, her hands full of waterproofed map-tubes.

"Right enough." She stood up; he nearly overset the chair in his haste to get to his feet. "Kasha, take Elder Landsman Jahvka down to the Lesser Hall and send a novice out for some food for him. Not even a barbarian horse-nomad is going to make a move in this rain, so see him fed and completely dry before you let him go back down the Pass. Tell Vider I want him to go along; the Elder says they've got some wounded. Then get Zorsha to do a supply inventory—yes, I mean *now*, I want it on my desk before I go to bed—and have Teokane see if the Library has anything to say about these steppes riders."

Kasha bowed—a little more deeply, this time—and ushered the Elder out with one unobtrusive hand behind his left shoulder blade. She closed the door behind them, and Felaras sank back down into her chair just as the first burst of rain pattered against the glass of the window.

Damn. Damn, damn, damn.

She reached for the thin pile of reports. No one would believe her three months ago when she'd figured these nomads wouldn't turn back when they reached the River. Half the Order had figured her for crazed, sending out Watchers to try to get information on the barbarians.

Now they'd be on her back to evacuate.

Evacuate to where? The biggest sister-house, the one at Yafir, is right in their path if we fall. The other one at Parda is there on sufferance; in no way are the Yazkirn princes going to let more "wizards" in at their back door.

She skimmed through the hastily written reports one more time, hoping to pry a little more information out of the barely legible scrawls, but didn't learn anything she didn't already know. No ideas as to the size of the "horde"; their habit of having four to six ponies each made them hard to estimate.

Their course was easy enough to follow. They'd cut their way through nominally "civilized" Azgun in a straight run west with Fortress Pass right on the line through to Yazkirn; didn't stop for much of anything and seemed to loot only the most portable of goods, mainly the foodstuffs and the horses.

Hm. Wonder why? Usual style is to pillage everything that isn't nailed to the floor, and round up the herds and the kids and women.

She made a mental note to herself to consider that question later, and went on with her gleaning. She chewed absently at her ragged thumbnail as lightning flashed by right outside the window and the stone walls vibrated to the thunder.

The leader was very young, by all accounts; a nomad going by the name of Jegrai. The group was not just a raiding party; their women and children were with them. But not their foodherds. Or their family tents and carts. Only their horses. Their riding horses, their pack horses.

Another anomaly. Strange. Very strange.

She came to the end of the reports with nothing more than questions, no answers.

She leaned her head back against the leather of the chair cushion, closed her eyes, and tried to take the whole mess she was facing down to its component parts. *If all things were wonderful and I wasn't having to fight my own people, what would our options be?*

Well, there's running.

There was always the option to escape; over her term as Master, she'd re-opened all the old escape routes and had enforced the rule that demanded every member of the Order have his escape-pack ready and to hand in his quarters, from the novices on up.

Oh, they truly thought I was crazed. I wonder what they're thinking now?

It wouldn't be the first time the Order had fled, the gods knew, although never in living memory had the Order been forced from their strongholds. But flight was how Duran and Keko had found this Fortress in the first place, in their own flight eastward away from the persecution of the Sabirn in the city of Targheiden. Although the interior was in ruins, it overlooked a strategic pass, and the walls were still sound. Most important of all, no one seemed to be claiming it. According to Duran's diary, the old Sabirn Dahji swore it was one of the original Sabir Empire border-posts. Well, that could be; it was surely built well enough to withstand about anything, including the centuries.

Still—this time there weren't many options.

Where to run to? East puts us in their laps; south may be cut off by now. West we aren't welcome, and north—gods above, I'd sooner face this horde than the savages up there.

They could just stay where they were, of course; a

fair share of the members of the Order were pretty complacent about their ability to withstand a siege. Felaras' policies of building the fortifications back up hadn't been popular with the Seekers and the Archivists, but at this point even her worst critics were probably singing her praises and telling each other that no barbarian horse-nomads were going to get past those walls, nor have the patience to wait out a siege.

So; they could sit tight and hope that Jegrai's horde never found out about them—

Huh. Not bloody likely.

—or indeed, did not have the patience to wait out a prolonged siege. Superficially, the second would seem quite likely, given Jegrai's actions so far.

So far. But what if our food runs out? We're at the end of our winter stores, and the Vale folk aren't going to be coming up the hill to trade food for made-stuff. Those nomads might get tired and go away, but they might not. They might decide that they like what they see, and settle down. Nomads don't necessarily want to remain that way. A good half the time they're wanderers because their land isn't fertile enough to support farms. I'll have to see if Teokane can dig anything up on their mythos. It would tell me a lot to know if their vision of paradise is a garden or an endless plain.

She opened her eyes long enough to make a note of that last, before closing them and settling back into thought.

The last option was her personal choice; treat with them.

Gods, will I be in for a battle over that idea, should I try it. Half of this ragtag lot will howl loud enough to hear in Targheiden—and that brings me back full circle to our internal problems, doesn't it?

She rubbed her tired eyes, sat back up, and blinked at the flame of the lantern on her desk. *Thank the gods I can count on most of the Watchers to stand by me,*

*from Watcher-novices to full Swords. I think I've man-
aged to brand the Oath into their souls.*

She looked up at the Three Oaths carved into the
living rock of the Fortress wall where the Master couldn't
avoid seeing them every time he raised his eyes from
the desk. There was no other ornamentation on that
wall, and each Oath was set in its own square, neither
above nor below the others. Farthest to her left was the
Oath of her chapter; when she read the Oath of the
Watchers she felt the weight of all her responsibilities
settling a little heavier on her shoulders.

"When the pursuit of knowledge requires the peace
bought at sword-point, I shall be the Watcher at the
sentry-post; I shall be the Sword that guards the gate.
Even unto death, I shall not fail those who Preserve
and those who Seek."

*They truly believe that Oath these days—even Zetren,
mad dog that he is. Thank the gods he's older than I
am. Even if he survives me he won't have time to undo
what I've done.*

Her eyes fell on the Oath of the Seekers next: "The
gods have given man a mind that he may use it. There
is nothing to bar the Flame of the mind of man. What
his mind can discover, his Hand can achieve. I shall
Seek, and I shall Create."

One corner of her mouth quirked up. *They should
have added, "and I will blow things up on a regular
basis."* Her eyes itched again. *Now there's a House
with internal divisions; Flame and Hand might be two
separate chapters. Thaydore will want to fling the gate
open wide the moment he hears that Jegrai's horde is
coming over the hill. If I hear him give me that lecture
about "all men can live together in harmony" one more
time—I may push him down the well and not wait for
him to fall in again. How someone with a mind that
keen can be such a fuzzy thinker when it comes to the
real world—well, the Flame will follow him—and if*

somehow I can placate him, I'll have the Flame on my side. And he will support me if I try to work something out with the nomads—that's right along his "peace-and-shared-wisdom" line. But the Hands—hm. A problem. That's Halun; I can't guess where he'll jump, except that he doesn't want the real world to even guess we exist. Let me think; I might be able to convince him that we can use the nomads as a shield between us and the rest of the world. And I've got Zorsha; that should give me a direct ear in the Hand camp. If I know what's coming I may be able to head it off.

"All knowledge is worth the preservation, all wisdom the dissemination" read the next and final Oath. "Mine the Book where it shall be recorded; mine the Book that shall preserve it. Mine the duty to bestow it wherever and whenever it is needed."

Kitri is going to side with Thaydore; which means with me, except I may have to tie her up to keep her from rushing out to the nomads with her arms full of books. And she's going to be on me again for not educating the Vale folk. Diermud, on the other hand, will be up in his room the moment he finds out about how close the barbarians are, to consult with the spirits and look for Signs and Portents. Another of my un-worldly idiots. If he wasn't such a powerful wizard—

The itching behind her eyes grew unbearable; and as she reached for the bottle of saltwater she kept to relieve late-night eyestrain, her arm barely brushed the half-full earthenware mug that Jahvka had left on the desk.

It promptly fell over, cracking in half and spilling red wine everywhere. The puddle headed straight for her notes—

And she finally recognized that itch at the back of her eyes for what it was—the sign she was being ill-wished.

She snatched the notes out of the way of the wine,

and angrily blocked the wish, flinging it back into the teeth of whoever had sent it.

Damn you to bottommost hell, whoever you are; I will not have internal politics jostling my arm!

The puddle slowed and stopped without harming anything. Felaras sighed and got a rag to mop up the spill and the pottery shards.

I wonder who that was, anyway? She chuckled nastily to herself. *Hope he or she got it in the teeth. Glad we've never put it about that one of the qualifications for anyone being considered for Master-candidate or Leader is that you have to be conversant with all the martial arts—including wizardry.*

A draft of high wind suddenly blew *down* the chimney, sending smoke and ash across the breadth of Halun's workroom. Halun bent over in a fit of coughing, and batted at the smuts heading straight for his book.

There was a glass beaker full of brown liquid being heated over an alcohol flame on the table. As Halun choked in the smoke and tried to clear his watering eyes, the flame beneath the beaker licked high in that wind, and the beaker was suddenly under stress of heat on one side, cold on the other, that it was never made to meet.

It shattered, spilling its contents all over everything on the bench. Brown liquid splashed and hissed on the metal of the lamp.

Halun cursed, and promptly canceled his ill-wish; the draft vanished, and the smoke began dispersing.

He stood and surveyed the wreckage with his hands on his hips. There was ash spread halfway across the floor. His good blue robe was now smutched with it. The lamp-flame was out, the lamp probably ruined; at the least it would need a new wick. There were shards of glass all over the workbench, and it was pure luck he hadn't had anything *on* that bench except the lamp, the

stand for the beaker, and the beaker itself. Brown liquid, full of ash, dripped down onto the floor. Thunder
growled overhead, sounding almost like laughter.

He sighed, collected an armful of rags from the pile
ready in the corner, and went to deal with the mess.

*Thank the gods all I was doing was heating some
chava. That could have been naphtha in that beaker.*

But he found himself grinning sardonically, as he
dirtied his robe further, down on his knees on the ashy
floor. *You're a worthy opponent, Master Felaras. Fore-
thought enough to have someone guard you, hm? Wonder who it is. Hm. Probably Diermud. He's good; better
at deflection than offense, but good. As I should know,
who trained with him.*

He swept the ash back into the hearth, then changed
his robe when there was no more sign that his wish had
been turned back on him. Last of all he picked up the
bits of glass carefully. Lisan would want the shards to
re-mold, especially with the barbarians out there bar-
ring the way to the best sand-pits.

*Well, so much for my hot mug of chava before I go to
bed—but I wonder—*

He padded across the smooth wooden floor, opened
the door leading into his novice's room and poked his
head around the edge of it. Jeof, a lanky blonde Ancar
boy of about fourteen in nondescript clothing three
sizes too big for him, was still awake, curled up beside
the fireplace with a book, oblivious to everything about
him. Halun cleared his throat. Jeof jumped, and went
crimson when he saw Halun looking in at him. Halun
got a brief glimpse of bright pictures before the book
vanished behind Jeof's back.

Halun raised one eyebrow. "If that's the book I think
it is—no, Jeof, don't tell me. I don't officially want to
know, that way I don't have to officially reprimand you.
Just make sure it's back in the Library before dawn,
hm? Come to think of it, the Library is on the way to

the kitchens, and I'd like some hot wine if there's any left."

"Yes, Master Halun." Jeof jumped to his feet, managing to hide the illustrated *Pillow Book of the Prince of Beshem* behind him as he rose. Halun would know that particular battered cover anywhere. . . . "I'll get you some; there was a messenger from the Vale, so they'll have put more wine in the kettle for him. Likely there's plenty left."

He backed up to the door, got it open with one hand, and slid out without ever letting Halun "officially" see his erotic prize.

Halun returned to his study, chuckling. It didn't seem all that long ago that *he'd* been the one hiding the Prince's Pillow Book from *his* Master.

But Halun's Master had also been the Master of the Order.

Which was the reason why Halun was not the Master of the Order now, instead of Felaras.

The Master of the Order could never be from the same chapter of the Order as the previous Master. That was the rule laid down by Master Vahnder, who had seen the need to divide the members of the Order into the three chapters of Watchers, Seekers and Archivists in the first place.

It was a reasonable rule, in that it kept the power from being concentrated in the hands of one chapter.

But it was an unreasonable rule when it put people like Felaras into the Master's seat in preference to someone with twice her qualifications.

And twice her sense.

Better her than Zetren. Halun shuddered at the thought. *He'd have turned us into an Order Militant and probably gotten us all killed doing so.*

He brushed the last of the scattered ash off his book and went back to his chair, to stare at the fire and brood. *Damn the woman anyway! Can't she see she's not the leader the Order needs, especially now? And if I could just get her out of the way—I am the only logical candidate for the seat, and if I'm following her, I'm no longer disqualified. I have got to think of a way—*

Before those barbarians out there leave me with nothing to lead.

Kasha pushed the study door open with her foot. "He's gone, Felaras," she said softly.

Felaras looked up from her rapt contemplation of the lamp-flame. Her high cheekbones were more prominent than usual; Kasha had suspected her of skipping meals lately, and now she was certain of it. The Master's clear hazel eyes were a bit darker than usual with brooding, and there were rings under them that told her Second she'd been skipping sleep, too.

Kasha waited in the doorway for the Master to respond, steaming jug in one hand, two clean mugs in the other.

"I hope that's more wine, girl. If it's chava, I'll never forgive you."

Kasha laughed. "Of course it's wine, I'm no fool. I know you—remember, I started as your novice. Besides, you need to get some sleep tonight, and chava would only keep you awake." She crossed to the desk and planted one of the mugs on the softly gleaming wood in front of Felaras, the other in front of the visitor's chair, and filled both without spilling a drop.

Felaras took her mug in both hands and sipped at it gingerly. Kasha took up her own mug, breathed in the cinnamon-scented steam with pleasure, then planted her rump in the visitor's chair and propped both her feet on the desk.

"Have you no respect for your Master, girl?" Felaras chuckled. "Zetren would have a litter of snakes if he saw you now."

"Zetren *is* a litter of snakes. I respect you; you know it. That's enough." Kasha dismissed Zetren with a shrug of one shoulder. "The Elder is on his way back down the Pass; Vider is with him, and he took a donkey-load of medicines; says he plans to stay with them until this mess is over."

"Good for him." Felaras rubbed her broad forehead with the heel of her right hand. "He'll do more good down there than up here, but I didn't think he had it in him to stick out an exile in the caves."

"He says he doesn't mind; says he wants to train some of the midwives the way you've been training some of the Elders." Vider's actions had surprised Kasha too; he was so quiet she'd mostly overlooked him. "Well, Zorsha is getting inventory from the cook; he's already been to the armory. Teo is ankle-deep in scrolls; he thinks he may have found something to give you an edge—if you still want to deal with these folk instead of holing up and pretending we don't exist or trying to fight them."

"So?" Felaras leaned forward eagerly; Kasha worried as the shift in light revealed more clearly the dark circles under her eyes and lines that hadn't been in her face a week ago. "What?"

Kasha snorted; Teo had been his usual obdurate self. "He says he wants to tell you himself; you know Teo— 'three independent sources or it's only hearsay.' "

Felaras sighed. "I know Teo. Thank the gods for him, too. He won't go raising my hopes for no reason." She leaned back and took another sip of wine, retreating into the shadow cast by the back of the chair until all Kasha could see were her eyes glittering in the darkness. "Thank the gods for you, too. And Zorsha. You're all sensible and I can depend on you, and you know this situation may prove to be the life or the death of the Order. And if everything goes to hell either one of the lads can train himself in this seat, and you'll help.

Because I surely won't have time to tell them everything they'll need to know."

Kasha shivered. "Don't say that. It sounds like you're ill-wishing yourself."

"Why not? It's true. We of all people should be able to face the truth."

They both took good long pulls at their mugs; Kasha as much to drive the night-fears away as for any other reason. It worked; she felt the wine going to her head.

Felaras brooded a while longer in silence until Kasha couldn't bear it. "Say something, Felaras. Anything."

"Like what?"

"What you're thinking."

Felaras coughed. "It's pretty selfish. I'm thinking it isn't fair. I am sixty-two damn-'em years old. I should be taking things easy, training the Terrible Twosome, enjoying a comfortable old age. I should be getting respect! What do I get? The Order playing politics under my nose, barbarians on the doorstep, and a Second who puts her feet on my desk!"

"If you really didn't like it," Kasha pointed out, "I wouldn't do it."

"I know it; and I was as snippy with Swordmaster Rodhru as you are with me," Felaras replied. "When you're snippy, I know I can trust you. Kasha, I wish I wasn't Master. And not just because I never wanted it. I wish I could pass the seat on to you. You'd make a better Master than either Teo or Zorsha."

The chair creaked as Kasha shifted uneasily. All this talk of passing on the seat—Felaras was fey tonight. It wasn't like her to be this gloom-ridden. "I wouldn't have your seat; Swordmaster I'd take under protest, but not that—"

"That's the point—you *don't* want it. The Master's seat goes to the most qualified person who wants it the least." The fire popped and Felaras took another large swallow. "That's how I got stuck with it. Ruvan frankly wasn't qualified—even he said so, when you could get his nose out of a book. Zetren wanted it too much. So did Halun, for that matter, but he was automatically out of the running. So it was me."

Kasha shivered in a bit of draft, and listened with half an ear to the fury of the storm outside the study window. "I didn't know that."

"You're not supposed to. Just like nobody outside the Watchers is supposed to know that a third of us are wizards." She coughed. "Kasha, how long have you and I been working together?"

"Since I was novice; um—twelve years, almost."

Felaras put her mug carefully on the desk and laced the fingers of her hands behind her head. "I've stayed out of your private life as much as I could—"

"I know—" Kasha began.

"Don't interrupt. I'm about to crawl into it with a vengeance. You and Zorsha and Teo have been a triad from the time you could crawl. Which one of them are you sleeping with?"

Kasha's face flamed, and she choked on her wine.

"Both?"

"*No!*" she exclaimed, trying to get herself back under control. "I mean we—you know kids, but—when it started to—I wouldn't—dammit, Felaras, you've got no right to ask that of me!"

"I know that," Felaras replied calmly. "I have a reason. You know them both better than I ever could. I need another perspective. Should I pass the seat to Teo, or to Zorsha?"

Kasha went from hot to frozen. That was the very last question she'd ever expected out of Felaras.

"You're drunk," she stammered, finally. "You're drunk, or you'd never have said that."

Felaras shook her head, gently curving grey strands just brushing the tops of her shoulders. "No, I'm not. Or not that drunk."

"Felaras—I—" She was at a total loss for words.

"Have either of them asked to be your permanent lover yet?"

"No!" She flushed hotly again. "We're . . . friends. That's all. I don't want to have to choose between them, not ever! Not for that, not for any reason!"

"You're a Watcher—"

"I know that. I'm a Watcher before I'm anything else, Felaras, and—"

"So focus and give me the answer to my question."

Kasha took a deep breath and focused down until her stomach stopped churning; stilled her mind and let whatever would come rise to the surface.

And when the thought came, it seemed an odd one, but she spoke it anyway.

"Zorsha has never had a nickname. Teo has never been Teokane to anyone except as a signature."

Felaras took her words, turned them around, and looked them over; Kasha could see it in the slightly unfocused eyes, the frown-line between her thick grey eyebrows.

"Meaning?"

Kasha followed her thought, as carefully as she would have followed a track over barren ground. "I'm not quite sure. Except that—nobody ever gave you a nickname either. Or me. Can people obey somebody they still think of as 'young Teo'? Can they trust the decisions of a man who is still bearing the diminutive he wore when he was a child?" She had to shake her head. "I'm not sure what it means; I'm not sure it means anything."

"Let me lead you down a side path, then; suppose I told you to choose, not for the Order, but for yourself. Told you that you would have to make up your mind between them. Then what?"

Kasha shoved the extreme embarrassment and the uncomfortable feelings that question caused down into a corner of herself and sat on them until they weren't getting in the way of her thinking. "If I were forced into choosing one of them as my lover, it would probably be Teo. And that would be because Zorsha would be hurt, but not as badly, nor as deeply, by my making a choice. Which is why I won't." Her mouth was dry, and she was feeling very off-balance and unsettled, and she didn't want to have to deal with it anymore. "Felaras, I don't like having to think about these things—"

"Enough of it, then. Drink your wine; you look like hell."

"Do I?" She willed her insides to stop fluttering. "I feel like hell. I've avoided just this topic ever since the three of us figured out that boys and girls were different. And that *I* wasn't a boy. Like I said, we—but when it looked like it might get into something other than a game, I started saying 'no' to that. I enjoy what we have and I don't want it ruined."

"But you've told me what I needed to know, girl. That Teo isn't as resilient as Zorsha. That other people view him—how to put this?—with a little less than the full respect the Master needs."

Kasha laughed, hearing the edge of hysteria in her voice and hoping Felaras didn't. "*You* talk about respect? With all the fights in Council—"

"They fight me; that doesn't mean they don't respect me." Felaras chuckled out of the dark depths of her chair. "Somebody out there respected my abilities enough to try and joggle my arm tonight. An ill-wishing. I sent it home with its tail between its legs."

Kasha sat bolt upright, mug sloshing. "An ill-wishing? But—"

Felaras waved her alarm aside. "Don't fret yourself. By tomorrow whoever it is will have other things to think about. We're going to have those blamed nomads at the door; that should keep *everyone's* attention, and—"

There was a tentative knock at the door. "Come,"

Felaras called, and Zorsha slid around the door-edge with his hands full of papers, his blonde hair and brown clothing dark with either sweat or rain, grey eyes looking a bit less sleepy than usual.

"Master Felaras, you said—"

"—that I wanted that inventory on my desk tonight, thank you. Yes, I meant it."

"Well, this is everything, down to the last straw in the stable." He put the neat pile of paper exactly in front of Felaras with a half-smile of pardonable pride.

"Good man; go get yourself some of that wine and get to bed; I'm calling a full Convocation tomorrow." She shifted her gaze to Kasha. "Finish yours and get yourself off. I'll need you tomorrow, and not muddled."

Kasha downed the last swallow in her mug, and left it on Felaras' desk. Zorsha waited for her just beyond the door in the dark stairway.

She stumbled over a rough place; he caught her elbow. Rawly sensitive after her bout with Felaras, she twitched away from him. Wisely, he let her go, and let her lead the way down the uneven stone steps.

"Is it that bad?" he asked her, about halfway down. "There's a lot of rumors below, but no real facts."

He had a very pleasant, rich voice; lower than a tenor, higher than a baritone. It unsettled Kasha in a way she did not want to deal with, and she simply nodded, forgetting for a moment that he probably couldn't see her gesture in the ill-lit staircase.

"Kasha?"

"It's bad," she replied shortly.

"The messenger was from the Vale, then? The nomads are at the Teeth?"

"They're at the Teeth," Kasha got out around her clenched jaw, exerting control over herself to answer. "They'll be in the Vale in the next few days. That's why the inventory. What we have now may be all we'll have for a while."

Zorsha made a soft little sound, like a cross between a sigh and a grunt. "I rather thought that was it." As they reached the bottom of the staircase, he gave her arm a squeeze, surprising her before she could pull away. "Go get some rest. You may not get any for a while."

She turned to glare at him. But he was already gone.

Chapter Two

Teo's eyes misted over, and he lost the sense of what he was reading.

Gods. He blinked; blinked again, but the old and fading words on the yellowed parchment page kept running together into illegibility. Teo rubbed his eyes with the back of his hand to clear them, but they wouldn't stop blurring. He glanced over to the corner of the scarred desk, at the time-candle he'd brought with him into the Library. He shook his head in mild surprise. *Half burned-down already?* It only seemed an hour ago that he'd started his search.

Is it really midnight? He sneezed and rubbed at his nose as another sneeze threatened; his eyes felt gritty and sore. He looked around, certain that the candle must have burned too fast, but he was alone; nothing but battered, empty desks and full, dusty bookshelves. His fellow Archivists and their novices had slipped away while he was deep in researches. *I guess it must be. I guess I got pretty involved.*

He closed his eyes for a moment; felt contented, rather than exalted, by his discoveries. But then, that was what being an Archivist was all about, anyway. Not the Seeker's sudden thrill of seeing something new arise out of your investigations, but rather the slow process of putting all the bits together until at last you could stand back and see the whole.

The whole—Hladyr bless, I have put together a whole indeed this time!

He opened his eyes again and contemplated the neat pile of papers before him with profound satisfaction. Each page was covered with notes in his own careful hand. He had put together a picture of the horse-nomads and their ways that had waited unnoticed in the Archives for a century—and that only Felaras had guessed (or hoped) existed. More than enough to inspire a soul-filling contentment.

An aged but still musical contralto interrupted his reverie.

"When I told you to burn midnight oil on this one, Teo, I didn't mean you to take me quite so literally."

He blinked, and came back to himself; not with a start, but slowly, carefully, as he did everything. He turned around to face the door, wondering what could have brought the Master of the Order down at this hour. Unless . . . unless things had gotten worse since this afternoon.

Master Felaras leaned against the frame of the open Library door, the only spot of color in the room full of dark wooden bookcases and leather-bound books. Her scarlet wool tunic and darker red breeches made her look like a flame in the light from the time-candle and the carefully shielded oil lamp beside the door.

No outward sign identified her as the Master of the Order. Not her age, nor her iron-grey hair—there were others in the Order who looked (or were) older. Not the sword at her side, nor her clothing; Masters wore what they pleased. Some Masters of the Order had gone robed in precious silks, and some in rags.

She certainly didn't look or act nobly born; if an air of

pedigree was a prerequisite for the Master's seat, Halun, (silver-haired, blue-eyed, holding himself with all the pride of his Ancas ancestors) would have had it long ago.

Maybe it was the aura of calm authority. Maybe it was the feeling she seemed to project that she would, somehow, get things done.

Whatever it was, it was obvious that she was the Master even without the tiny badge on the shoulder of her tunic, of Sword, Flame, and Book—the badge that only the Master wore.

"Dreaming awake, lad?" Her generous mouth quirked in a smile. "Hadn't you better be doing that in bed?"

He gave himself a mental shake, and returned the smile. "I'm sorry, Master, I was wool-gathering."

"I hope you were gathering more than that." She sniffed, and rubbed the side of her nose with her knuckle. "I hope you gathered me some answers. I need them; we've had bad news. The nomads are at the Teeth."

"I have what you wanted, I think," he said cautiously. "I found a whole set of Chronicles taken from some silk merchants who came through the Teeth about a hundred years ago."

"Isn't that a bit old to do us any good?" she asked doubtfully, pushing away from the door-frame and walking over to lean on his desk instead.

He shook his head as she planted both palms on the desk top and looked over his shoulder. "No, not really. Things don't change much for the horse-nomads. Not that much to change, really. They would probably be much the same today as they were when the Sabirn Empire collapsed . . . except for one thing."

He launched into a fairly concise summary of what he'd gleaned, pausing now and again to check his notes. Felaras followed his speech with narrowed eyes, nodding now and again when something he said seemed to touch on something in her own mind.

His throat was dry and his voice cracking a bit as he built up to the really choice bit of his gleanings. " . . . so this wandering healer, whoever he was, and the merchants seemed to think he was one of us, made one really important change in their outlook. Almost in their religion. By the time the merchants came through, he'd risen in the legends of the Clans to something like a saint or a demi-god."

"Which means what? That a scholar gets nearly the same treatment as a shaman?"

"Oh, better," Teo hastened to tell her, not concealing his glee, the glow of discovery making him forget his aching shoulders and burning eyes for a moment. "A man that's a scholar or a healer is sacrosanct. It's assumed that the Wind Gods have him under something like divine protection. If you molest him, you bring the gods' anger down on your whole Clan; if you shelter him, you bring their blessing. A scholar can move about among the Clans pretty much at will, and virtually unmolested. All he has to fear is outlaws."

"What if this bunch is—"

"No," he interrupted, "these aren't outlaws; they have their horsetail banner with them, so they're a real Clan."

"Gods bless." She gripped the edge of the table and closed her eyes, leaning all her weight on her hands; and suddenly Teo saw not her strength, but her bone-deep weariness.

It frightened him. They *depended* on her.

"Master Felaras?" he said, reaching out to touch the wool of her sleeve with tentative fingers. She sighed; and he saw not the Master, but an old, tired woman. One with terrible weariness behind what was no more than a facade of strength. "Master?" he faltered again in dismay.

She opened her eyes quickly, and the strength was

back; real, and not an illusion. It was surely the weakness that was the illusion—

She was looking at him measuringly, and he wondered why.

"Teo," she said, slowly, "Would you . . . ?"

When she didn't finish the question, he prompted her. "Would I what? Anything you need, Master Felaras. Just tell me what to look for."

"Never mind." She favored him with another of her half-grins; back to being the Master Felaras who was as predictable and dependable as the stone of the Fortress. "Get on to bed, there's a lad. I'm calling a Full Convocation in the morning, and I want you to have a clear head for it; as one of my three pets, you'll be in for a lot of questioning, after, from your own chapter. I want you in shape to answer clearly and remember who asked what for me." When he hesitated, she jerked her head impatiently in the direction of the door. "Off with you! I'll secure the Library."

He nodded obediently, gathered up his paper and his pens, and handed her his notes on his way out the door.

But as he left the Library he thought he could feel that penetrating stare on his back—as if she was looking for something in him. It seemed that her eyes followed him all the way back to the door of the Archivists' Quarters.

The boy slept uneasily beneath his blankets of felt and horsehide, his face pale and haggard in the light from the clay-lined fire-basket, his dark hair matted with sweat. From time to time he moaned in his sleep, as the pain of his wounds and of the injury to his head passed the drugged wine he'd been given; it bit at him and made him toss his head on the hard, flat leather pillow. He shivered too; and that was a bad sign, for the round felt tent was as warm as a sunshine-gilded spring day, so that meant that the last of the mold-powder had done him no good. Yuchai was undoubtedly in the first stages of infection, and the Healer-woman Shenshu might not be able to grow what he needed quickly enough to do him any good.

Shaman Northwind (he'd borne the name for so long that even he had difficulty recalling the time when he'd been Taichin, or sometimes Taichin Wanderer) sighed and began unpacking his medicine rattles and sacred incense from their basket. The scent of precious sandalwood rose from the packing; nothing less would call the Wind Lords' attention to their need. He'd helped clean and bind the boy's injuries; he'd well-wished him with all the strength and skill at his command. When all else failed, there was always prayer.

At least the storm has stopped, he thought. *But everything else . . . it's as though the entire world was ill-wishing us. And now Yuchai—lightning spooking his horse, sending both of them into that pit-trap—it was the worst possible ill-luck. The people are reading it as an omen. Wind Lords, have you deserted us too?*

Someone coughed politely outside the tent-flap; Northwind identified the cough without thinking. "My tent is always open to you, Khene Jegrai," he called softly.

The felt tent-flap was pushed aside by a strong, slender brown hand; the rest of Jegrai followed his hand in short order, and was, like the hand, strong and slender. The Khene of Running Horse Clan cast a worried look at the wounded boy, then seated himself cross-legged on the layered carpets of the tent-floor with a grace that was almost boneless.

There was something about the young man that commanded attention, demanded loyalty. Northwind sometimes thought of him as a pure flame in a fine porcelain lamp such as the Suno made and used; his spirit seemed to shine through his flesh. That spirit was powerful enough to make one forget Jegrai's patched and faded clothing, garb that was more suited to a beggar than a Khene and the son of Khenes.

"How is the boy?" That voice, as flexible and obedient to Jegrai's will as his horse, held only concern now. For once—with no one about to see him—Jegrai was not being Khene. Jegrai was being young Yuchai's adored—and anxious—cousin.

The Shaman shrugged eloquently, rippling the fringes decorating his suede leather garments. "He lives. Whether he will prosper I cannot tell you, but it is now in the hands of the Wind Lords. Both I and Shenshu have done all we can."

"The Wind Lords do not hear us," came the bitter reply.

Twenty years ago Northwind would have rebuked Jegrai for blasphemy. Ten years ago he would have delivered a lecture on the folly of man attempting to judge the will of the gods. That was in the days when Running Horse held their territory in relative peace. Before the Suno Lords chose to conquer the Clans from within, by setting Clan against Clan, turning what had been friendly contests of honor into blood-feud and death. Before Khene Sen of the Talchai turned upon them. Before their flight into this strange land where the earth rose to block the sight of the open sky. Now he only sighed.

"I do not know that either, Jegrai. It certainly seems that nothing we have done has prospered."

"Except our running," the young Khene spat. "*That* we do well enough, it seems."

Northwind looked up, and his eyes locked with Jegrai's hard, black ones. There was no doubting the power, the will behind the Khene's eyes. The tent seemed too warm of a sudden, and the Shaman was the first to drop his gaze.

"I do not know what to tell you," the Shaman said, after silence thick enough to choke upon filled the tent.

"I truly do not. You know what I know; that the omens have told me that the Winds say our fate lies in the West. And truly, these people of the West cannot seem to stand before us."

"That is at least in part because we move so quickly that we outpace the rumors of our coming." Jegrai's tone was still bitter, and he played with the end of his sash, plaiting and unplaiting the faded fringe. "We are down to half the strength we had when we fled the Talchai, Shaman. At this rate . . . Tell me, should I stop this senseless, cowardly fleeing? Should I give myself over to the hands of our enemies? Will that save my people further suffering?"

To his people, the Khene was as strong, as cold, as a living blade—as fierce as a wind-driven fire. He was none of those things now; the mask was gone before his teacher and oldest companion. Northwind could not meet that burning, agonized gaze, but for that question he did have an answer.

"It was," he said slowly and carefully, "the Talchai who broke faith when your father died. It was the Talchai who allied themselves with those Suno dogs and began gathering or destroying the Outer Clans. More specifically, it was Khene Sen, who would make himself Khekhene over all the Clans. And he did so because you dared to speak the truth of him in Khaltan, the Great Council. Would you have us bind ourselves over to one who licks the spittle of dogs so that he may bear the Banner of Nine Horsetails, so that sons of dogs will call him Khekhene?" His voice strengthened. "You kept honor; Sen has destroyed his."

"What good is honor," Jegrai cried, his voice tight with anguish. "What worth is honor when it is bought with the lives of Vredai children? When the First Law of the Wind Lords is 'Cherish the children, for they are the lifeblood of the Clan' and what I have done has spilled that blood as surely as the swords of the Talchai?"

He says "Vredai children," but he means Yuchai, the Shaman thought. Then he rebuked himself. *Nay, that is less than the truth. I have never seen any but a healer or shaman take the First Law so to heart as Jegrai. Yuchai is the first youngster to be so badly hurt since the raid that near destroyed us—and Jegrai knows full well that it was because Yuchai was striving to emulate him. Jegrai would feel the same guilt over any other child suffering what Yuchai has.*

Yet another thought occurred. *And the boy lived in his shadow. He is the son Jegrai longs to have. . . .*

"What worth is freedom?" he replied softly. "I tell you, it is everything. And if we bought safety at the expense of our freedom, then the Wind Lords *would* turn their backs upon us."

"But—" Jegrai began.

The Shaman cut him off ruthlessly. "And what if you turned back and faced the wrath of Khene Sen alone? What good would that do Running Horse?"

"You would live—"

"We would die," Northwind said fiercely. "Vredai would be no more, her banner trampled, her women and children distributed to Sen's hangers-on, her men sold in the slave markets of Kalandu. You know this, Jegrai. There is not enough grazing for all the Clans since the drought, and that has continued for three years; that is what allowed the Suno to twist fear into the quarrels that began this. That is why when we fled, we fled west, where no one goes. Because there is water and grass in the West, and because Khene Sen will destroy us if he takes us."

Jegrai bowed his head, and his shoulders sagged. "And that too is my fault. If I had not stolen the Talchai shrine—if I had not thrown it into the path of those who pursued us so that their horses trampled it into the dust before they knew what had happened—"

"You called your 'council.' You asked me; you asked all of us before you did it," Northwind reminded him. "And all—myself, Ghekhen Vaichen, your mother Aravay, and Shenshu—we all agreed. Khene Sen had already trampled his Clan's honor into the dust; it were well to remind his people of that. For them to trample and destroy their own shrine was a terrible omen, and we hoped it would shake them deeply. And besides that—"

"We had thought there was no way to escape him; we thought we were doomed," Jegrai finished for him, dully.

Northwind did not like this lifelessness that had come upon his Khene. Even Jegrai's fire could not burn forever, and it seemed he was coming to the end of his will. Northwind put force behind his words in an attempt to shake him from this sickly mood. "Think, Jegrai! We all thought—you and your advisors—it was the only chance we had to distract them from the chase long enough to have a *hope* of eluding them. The Wind Lords favored us, Jegrai. They favored us then; and I—I somehow have the feeling that I *am* reading the omens aright. There is something they wish for us here . . . . " Shaman Northwind sighed. "And we have not done much to find it."

Jegrai shook his head. "Now *that* I shall take blame for. A winter's march, a spring campaign—we have not done much but trample the land-folk beneath the hooves of our horses. And the crops."

Northwind felt the pain any of the Vredai felt at the abuse of good land. It was not through will that Running Horse Clan wandered—it was through lack of good grazing lands. Any of them would as lief gone back to the settled, pastured life of their ancestors, before the Suno drove them into the steppes.

"This land is leaderless, and I cannot see how these folks have lived all this time without a leader to rule them. It is a good land, ill-used," Jegrai continued, "but we are hurting it further—I can hear it groaning, Shaman. It is spring, and there should be, there must be, planting. But we, *we* are keeping the land-folk from that planting. We rob them, when we should be trading with them. Now they will starve, and then there will be nothing and we will starve—"

"But we are starving now," Northwind said with reluctance. "What choice have we but to live off them? And the Talchai may be yet on our track."

"I think . . . I need a council, Shaman." Jegrai finally seemed to have regained some of his resolve. "Tell the others; speak to the warriors, the scouts, then come to me at midmorning. We need, perhaps, to change direction. Perhaps the time has come to stop running."

"I shall," Northwind replied, heartened again. "And I shall speak with the Wind Lords this night. If there be any thing I may do to gain their aid . . . "

"So long as you gain Yuchai's healing—and an end to the deaths of my people—that is all that matters to me, Shaman." Jegrai rose, his head brushing the roof of the tent. "The rest must be, as you have told me, done or undone by our own actions. Tell the Wind Lords that when you speak to them."

"I shall," Northwind replied soberly, as Jegrai slipped back out into the cold, damp night. "Believe me, I shall."

Felaras surveyed the Convocation with what she hoped looked like calm authority. Every person in the Fortress truly a member of the Order was here, in the Great Hall. Once this had been some huge assembly room, perhaps an armory or training-room, or a dining hall, but Master Duran had caused it to be altered so that it matched his memories of the great lecture rooms in the colleges of Targheiden. It was useful to have one place within the walls where all members of the Order could gather at one time. Tier after tier of wooden benches built like three huge staircases, one on each of the three blank walls, rose to the ceiling, so that the room had taken on the look of a lopsided bowl, or half a bowl, with the lectern at the bottom of it.

It was a perishing *cold* bowl, though. No fireplace, and mostly stone. Her nose was cold, and her fingers, and she hoped her nose wouldn't start dripping. That would surely put paid to the little dignity she could muster.

The room buzzed with the sound of those assembled muttering to one another. The room was nearly full, and the folk on the benches hardly looked to be members of the same organization. There was no "uniform" for the Order, not even an approximately uniform way of dress.

That was the legacy of Duran; their diversity. They came to the Order from every class, every race, every nation. Half of those here in the Fortress had been born here—but there were plenty, like Felaras herself, who had come from far away, hot on the scent of learning. Some had come seeking a legend of magic; some, like Halun, had come on the advice of their teachers. All shared the same dream: to learn, to teach, to preserve old knowledge and seek new.

That was the *only* commonality within the Order. And the varied dress of the members reflected this.

Those of the Watchers tended to wear breeches and tunic regardless of sex, but the cut, color and style of those garments ranged from the dark cotton gabardine garments typical of the island kingdom of Bergem that Kasha wore, to the heavy, brightly dyed, fur-trimmed wool of Albirn that she herself favored. The Archivists tended to robes, with deep pockets and wide sleeves that could also serve as pockets, but that did not even hold true throughout the chapter. And the Seekers wore anything and everything; Flame tended to knee-robes and breeches and Hand to short tunics and breeches—but there sat Halun in a rich blue robe more suited to an Archivist, and beside him was Zorsha in a dark-grey tunic that could have come from Kasha's wardrobe. And the minds and souls about her were as varied as the clothing their bodies wore. Felaras wondered how in the name of all the gods she was ever going to get this motley crew to agree on anything.

She had never enjoyed lecturing, nor holding these Convocations. She always felt like a Seeker's prize specimen of new insect under all those eyes. She'd held Full Convocations perhaps four times in her twenty-seven years as Master. This would be the fifth—and the most important.

She cleared her throat, and the dull hum of voices ceased. Silence fell over them all, a silence that seemed fragile, and prone to shatter at a breath.

"You've probably heard the rumors," she said, deciding that blunt directness would serve her better than anything else now. *Tell them the bad news, get the shock over with, and then get those fine minds* moving; *that's what I need to do.* "I called you all here to tell the exact truth. There's a Clan of horse-nomads out of the East that's been pounding through Azgun since fall. Nobody's managed to hold them, or even make an effective stand against them. Now they're here; just on the other side of the Teeth. I've been warning the Yazkirn Princes and the Court of Ancas that they're coming; I wasn't believed, and I see no reason why they should suddenly send an army to rescue us. They won't lift a finger to help us; they will move only if they see a threat to themselves. As you should well know. So we're alone in this."

Near two hundred pairs of eyes were on her; brown, grey, blue—some shocked, some frightened, some thoughtful—and some, still, full of an arrogant contempt for the danger on their doorstep.

"There are, at minimum, nearly a thousand fighters. That's a guess, but probably a low one—*I'd* reckon more, and you all know what *my* chapter was. And that's assuming their women don't fight, or their youngsters, which may be a stupid thing to assume. The Vale folk are running for shelter; I sent them to the caves—"

"I thought the caves were supposed to be *our* shelter!" shouted an angry voice from the back.

"Would you rather they came here for refuge?" she replied sharply. "There's at least *room* for them in the caves! Tell me where in Hladyr's name we'd put them if they came here, why don't you?"

The tense silence fell again. This time the silence held a strong note of fear. They were beginning to see the danger. And take it to heart.

"All right, now you know the worst of it. There's no doubt in my mind that we can keep them off the Pass. The question I have is if we can—or should—try to do anything, and in that I include trying to outwait them. We've got supplies enough for about two months, but no way of getting more except from Yazkirn, and that means trading. And you all know the only coin we have to trade with."

She paused, but it seemed that there was no one else ready to make any protests yet.

"I want you all to think about this problem; we've a couple hundred of the finest minds in the world here. I want to hear if any of you have any answers *or* questions. We all know that sometimes it's the questions that make the answers. I'm including you novices in this—sometimes what seems to be a stupid question or answer turns out not to be so stupid after all. When you leave this room you'll be given duties to cover so that we can get the Fortress ready to withstand a siege. But while your hands are busy, I want your minds busy too. Whatever you come up with, put it in writing. Leave it in my study. Sign it or not, I don't care. I want your thoughts, men and women of the Order. I can't make a decision that will determine the fate of the Order without knowing those thoughts."

Once again she raked the room with her eyes.

There was very little fear there now. Some dismay, but very little fear. And a great many faces that had gone quiet and inward-focused. She began to hope.

"All right, then; see your chapter Leaders about your duties—and remember what I told you." She made a dismissing motion. "You may go."

"So." Jegrai settled himself on a thin pad of stuffed felt beside the cold fire-pot in his tent, and surveyed the faces of his four councilors. Light came through the white felt; it was shadowy within, but not at all dark. Beyond the felt walls he could hear the sounds of the camp; children playing, folk talking, normal and sane sounds that had not been heard among the Vredai tents in far too long. He hoped that what they decided here might bring those sounds back again.

He had trusted the wisdom of these four since he first took the reins of Running Horse at fifteen. Then, they had ruled him. . . .

Now he ruled them, and the change had come about so gradually that no one of them could put a finger on a particular moment and say, "That was when things changed." But the change was there. And he had thanked the Wind Lords that they had been great enough of soul to accept that change.

On his right, Shaman Northwind; a man so old he had outlived Jegrai's grandfather. He looked as fragile as one of those pampered little birds the Suno Emperor kept in gold cages. In some ways he was as frail as he seemed, but not in any fashion that had any significance to his duties. His eyes were oddly gentle, and full of good humor even at the worst of times; his face was as wrinkled as a dried berry. His silver hair, worn loose and as long as his waist, marked his calling, for no warrior would have grown such a convenient handle for an enemy to seize. His moustache and neat little beard were as silver as his hair, but not nearly so long. Today he was wearing his fringed ceremonial robes and his buffalo-skull helmet, which indicated to Jegrai that he, too, felt this council might well decide the fate of Running Horse Khenat.

To Jegrai's left sat his mother, Aravay, as she had sat at the left hand of his father. She was like an antique carving of fine ivory; nothing could be read upon her face, which was a serene, feminized version of her son's. *After all these years*, Jegrai thought in sudden wonder, *after all she has been through, suffered through, she is still beautiful.*

But she was more than beautiful; she was clever and cunning and wise. She heard everything that any woman of the Clan said; knew within a day what any of them did. She knew entanglements of kinship and honor-debt going back generations; remembered things Jegrai would have long since forgotten. She had advised his father, and he had had the sense to listen to her. Some had scoffed at Jegrai for keeping her on his council, but Jegrai had no intention of *ever* letting her go. The man who put away the gifts that Aravay had to offer simply because she was his mother was a fool who did not deserve to be called "Khene."

To the Shaman's right sat Shenshu, the chief of the Healer-women. Where Aravay was an ivory carving, Shenshu was a round little earthenware statuette; everyone's favorite aunt, the person who heard everything troubling anyone. Nor would she reveal those secrets—not directly, at least. But Jegrai could depend on her to tell him—indirectly, if need be—what he needed to know.

To Aravay's left was Vaichen, the warlord of Khenat Vredai. Dark as old leather, aged, wrinkled and weathered, and bald as a stone—but he sat straight and tall, and met his Khene's level gaze with perfect fearlessness. Injured in a fall that killed his horse this past winter, his right leg stiff and without feeling. There were those who said he had outlived his usefulness, for what good was a warlord who could not lead the charge? To which Jegrai would immediately reply, "What use is a warlord who does not know his brain from his buttocks?" So long as Ghekhen Vaichen could use that brain and speak his mind, Jegrai would see that the horsetail banner *remained* in front of his tent. . . .

"So," he said, looking from one to another of his advisors. "We are met. I would hear what the people will not tell their Khene."

Shenshu cleared her throat and began, with an apologetic side glance at the Shaman. "They are frightened, Jegrai. They say that the Wind Lords have either abandoned us, forgotten us, or can no longer hear us in this land where the earth blocks the sight of the sky. But they are also afraid of the Talchai." She ran a string of wooden beads through her fingers, as if the feel of the carved wood in her hands soothed her; they clicked softly in the pauses between her words. "They say we must not stop; that we must keep running. They think that the Wind Lords will not be able to hear the Talchai either, in this place, and that . . . you have seen, perhaps, the consequences when a rabbit is chased by a dog through camp? The rabbit, running swiftly, may overturn waterskins, may frighten the horses—but he surprises the encampment and they do nothing to *him*. But the dog, following after—ai, the women chase with sticks, the men with whips, children throw stones, and every hand is against him. So they think it may be with us, as the rabbit, and the Talchai, as the dog. We scatter these land-folk before us, but when the Talchai come they shall be aroused and they shall have rega-

thered their wits. We must let nothing stop us but the
Great Western Ocean. So say the frightened."

Jegrai nodded; in some ways that turn of thought had
a great deal of merit. Surely it was true that they had,
so far, met little resistance. But there was no guarantee
that this fortunate state of affairs would continue. He
did not know what lay beyond the mountains. At this
point, none of them knew. If it was another organized
empire such as the Suno ruled, they would be crushed.

He reached beside him for the skin of *khmass*, and
poured each of his councilors a full wooden cup of the
powerful fermented milk. He had no fear that any of
them would lose his or her head to it, and he wanted
them to know he truly wished to hear everything, however distasteful. And indeed, there was a slight relaxation of posture in everyone around the circle at this
gesture of hospitality.

"So, the frightened would continue to flee, and hope
we may still outpace the rumors of our coming." He
sipped his pungent *khmass* and nodded thoughtfully.
"There is merit in such a thought—but we have not yet
met a people who can stand against us. And when we
do, we may find ourselves trapped between the grass
fire and the raging torrent."

He rolled the cup between his palms, the wood
silken and warm under his fingers, and waited to hear
what this observation would elicit.

"That is the more likely as we force deeper into the
West," rumbled Vaichen. "The warriors have a liking
for this valley beyond the Pass, what they have seen of
it. They say it is a good place for defense. They are
saying that we should take it, and make our stand here.
Then, when the Talchai come, we should die in honor
and glory, making them pay, and pay, and pay."

"And you, Ghekhen?" Jegrai looked at his warlord's
hands, clenched around his wooden cup.

"To survive and prosper is a better revenge," the old

man said reluctantly. "To take this valley—if we can—would be no bad thing. It is defensible—and is like the old tales of the home the Suno stole from us. But I cannot counsel making a stand; I would not care to have our banner in Khene Sen's tent, no matter how many lives it had cost him."

"Can we take this valley?" Aravay spoke softly. "I do not know that we can. You know that my care is the scouts. The young scouts have brought tales to me, of wizards on the western pass. They say that it is only because they are vowed not to meddle in the lives of lesser men that we have not been struck down before this. They say that the storm of last night that sent Yuchai's horse shying into the pit-trap is a warning not to go further. They say that the wizards of the mountain can call upon the lightning—"

"Any man can call upon the lightning," Northwind said skeptically. "The question is, will it answer him?"

"They say that the lightning has answered the wizards, and out of a cloudless sky and bright day," Aravay replied. "They captured those who had seen it with their own eyes."

"Men will say anything," interrupted Vaichen.

"But these were not men, they were children. And they had seen this less than a year ago."

Jegrai clenched his jaw, anger at the thought that his orders regarding youngsters had been disobeyed. "Children? We took children? How? What became of these children?" Jegrai asked sternly. "We are burdened enough with Vredai children, but—I gave orders that there was to be no slaughter of women and young things. Vredai has *honor*. We fight only those who will fight us—and we make no warfare on the helpless."

"The scouts surprised and scattered a party of fleeing land-folk in the pass itself," his mother answered serenely. "And two children were left behind. As you ordered, the scouts took counsel of me. Upon my advice, Obodei, who has some of their tongue, took them blindfolded through the valley pass and released them." Aravay smiled a little. "But only after telling them to tell their parents that we numbered in the tens of thousands and ate babies, and that they were fortunate that Obodei was not hungry at that moment."

The Shaman grinned, Shenshu snickered, and Vaichen shouted his laughter. Even Jegrai had to chuckle.

"Old schemer, well did your husband name you Fox-woman!" Vaichen snorted. "I think perhaps I should take the horsetail banner and have it placed before your tent!"

Aravay inclined her head to him, her eyes twinkling.

"These wizards," Jegrai prompted. "Did the children have anything else to say of them?"

"That they are very strange; more scholar and healer than wizard. They sound something like to Holy Vedani. That they keep mostly to themselves, but have been known to take a very clever child into their ranks should the child wish to become a wizard. That they have lived upon the mountaintop for time out of mind, and trade wondrous devices for food and the like, but have otherwise little to do with the folk of the valley."

Jegrai whistled between his teeth, softly. "So," he said, after turning all this over in his mind, "we have one choice: to make a stand. And another: to continue to flee. I think perhaps we have a third. We might seek allies and settle here, so that if the Talchai follow, they find us in the position of strength."

"Allies from among the wizards?" the Shaman asked, one eyebrow rising high. From his expression, Jegrai judged that he was surprised, but cautiously approved. "What of the land-folk, then?"

"I do not know; I do not think it matters for now. Eventually we must win them if we are to remain, but first we must win the wizards. It would be best to come at the wizards with at least the appearance of strength, hm? It would make an alliance to their advantage, I think."

"Aye," Vaichen said, slowly. "What say you to this: let us harry these land-folk, but gently. If they flee, pursue only so as to let them know we do pursue, but allow them to escape. Raid only to take what we need, no wanton wastage, no despoiling, no burning. Most of all, take this end of the valley and hold it, so that we have a secure camp to work from."

"Good." Jegrai nodded, and felt a rising hope. This might well work. "The warriors are weary enough to accept this, I think. Listen out there—I think the Vredai are equally tired of running and warfare. I think they would welcome the chance to rest. All of you—pass the word that we *do not* harry the wizards; we will tell the people that they are dangerous, and probably quick to anger—"

"And like to Holy Vedani," his mother interrupted. "That will hold them when naught else will. The Wind Lords would surely curse a man who caused harm to such a wizard. Fear of the Wind Lords will stay their hands where fear of magic would not."

"Very good." He put his cup down on the carpet and leaned forward. "This is what we do not want the wizards to learn; that we are fleeing the Talchai, that we are not here to conquer, but in retreat. If they rally their folk and cause them to come upon us from behind, we *surely* will be caught between fire and torrent. If the Talchai do not come upon us this summer, they surely will the next."

All four of his advisors nodded at that, faces sober. "Is there anything else?" Shenshu asked.

"I need to learn more of these wizards," he replied, chewing his lip. "Much, much more."

Though Jegrai had his own tent, he had neither wife nor sister to tend it for him. Though Aravay had her own tent, which had been his father's, she found time to tend to his. The arrangement worked well, for she could bring him the scouting reports—if they were less than urgent—with his dinner.

So she had tonight. The light from the lantern hanging from the centerpole cast a gentle glow that made her seem as ageless as a Wind Lord. She handed him the covered bowl of thin stew she had brought from her fire, and knelt beside him while he ate.

"The wizards are of a surety aiding land-folk over the pass," Aravay said softly. "So all the scouts say."

Jegrai flexed his aching shoulders and leaned back against the tentpole. He had ridden out with a raiding party, but what they had brought back with them was firewood; a singularly awkward prey to carry. "These land-folk either will or will not return; it is of no consequence. If we do settle here, our own folk will make up for those who flee. How do the folk care for this new camp?"

"They do not like the mountain at our back, but the pasturage and good water make up for it," his mother replied. "My son, you are worried. Have you learned something which troubles you?"

"Aye," he brooded for a moment, then concluded that Aravay might as well know the worst. "We can go no further. It is as I feared. Beyond the western pass lies a land that is well ruled, and strong. It is called Yazkirn, and governed by princes. They have ignored our presence because they care not overmuch for these lands; they are hard to reach and tax, and besides, contain the wizards. But—should we force our way over the pass, it would be up with us. They *would* come to the defense of their land, and crush us. If they even think we have become a threat, they will come to us, and I think we would have no chance."

The fire in the fire-pot flared, and Aravay's eyes

showed her alarm, though nothing else did. "How came you to learn this?" she asked, cautiously.

"That merchant we let pass. I questioned him myself; promised him no despoiling in return for truth." Jegrai sighed. "I have some skill at reading men, I think. He told truth. We are in the cooking pot. . . . "

"Unless we can gain the favor of the wizards."

"Aye." He bit his lip, and told her what he would tell no other living soul. "They frighten me, mother—and they fascinate me. They *can* call the lightning, for every prisoner we have taken has tales of it, tales so unlikely I think they can only be true. They have used it—imagine this, mother—to gain metals, and to level great rock outcroppings, and to change the lay of the land about their fortress! And if they can call lightning to do that for them, it should be the work of a single thought to use it to start a fire in the grasslands where we cannot escape it."

Only once in Jegrai's memory had the Vredai been caught in a grass fire. They had lost a third of the herds, and many lives, and there were men and women among those left who still bore the ugly keloid scars from it. It had been in the first year of the drought, and the memory still gave him nightmares when storms passed overhead.

"The stories I hear say they are very wise," his mother replied thoughtfully, her hands busy with plaiting a new riding quirt. "And that they do nothing without good reason. *And* that they are no friends to the kings over the mountains."

Jegrai sat straight up. "That is something I had not heard!" he exclaimed.

His mother looked up and smiled at him. "The kings over the mountains drove them here, or so it is said," she told him serenely. "And wizard or no, I have never yet seen the man who does not thirst for revenge."

"So-ho. A reason to ally to us. Their magic—and our

warriors . . ." Jegrai fell silent, considering the possibilities.

"You have ever been a Khene who respects good advice when you can get it, my son," his mother said demurely, breaking the long silence.

He roused from his thoughts and gave her a half smile. "If there are strange gods to have the blessing of, and wizards to come upon my side—it would be folly to foul my chances, no?"

"And you have never been foolish, not even as a child." Her eyes darkened with affection; then a sadness passed across her face. "The Shaman wished me to tell you that there is no change with Yuchai."

Jegrai cursed under his breath, and his food lost its savor. He started to push his bowl away, then recalled how little they had, and finished it grimly.

"My son—I speak as a mother." Aravay put her hand over his, and her eyes were soft with concern. "I cannot see how Yuchai's hurt is your doing, nor does his mother blame you for it."

"You cannot—but I can," he replied harshly. "The boy follows after me with his heart in his hand. He strives to copy all I do. He wishes so much to have my approval that he would do anything to get it. There was no need for him to have joined the scouts. He was barely within the age. I could have told him he must wait a year. But I was a scout at fourteen summers, so therefore he must do likewise—I should have forbade it. He is not the rider nor the fighter that I was at twelve, much less having the skill I had at fourteen. But I could not find it in my heart to tell him no. And this is the result of my ill-judgement. Bones broken, and flesh torn by the stakes in that pit, and a blow to the head from which he may never awake—and it is only by the grace of the Wind Lords that these people have honor enough not to poison the stakes. It is only by their grace that he is not dead already."

"Jegrai—" Aravay said, after a moment of brooding silence. "I wonder—the Holy One was a healer—and if the wizards *are* of his kind, could it be that they could help young Yuchai?"

He started, for the thought had not occurred to him. "It may be—it just may be. All the more reason to ally with them. And may the Wind Lords grant it be not too late!"

Chapter Three

Kasha shaded her eyes from the brilliant afternoon sun with one hand while she clung to the polished wood of the Fortress flagpole with the other, and strained up on her toes as high as she dared.

"I wish you wouldn't do that," Teo complained from the window below her, his uneasiness plain in his voice. "It makes me dizzy."

She grinned down at him, perfectly comfortable on her tower-top perch. He squinted up at her; from here his blocky face and wide shoulders made him look a little like a granite statue that had never been completely finished. *Hladyr bless*, she thought impatiently, *I've got both feet planted on the pole-socket. What's to be nervous about?*

"Why should it make *you* dizzy?" she asked mockingly. "It's not *you* that's up here!"

He shivered visibly and looked away. "I can't help thinking about how Benno fell from up there."

"Benno was a thirteen-year-old fool who didn't live to see fourteen *because* he was a fool," she retorted, reveling in the brisk east wind that was playing with the short strands of her hair. "He climbed up right after a

51

storm when the slates were slippery, and he didn't have
a rope on him. I do, because I'm *not* a fool."

"We know you aren't a fool, Kasha," Zorsha replied.
"You keep forgetting Teo saw him fall."

So did I, and so did you, she thought, but didn't say.
*People die; it happens. You learn from it, but you try
not to let it live in you forever.*

"Now that you're up there," Teo said, carefully not
looking at her, "can you see them?" He tugged at his
neat little beard with his right hand; an unconscious
gesture that showed how nervous he was.

She squinted at the eastern end of the Vale. "Maybe
. . . I can see a big dust-cloud, anyway. That'll be their
horse-herd." She groped for the far-glasses looped around
her neck, and put them to her eyes. It wasn't easy
adjusting them with only one hand, but unlike Benno,
she wasn't out to prove what a great daredevil she was.
The blurs of green, white, and brown finally leapt into
clarity.

"Well, I sort of see them," she called down. "Too far
away to make out people, but there's a bunch of white
things that are probably tents. And if there's as many
people as there are tents, we've been undercounting."

She swung the lenses slightly right, to see if she
could make out anything under the dust-cloud. "Hladyr
bless—" she said in awe, the word trailing off.

"What?" Teo asked anxiously. "Something—something
wrong?"

"No, nothing like that. It's just—I've never seen so
many horses before in my entire life." Even with the
far-glasses they were just tiny dots—but so *many* of
them!

"There must be hundreds—thousands. No wonder
they move them every day; they'd eat the grass down to
the ground if they stayed put for long." She let the
glasses fall, and felt for her footing on the slates of the
peaked roof. "I've seen enough; I'm coming down."

*   *   *

The window in Halun's study stood wide open to the balmy breeze, and it faced westward, down the side of the Pass opposite the Vale. It was seductively easy to believe that the danger posed by the nomads simply didn't exist. Even the sight of the novices beyond the walls (cutting back all brush that could conceal anything bigger than a rabbit) didn't break the illusion of safety.

Halun was swiftly coming to the conclusion that he had been as much a prey to that illusion as anyone else. Young Zorsha's report of the afternoon's observations had been unsettling, to say the least.

"That many?" he asked again, still surprised. "Truly that many of them?"

"That many," Zorsha replied grimly, pushing his hair out of his grey-brown eyes. "Felaras was not exaggerating the danger, I can tell you that. We haven't heard from the Watchers she sent out to try and get a closer view, but from the size of the encampment these nomads are traveling with a population the equal of a small city."

"I never said she was exaggerating, lad," Halun answered, crossing his arms on the table between them and leaning his weight on them. "I just thought she might have been misinformed, or have miscalculated. She was right; I was wrong, and I should have known better than to challenge a Master in her own specialty." He produced a rueful chuckle. "Serves me right, too. Pride begins, a stumble follows."

Zorsha half-smiled, but his deep-set eyes were still shadowed with unvoiced worry. "Kasha thinks we're in even deeper trouble than Felaras has let on. It could be; of the three of us, she talks more openly to Kasha than to Teo or me, but even I can see she hasn't been sleeping much or eating regularly."

"I don't suppose you have any notion of what her plans are, do you?"

He was faintly disappointed when his former novice shook his head. "She's still collecting opinions," Zorsha told him.

There was silence for a moment. Sunlight was beginning to shine in through the window, and it made a square of bright gold on the satiny brown wood of the floor. Halun watched dust-motes dance in the sunbeam until Zorsha spoke again.

"I can tell you about those. Since they seem to fall into categories, she's been having me tally them. About a third of the ones we've gotten so far are variations on the theme of running and hiding. About a third want us to stay where we are and pretend we're invisible. Another third are variations on negotiating with them—"

"Do we have any notion of what we're dealing with?"

"Well, Teo says they're definitely the Clan called 'Running Horse'; that's *Vredai* in their tongue." Zorsha managed the strange name with an ease Halun found enviable. He'd never been much good at speaking languages, although he'd mastered the written version of several. "He says this is a real Clan and not some outlaws, and something he uncovered in the Archives has Felaras a little more hopeful. But whether it's to give us an edge in frightening them off or in talking to them, I don't know."

"My personal choice would be to remove ourselves to one of the two sister-houses," Halun replied, "but I can see the difficulties. The only conceivable way we could get by with it would be to slip in a few at a time; otherwise the Prince of Parda or the Duke of Albirn would forbid any more of us within their borders. Failing that, we *could* pack ourselves up wholesale and try somewhere else, I suppose."

Zorsha sighed and shook his head, and his straw-gold hair tumbled back into his eyes. "I told that to Kasha," he said, raking it out of the way again. "She pointed out that more than half of our members are over forty; a third are over fifty. Can you see yourself making a trek across the mountains, when you've never been outside the Vale since you were a novice?"

Halun was forced to admit young Kasha had a point. "I suppose not. It is altogether galling, but I am afraid I must admit I couldn't make an unassisted trek to the caves, these days. And even with the help of you younger folk—Hladyr bless, but we'd have to devote four of them just to keep Diermud from following a portentous cloud-shape or mist-wisp right off the side of the mountain."

"And he's not the only one," Zorsha agreed. "Halun, at this point leaving is right out of the question. Kasha *has* been out of the Fortress this past month, out on the peaks, and she told me what a trip would be like if we tried to make it—"

"She's been out on the mountains? Why on earth would a woman—"

"She told me it's one of the duties of all the Watchers to take a kind of long-range patrol in rotation even when nothing's threatening us. She's gone out at least twice a moon since she was promoted from novice."

Halun was briefly annoyed at himself for forgetting something so basic; if he intended to take the Master's seat away from Felaras, he should at the least keep in mind that the women of the Watchers were not the sheltered creatures his mother and sisters had been! It would behoove him to keep that factor ever in mind when dealing with his rival.

Zorsha was continuing. "Anyway, the point is that while it's pleasant enough here in Fortress Pass, she says that those thunderstorms we see over the mountains can literally be killers even for the young and fit. For the old, the sickly—it would be suicide."

"It would be folly to think we could hide from these nomads," Halun mused, drumming his fingers on the wood of the table. "If we know about them, they most assuredly have learned of us. And while some of my less worldly colleagues may have forgotten the fact, we are hardly self-sufficient. While our Vale land-folk are hiding in the caves, they are not out planting crops. And if they are not planting, there will be nothing to harvest. I have seldom seen foodstuffs coming to us from the west side of the Pass. . . . "

Zorsha nodded tiredly. "Exactly. That's exactly what Kasha said."

"A bright young woman, is Kasha," Halun said absently, then saw a tiny twinge, almost too insignificant to be called a reaction, pass across Zorsha's thin, bony face at the sound of her name.

Hm? Something odd there, Halun thought. *I think perhaps a change of subject is in order.*

"Zorsha, I hesitate to interfere in your personal life— but I *was* your Master when you were a novice, and I feel a certain—ah—proprietary interest in your life. Is there some trouble between you and Kasha?"

Zorsha flinched a little. "No . . . well, not precisely trouble . . . "

"Something troubling you, then?" Zorsha had been Halun's favorite among all the dozen or so novices he'd trained. The cheerful young orphan passed up from the sister-house in Albirn had quite won his solitary heart, and was the nearest he had to a son. "Would you care to talk about it?"

Zorsha sighed. "You know how long we've been friends, Halun; practically since the first moment I arrived here."

Halun nodded. "The Unholy Trinity, we called you— Zorsha, Kasha, and Teo. We never saw one of you without the other two somewhere about." He shook his head with a reminiscent chuckle. "You children!"

"We aren't children anymore," Zorsha said glumly. "And—I would like to have more from Kasha than to just be a friend. And she's not interested."

"Why?" Halun replied with amazement. "Hladyr bless, I thought every young woman wanted—well—" He coughed. "Well, a marriage and a family, anyway."

"Not Kasha, at least not from me—and the worst part of it is, I have to agree with her reasons." Zorsha looked as forlorn as a lost spaniel puppy. "She says that if she—favored me that way, Teo would be hurt. And if she favored Teo, I'd be hurt. And no matter which of us she favored, we'd never be the same kind of friends again, afterwards. So she isn't going to favor either of us."

Halun was totally dumbfounded. "Hladyr bless. I didn't think there was a young person in the world capable of thinking past his cr—ahem. Past his primal urges. She could be right, you know. At least for now."

"Oh, she is." Zorsha's thin face grew longer. "That doesn't mean I have to *like* it. I know very well that if I knew she and Teo were lovers, I'd—I'd—well, I'd be angry, and pretty hurt. And it would take an awfully long time to get over that hurt. And even if I could, well—they'd always be two, and I'd be on the outside. We'd never be three again. And the same would be true if the positions were reversed for me and Teo, only worse, because Teo would be terribly hurt and try not to show it. He'd probably just sink into his books like Master Diermud and we'd never see him again except at meals. But—" He colored. "—sometimes I can't help but wish he'd fall in love with somebody else, or—have a religious conversion or—or—something—"

Halun nodded sympathetically, and put one paternal hand on the boy's—or rather, young man's—shoulder. *So my Ancas imp is grown up enough to think beyond the moment. I shall have to cease thinking of him as a boy.* "Well, never having been afflicted with your problem, I can't very well advise you. I fear I never was that attracted to anyone, inside or outside the Order. But you have my empathy, if nothing else."

"Thank you." Zorsha smiled wanly. "At least if you'll let me wear your ears down about it, now and again—?"

"Of course."

"Well, that'll help."

"But the cost to you, young man—" Halun wagged an admonishing finger at him "—is that you are going to have to keep me informed. While I can understand Felaras not wanting every bird-brained flitter-head in the Order to go flying off on tangents because of a little bad news, I rather resent that she feels she needn't tell those of us who are level-headed until she's ready for us to hear things."

Zorsha grinned. "Well, I kind of tend to agree with you there. No fear, Master Halun. What I know, you'll know. But right now, I'm afraid I've got brush-cutting detail, so I'd better get to it."

Halun stood up with a scraping of chair legs across the wooden floor to let him out, and thought with some little satisfaction that Felaras hardly reckoned on his having an ear in her camp.

Yes indeed, my dear rival, he thought, shutting the door behind his former pupil, *I know very well you've been getting information on the Seekers from Zorsha. But this time* you *have forgotten something. A window like Zorsha can let you see* out *into the Seekers—but he can also let me see in—to* your *plans. And I just may be able to turn those plans to uses you never imagined.*

Young Vredai riders showed off their horsemanship and high spirits, yipping and catcalling each other as they milled in an eddy of barely controlled chaos with Jegrai in the center. The raiders were all of them Jegrai's age and younger, but tough, and far from inexperienced.

The pity of it was that there weren't any inexperienced fighters over the age of fifteen in the Vredai. Not anymore.

Jegrai raised his fist high over his head, and the

riders reined their mounts in with instantaneous obedience. Quiet hung in the air like the dust they'd stirred up. Now there were only the camp-sounds, the clink of harness, the occasional stamping of an impatient hoof.

Then, when he thought he'd held them long enough—

"Hai *ya!*" Jegrai shouted, bringing his fist down, and digging his heels into his own mount's sides.

The entire party swirled out of the encampment in a tangle of tails and legs and dust, with Jegrai in the lead on his tough little roan gelding.

Jegrai had taken charge of this raiding party himself with two purposes in mind. The first—well, his people required frequent reminders that their Khene was also a warrior. His father had led raiding parties—

—yai-ah, and it was a raiding party that killed him—

But that was a thought Jegrai would not dwell on for long. There had been other reasons for the failure of that raid, and none of them applied here and now. This was a different set of circumstances, and a different sort of raid.

The fact was that the Khene of Vredai had best be prepared to prove himself on a regular basis, and it had again come time for Jegrai to do just that.

The other reason for leading this raid was more personal. Jegrai was hoping, in his deepest heart, that in the excitement of the raid he might forget the spectre of Yuchai moaning in pain and delirium in the Shaman's tent. At least for a time.

But at first there was little to distract him. There was no one and nothing at the first few farms they came upon, only the fields and deserted buildings. It was a good land they rode across, and Jegrai felt a twinge of guilt at driving the land-folk from it. Rich black soil, well watered, but now going to grass and weeds; windbreaks of strange, tall evergreen trees with pungent needles. And all of it deserted, forlorn in the morning sun.

Still, that was hardly surprising; the scouts had been reporting for days that the land-folk were packing up and fleeing—westward somewhere. Some—few—had gone over that far pass guarded by the wizards.

Ah, but the rest had just disappeared, as if the ground of the western mountains ate them, their goods, their livestock. They simply vanished, leaving neither trace nor track. It was a mystery. It was one Jegrai did not care to have solved, particularly. He would just as soon not slaughter defenseless farmers; such a slaughter had no honor in it, and bought Vredai nothing but the possibly dangerous ill will of the land-folk that remained.

And it felt too much like the time the Talchai had ridden through the camp, slaying combatants and non-combatants indiscriminately. Riding down children. No, Jegrai wanted no such stain on his hands.

He shook off the dark thoughts and listened instead to the jokes and jibes of his followers. They rode in sun-gilded high spirits for most of the morning, without seeing a single thing worth stopping for. As morning turned toward noon, they penetrated deeper into the valley—much deeper than any Vredai party had ever passed before. And as they topped a rise, they found themselves riding into the yard of a dwelling-place that bore the unmistakable signs of having been abandoned mere hours ago.

Possessions had been dropped on the roadway, strewn as if kicked out of the way, and discarded by those in too much haste to bend to retrieve them; a thin tendril of smoke still curled up from the chimney of the house.

With the wariness of long habit, the raiders scattered and took cover. But when there were no sounds of life, they crept from shelter and began prowling the abandoned buildings.

They found a few animals still remaining, two nursing sows in their pens and a couple dozen half-feral goats and chickens; the former too large and too protective of their young to move from their styes with any speed, the latter too stubborn and wild to catch. The warriors made fine sport with what they found, slaughtering the pigs to take back to the camp, rounding up the goats, decorating themselves with the strange garments and utensils. One young warrior flung a bright quilt about his shoulders like a motley cape; another topped his helm with a foolish-looking cap, and a third traded his helm for some kind of metal basin. Jegrai sat his horse, aloof from it all, checking for signs of which way the land-folk had fled—until his sharp eyes caught an unmistakable sign on the soft ground of one of the empty pastures.

The print of horse-hooves!

He whooped to get the raiders' attention; they abandoned their foolishness and joined him in following the tracks all the way to the western fence.

One panel of the fence was down; had been *taken* down. "What do you make of this?" he asked Abodai, the best tracker of the lot of them.

Abodai pursed his lips, which made his moustache squirm on his upper lip as if it had a life of its own. "I would say that this was a true herd, mares, foals, and a stallion. I think perhaps the fear of the land-folk spoke to the herd, made them spooky and impossible to catch. This may be what delayed these folk so as to abandon so much. So. It may well be that the herdsman felt that to let the horses free would keep them out of our hands, no? Or it may well be that the herdsman is with them, mounted, driving them before him. And he thinks we cannot catch them."

Jegrai grinned. "Foolish herdsman!" The shiny copper, brass, and silver trinkets, the other booty they had picked out of what had been abandoned, was now cast away. The goats were left in the care of the youngest, least experienced member of the raiding party to be driven back to the Clan. He would lead a foraging party back for the pig carcasses and the rest.

But the remaining members of the raiding party would be going after the booty that truly mattered: the horses. Gold and silver were fine for ornamentation, brass and tin useful, but horses were life itself. So far they had captured only two old mares, both too old to breed, and one half-broken gelding. The young gelding had called up a fire of lust in the heart of every person of the Vredai that had seen him; nearly four hands higher than the sturdy little steppes horses, he was clean-limbed and strong and swift. Jegrai badly wanted a stallion of his kind to breed into his herd, and mares to breed to his stallions. With such tall, swift horses, they might hold even against the Talchai.

"*Hai-ya!*" he cried, giving his gelding his head and urging him with his legs into a gallop. "Let us ride!"

They pounded after the vanished herd, the excitement of the chase building as the trail grew fresher and fresher; they urged their mounts over pastures of lush grass of a thickness and luxuriance that no one of the Clans had seen since before the drought. And their building excitement was such that they hardly noted the rich pasturage except as something to cross. They raced through orchards of tall trees covered in white and pink blossom without a backward glance. All that mattered was the trail, and the quarry at the end of it.

Jegrai was the first to actually see them, so far in the distance and high up on a mountain road that they were little more than moving dots beneath a cloud of dust. He gave a whoop of victory, and the others looked up almost as one to see what he had spotted. Their fierce warcries must have been loud enough to carry up the side of the peak, for the little group of dots sped up a moment later—sure proof that they were being herded.

It was only when they were halfway up on that trail

themselves that Jegrai realized with a shock of dismay just where that unseen herdsman was taking his horses.

This is the wizards' mountain! he thought with a chill, and fought down the urge to rein in his gelding there and then. *Wind Lords—he's heading right for the wizards' pass! If they see us—oh, Wind Lords—what if those are the* wizards' *horses?*

He wanted, with a desperation the like of which he had not felt except when faced with Yuchai's illness, to turn the party back around and give up the chase. But one look at the faces of the others told him that he dared do no such thing. He would lose face before them—and they would go on without him.

And when they all returned to the camp, there might well be a challenge for his rank of Khene. Probably from his half-brother, Iridai.

So he whipped his horse up to the front, and prayed to the Wind Lords that the raiders would be able to overtake the herd before they passed into the wizards' protection.

The Wind Lords were not listening.

The track turned into a trail cut into the very face of the cliff. Their quarry had vanished somewhere up ahead, but the dust of the herd's passing still hung in the air, and the nearness of their goal heated their blood still more. They pounded around a bend in the trail in a cloud of dust and sweat. . . .

Only to pull up in startlement at the sight of what lay across the place where the main road joined the trail they had been following.

They had scarcely a moment to take in the incredible size of the structure before them—larger than anything any of them had ever seen before, even Jegrai, who had been to the Suno Lords' city once as a child. They had just enough time for their hearts to stop dead and start again with the astonishment of it.

There was an eerie whistling that seemed to come from somewhere above—

And Jegrai had a fleeting impression of something large and boulderlike thudding down into the trail before them—

Then the wizards called lightning down upon them out of the clear and cloudless blue sky.

Thunder roared in their ears, flames and dirt sprang up before them; the trail itself was torn and flung into the air in front of their panicked horses, and scarcely ten horse-lengths away.

The horses screamed and fought their bits—but not for long. As one man the raiders let them have their heads, and turned tail and ran for the shelter of the cliff-face they'd just come around. There they did rein their panicked, sweat-sodden beasts in, before they could break legs in their headlong flight. Afraid to move lest the lightning find them, the Vredai cowered under the cliff and looked to Jegrai to get them safely out—

—Jegrai, who had no more notion of what to do than the rest of them did.

"Felaras!"

Teo burst into the Master's study, white-faced and breathless. Kasha dropped the mug of chava she'd been drinking, and the pottery cup shattered unnoticed on the floor.

"Fe—Fe—laras—" Teo panted, clinging to the door-frame. "Zetren's—on the—wall. With the—gunners—"

"*Damn!*" Felaras spat, "that mad dog will ruin everything!" She leapt out of her chair and vaulted over the desk, but Kasha beat her to the door. Kasha sprinted down the dark staircase as fast as she dared, with Felaras right behind.

Gods above—Kasha thought angrily, —*we go to all this trouble of* setting *this trap, risk young Eldon and the horse-herd—if Zetren ruins it for us*—

She hit the entrance to the hallway with enough momentum to have bowled over a dozen tall men, had there been anyone blocking her way. The stone floor was slippery; she skidded, bounced off the wall opposite the staircase, and kept going. Behind her she could hear Felaras making the transition from stairwell to hall with a little more control.

At the end of the hall was the wooden door to the outer yard that lay between the Fortress building and the wall. She hit the door at a dead run, and it slammed against the stone. The sun nearly blinded her, but she didn't stop to give her eyes time to adjust, just ran, scrubbing at her watering eyes, and trusted to memory and habit to put her feet where they should go.

She ran up the stairs to the top of the Fortress wall still half-blinded, just a little ahead of Felaras, hoping Teo's breathless warning hadn't come too late. At the top of the flight of stone steps were three of the six permanent mortars, their Watchers—and Zetren.

As she ran through the gap in the waist-high barrier on their side of the wall, she could see Zetren talking to the gunners. He was facing her, a wall in human form, and his dark eyes glittered like a half-mad bear's. He ignored Kasha's presence entirely. The bloodthirsty glee in his voice could not be concealed, and the Watchers manning the mortars on the wall did not look to Kasha's eyes to be comfortable hearing it. "When they reach the first mark," he said, "touch off the—"

"*What in hell is going on here?*"

Felaras climbed the last of the stairs two at a time, her eyes cold with anger. The Watchers had been uneasy at what lay in Zetren's eyes; they shrank desperately away from the look the Master was wearing. She hadn't worn that look often in her tenure as Master, but out of the half-dozen times she had, twice she'd killed a man with her bare hands. For good reason, admittedly; and she only hastened the sentence that would have been delivered anyway—but none of them had ever forgotten the incidents. Felaras in full wrath was not something any of them faced willingly.

Except Zetren, who feared nothing. He drew himself up to his considerable height and stared down at her.

She ignored him, going straight to the mortars. "What in hell have you got these set for?" she asked, with icy calm.

"Last notch, Master," said old Amberd, the most senior.

"Which plants our little eggs right at the mouth of the trail." She wasn't asking; she knew exactly what that setting meant, as did Kasha. "You know what my instructions were. Reset them the way I ordered."

Zetren gave an inarticulate, angry little growl.

Felaras turned and gave him a long, measuring look—

Then shrugged, and turned her back on him, plainly dismissing him as something of no importance.

Whatever he'd been expecting her to do, it wasn't that. He was left staring impotently at her back as she ordered the mortars reset by two notches so that the explosive shells would land considerably ahead of the mouth of the trail. He went red, then white; clenched his fists as if he would like to strike her. . . .

Then did the unforgivable; made one step toward Felaras' undefended back with his hands coming up.

That was why Kasha was there.

Sweating with fear—for this was the first time she'd ever done this outside of lessoning—she *ill-wished* with all her strength. And got ready to move in case it didn't work, or Zetren was protected.

Her vision narrowed, as if she was looking down a long tube, and things seemed far away and ill-defined, like in a dream. Well, that was fine; that meant she was directing the power correctly. And there was a sharp pain between her eyebrows which meant she was focusing right. . . .

She put every bit of her concentration into it; her entire universe narrowed to one thing. Zetren.

Zetren made another step.

His foot came squarely down on a piece of round shot from the loading of the mortars that *shouldn't* have been there. His foot skidded, flew up and into the air, right out from under him. He flailed, both his arms windmilling wildly for a moment, wearing an expression of such amazement that Kasha almost laughed and broke her concentration.

Then he landed on his back, hitting his head on the stone of the wall and knocking himself unconscious.

Kasha cut off her *wish*.

Sight went back to normal, although she was as tired as if she'd just gone a full ten rounds of hand-to-hand with one of the senior Watchers.

She daren't show it, though; she took a deep breath, steadied her legs, and went to Zetren's side. She studied him for a moment, then knelt and pried open one eyelid.

Perfect. Out like a snuffed candle.

"He tripped over something," she said with feigned innocence, looking over her shoulder at Felaras. "I think he must have hit his head."

Felaras sighed, as if she believed her aide. "Amberd, I think the sun must have gotten to him. Get him on his feet and back to his quarters, will you?"

Amberd snorted, but obeyed. The others sighed with relief and went back to resetting the mortars.

No one seemed to have an inkling as to what had really happened at that moment—which was precisely as both Kasha and Felaras wanted it.

They got the mortars reset just in time; for a few moments later Eldon pounded up the trail driving the weary herd of horses belonging to the Order before him. They poured in through the Market Gate with a sound like distant thunder, streaming sweat that ran in muddy runnels through the dust covering their flanks, and Watchers on the gate slammed and locked it behind them. Now . . . it shouldn't be more than a few moments . . .

Kasha strained her ears and eyes both, but it wasn't until the Watchers below got the weary horses safely away into their stabling for a deserved rest that she heard it—the drumming of more hoofbeats on the herd-trail coming up the mountain.

It seemed to take forever; her heart was pounding in her ears, she clenched her hands on the stone of the parapet before her, and her breath came harsh and panting. Would they turn back? Would they sense the trap?

Then, suddenly, there they were—hauling up short at the sight of the enormous structure that guarded the Pass.

"*Fire!*" Felaras ordered—and the mortars spoke as one.

The trail between the Fortress and the nomads erupted with thunder and flying debris. It was much too far away to do them any harm, but it was virtually guaranteed to make the most hard-headed of horse-nomads believe in wizards with sky-fire magic.

When the dust cleared the nomads were nowhere to be seen.

The horses stood, spent, heads down, exhausted. Sweat collected on their flanks, the sweat of fear as much as of exertion; they slobbered around their bits, and their eyes still showed white around the lids. His raiders said nothing, but there was that same stark fear in their eyes, and pleading. *You are Khene,* said those eyes, white-rimmed in their sun-darkened faces. *Think of some way to get us down off this mountain alive!*

Once his heart stopped racing with fear, Jegrai felt oddly calm. He dismounted, handed his reins to Abodai (whose face was drained nearly bloodless), and walked cautiously up the trail to peer around the side of the escarpment protecting them.

There were three truly enormous holes in the trail.

Whatever those wizards had, it wasn't lightning; it was *worse* than lightning. Lightning didn't leave huge, smoking holes in the earth. Lightning didn't reduce boulders to a pile of fragments and pebbles.

He considered the Fortress, the trail, and the craters in it with a strange calm and detachment. *They could have killed us easily,* he decided after a moment. *They probably could kill us now. If they can do that—there's no reason why they couldn't reach all the way to the camp if they wanted to—*

His heart began racing at that, and he sternly told it to calm itself.

It wasn't listening. It was convinced that if the wizards cared to, they could keep them from ever getting off this damned mountain.

And the worst of it was, Jegrai's head agreed with it.

That had him in a panic, until he turned the thought around and looked at it from the other side. *They could have killed us, and probably still could. So why didn't they?*

That thought seemed to ease the tightness in his chest, the panic that squeezed the breath from his lungs.

Maybe they are *like the Holy One,* he thought in a burst of inspiration. *Maybe that was a warning? Maybe— maybe this is the chance to speak with them—*

He waited for a moment more, to see if lightning was going to strike him down, either from the wizards or the Wind Lords, at the audacious thought.

Nothing happened.

Taking that as a sign, he turned to call the others to him.

*   *   *

"Where in Hladyr's name is Teo?" Felaras growled under her breath, watching the spot where the nomads had hidden with far-seeing glasses. "If these flea-bitten nomads make a move, I need to know what it bloody well means!"

The Fortress sat in a kind of shallow depression split by the Pass; it was screened on the east by rocky outcroppings that rose about half as high as the Fortress walls themselves. The main road ran straight through those outcroppings, but the wilder trail the nomads had followed ran beneath them before joining the road at the point where it crossed the rocks. She could see the barest edge of a head peeking around the side of the boulder-face from time to time, then pulling back quickly. It looked like the same head each time, provided those nomads weren't all wearing identical fur hats.

So they aren't running away—gods, I would give five years off my life to know what they're thinking! Are they staying put because they're afraid I'll blow them to Yazkirn if they move? That's got to be at least part of it, but that wouldn't account for that head that keeps poking around the rocks.

The watcher was getting bolder; he put his head above the rock almost to the chin and kept it there.

"Master?" asked one of the gunners, nervously.

"Stay quiet," she warned. "Let's not startle them."

"But, Master—what if they charge?"

She took the glasses away from her eyes and turned to stare at him incredulously. "Reder, there are maybe two dozen of them. They have bows. No siege engines, no armies. And we just brought magic lightning down on their heads. Would you mind telling me just what you're worried about?"

The Watcher looked sheepish; Felaras remembered now that this man had been one of the few Watchers who had been truly spooked by the presence of the nomads in the Vale below. *Well, he'd better get over*

his fear of barbarians, and fast, she thought to herself.
Because if this works he's going to see a lot of them.

"Sorry, Master," he mumbled, shamefaced. "I guess
I just wasn't thinking."

Felaras snorted, and put the glasses back up to her
eyes. "The gods gave you a head, Reder, and they
didn't intend it only for ornamental use. You might try
using it now and again."

His fellow gunners chuckled; evidently they were a
little tired of Reder's nerves. "Yes, Master Felaras,"
Reder said, unhappily.

"Kasha, would you see what's keeping—"

"He's coming up the stairs," Kasha interrupted.

"And just in time," she growled, trying to fine-focus
the lenses of the far-seeing glasses. "I think we're getting something happening over there. Teo—"

"Wait a minute, Master Felaras." She glanced over
her shoulder to see that Teo had somehow pried the
only other really good far-seer in the Fortress out of the
hands of Diermud; this one was a single tube rather
than the linked pair of tubes Felaras was using. "All
right, I can see him."

The man was making his way out of the cover of the
rocks; he was a bright as a splash of dull scarlet paint
against the dun of the boulders.

"He's got—yes—he's wearing the right sort of hat to
be a leader, Felaras!" Teo said excitedly. "I think he's
either the Clan Chief or the warleader!"

The lonely figure just stood there in the middle of
the road for a long moment, and even this far away
Felaras thought she could read a bowstring-tight tension in his stance.

You do have courage, stranger, she thought wryly. *I
hope you have sense as well.*

"Is he waiting to see if we take another shot at him,
do you think?" she asked the young Archivist at her
right elbow.

"I'd say yes—wait a moment—they're handing him something from behind the rocks—"

That "something" was long and thin, like a spear or lance, but Felaras' glasses weren't good enough to make out any details.

But Teo's tube *was*.

Felaras looked to him for enlightenment, dropping the glasses to hang around her neck.

"Well?" she asked, tightly.

And as the figure raised the stick over his head, and began walking slowly and cautiously—but with evident determination—toward the Fortress, the young man let out a long sigh and took the far-seer glass away from his eye.

"Master Felaras," he said, grinning at her so hard she thought his smile was going to meet at the back of his head. "I think you just got your wish. That's a peace-staff he's carrying. They want to talk."

Chapter Four

"Don't get too excited," Felaras said warningly, watching the envoy with one eye, half afraid he'd vanish if she turned her back. "Just because they want to talk, that doesn't mean we're going to come to any kind of an agreement. But they made the first move; that's hopeful."

She looked to Teokane, and reached up and tapped him on the shoulder when it was obvious that all his attention was still on the nomad. He started a little, and took the far-seer tube away from his eye.

"All right, Teo," she said as calmly as she could. Half of her wanted to run right down onto the road. The other half was looking for hidden traps. "You're the closest thing I have to an expert. How do I answer this truce-staff?"

He frowned, but not with anger; it was only because he was concentrating, Felaras knew him well enough after having him under her eye for the past two years to know that. "You either send somebody else out with a truce-staff, or you go out yourself," he said finally. "The staff is just a spear with the head wrapped. It'll be easy enough for us to make one to match it."

"Which would you do?" she asked him, sensing the

answer might be important. "If you were me, would you go out yourself, or send someone?"

"Are—are you asking me for advice?" he faltered, his eyes widening with alarm. "I'm not—I mean I don't—"

She restrained herself from sighing with exasperation. "Yes, Teo, I am asking you for advice. You know more than I do about these people. You can make an informed judgement; I can't. Should I go myself, or send a proxy?"

He gulped, but finally gathered his scattered wits and answered her. "I—I think that's their leader out there. It would show that you consider us to be very much their superior to send a proxy. They put a very high value on 'face,' and while that might be a good thing in the short run, in the long run it could make for resentment."

She nodded. He hadn't answered her question, but he'd given her the information she needed to answer it herself. "All right. How do I go about showing that I'm the Master here, that I'm the equivalent of their Clan Chief?"

He shook his head. "I don't know, Felaras. Clan Chiefs usually have those foxtails on the sides of their hats, but you don't have a hat, and I don't know where we could find a pair of foxtails. . . . " He faltered, and she kept the sharp rebuke she wanted to give him behind her teeth. More and more she was coming to the conclusion that her choice between the two candidates was correct. Teo was crumbling under the first real pressures the Order had seen. Now if Zorsha responded positively under pressure . . .

Teo finally finished his statement. "I guess—I guess you'll just have to tell them and hope they believe it. They speak Trade-tongue; at least, that's what the chronicles said."

She thought about the risks for a moment, rubbing her aching head with her hand. *This could be a trick, a trap. On the other hand, if I move now, before anyone knows what's going on, I can get the Order so firmly on the road I want that my rivals—like Zetren—won't be able to fight me as effectively.* She looked out over the wall to the road, white in the bright sunlight, and the dull scarlet figure standing patiently halfway up it. *Gods, what am I worried about? I'll be within bowshot of the walls!*

Then she thought of the converse. *Gods. I'll also be within bowshot of his people.*

The sunlight seemed weak, and a chill went up her back.

Oh, hell. There's no living without taking chances. Time to trust to luck-wishing and take one.

"Kasha, go open the night-gate," she said abruptly. "I'm going out."

The terrible, bloodthirsty nomad came as something of a surprise.

He's so young! Great good gods—if this is their leader, their warriors must be babes in arms.

Felaras studied the young man standing rigidly before her, every fiber of him projecting dignity and a fierce pride. Thin, dust-covered, and shabby. Frightened, but that wouldn't be evident to anyone who didn't have her long years of experience at reading the tell-tale signals people's bodies showed. Not inexperienced, one could bet on it, but still very young, perhaps all of twenty or so. That was a very tender age to be a Clan Chief. Quietly handsome, in an intriguingly exotic way, with his almond-shaped eyes and dusky gold complexion. Beneath that round fur hat with fox-tails falling on either side of his face, he wore his straight black hair very short, which wasn't surprising in a warrior; she wore her own nearly that short for the same reason.

He was dusty, yes, but not dirty. He didn't smell of

anything worse than clean sweat and horse. *Points for his people; anybody who reckons being clean is important is a leg up on civilization. Bet they don't lose many people to disease.*

She grounded the butt of her truce-staff on the road at her feet, feeling very much aware that they were both within bowshot of the opposition. "I'm Master Felaras," she said in Trade-talk. "I'm the leader of the wizards, something like a Clan Chief. You have something to say to us?"

The slight twitching of one black eyebrow was all the reaction he showed. Her words had surprised him. She couldn't tell if that indicated surprise that she was the leader and not a proxy sent out to meet him, or surprise that the leader was a woman.

"I, Jegrai am. Khene Vredai. Master for Vredai." He regarded her for a few moments, scarcely blinking. "You, killed us could have," he replied slowly and carefully, enunciating each syllable exactly.

Was that a question?

He seemed to be waiting for a reply.

"Yes," she said shortly.

"You, killed us not."

"Yes."

"Why?"

She shrugged. "Dead men cannot speak." She paused. He waited patiently for more, his face as calm as a stone, his posture outwardly arrogant. "We want to know why you come here, why you raid our land-folk."

His turn to shrug. "Need. Food, grass. Both there, we need, we take."

"Take any more and we will grow angry," she growled. "Take more, and we will not be patient."

His eyes widened just a trifle, and he covered a flinch, but said, "Many are we. Strong in warriors are we."

Felaras snorted. "We have the lightnings to answer our call."

He remained silent.

"There may be," she said slowly, "another way."

While he pondered this, she considered him a bit more carefully. There was a charisma, a power about this young man that made you forget his relative youth and the shabby and threadbare state of his clothing. As a fighter herself, she could evaluate the implied ability in the way he moved and stood; balanced and controlled, very like a powerful predator at rest.

It's a damned pity I'm not thirty years younger, she thought wryly. *I'd see what else he can do besides fight. . . .*

"There other Clans are," he said abruptly. "There is—there is no rain in Clan country many summers. We look here, for grass. Maybe others grow hungered, maybe they come, look here."

"*We* have the lightning," she reminded him.

He took a deep breath, and braced himself. "Then why not you call lightning when Vredai on east pass? Why not call lightning when Vredai take from land-folk?" He scowled, and Felaras stifled a smile.

Very good, young man, she thought. *My bluff is called—maybe.* "Dead men," she repeated, "cannot speak." *Time to drop the hot rock in his lap.* "We seek new knowledge above all else. You come from the East, a place new to us. We do not kill what we do not understand."

"You—" There was something like wild hope in his eyes for an instant before he shuttered them. "—You seek new learning? You heal too?"

"Sometimes. When we can. So?" she said, raising one eyebrow and attempting to look as if his answer was of complete indifference to her.

"Maybe we keep other Clans out of valley?" he

offered, tentatively. "Strong Vredai warriors be good to guard."

"Maybe," she answered, trying not to show her elation. "The lightning is not to be wasted on foolishness. Maybe we could have a bargain? Trade grazing for learning and use of your warriors. Such a trade would save us tedious work."

He pulled himself up higher. "You call not lightning, we raid not valley? We meet three days? Have trade-talk? Trade learning, maybe? Speak treaty?"

She nodded slowly, after pretending to think about it. "You move your Clan here—to the bottom of the road. Where we can watch you." *Which should make you think twice if you aren't serious.*

His eyes widened again and he swallowed once before he replied. It took him a moment to recover his arrogance. "We move," he agreed reluctantly, and not at all happily.

"Three days," she reminded him. "Here."

He nodded again. "Three days."

Her back itched all the way back to the gates, just waiting for an arrow to come winging out of the rocks, and it didn't stop until she was safely back inside.

She leaned against the closed gate and breathed her first easy breath in days—and, she suspected, her last.

Then her knees went to water as she realized just how easily she could have been assassinated down there; how simple it would have been for those horse-nomads to have taken her prisoner. All she'd had to go on was the assurances of Teo that this "truce-staff" of theirs was sacrosanct, and the hope that they were too frightened of her wizard's power to try anything so close to the walls of the Fortress.

Hindsight-nerves. Damn, thought I was over that. Guess not. Now I'll wake up in a cold sweat for the next three nights.

So she just braced herself against the rough stone

wall, feeling every bump and raspy spot on the skin of her back through the cloth of her tunic; closed her eyes, and shook from hair to toenails.

All three of the "Unholy Trinity" came clattering down the stairs leading to the top of the wall within moments of the closing of the gate. She opened her eyes as they surrounded her. She expected an avalanche of questions, but they kept silent, and kept everyone else at a distance. Kasha's idea, she suspected. When she was over her shakes, she got hold of herself and looked over that blessed barrier of protective shoulders at the double handful of curious and apprehensive Watchers and Seekers that had gathered, not even really noting the varying expressions they wore.

"Pass the word," she said briefly. "Convocation tonight at sunset. The nomads gave us a three-day truce, and they want to talk about a permanent truce and maybe an alliance. I'll tell you all everything then. Meanwhile you've all got things to do. Go do them."

The small crowd did not immediately disperse—and it was Zorsha who drew himself up to look much larger than he really was, took on an air of authority, and growled, "You heard the Master's orders. Let's see some backs!"

Felaras blinked in surprise at his sudden show of strength, but didn't have much time to think about what he'd done; Kasha gave her a gentle shove and she headed for the sanctuary of her study, where she could think.

"Here," Kasha shoved a mug of chava into her hand and pushed her down into her chair. "What happened out there?"

"Truce, at least temporary, like I said." She looked from one to another of her favorites. Kasha had perched herself on the side of the desk, Zorsha had the chair, and Teo was draped over the back of the chair above

Zorsha's head. "That man I spoke with—Teo, what's a Khene?"

"Clan Chief," he said, and grinned shyly. "So I was right?" His blocky face brightened when she nodded yes.

"There's something going on with them, but damned if I know what," she continued, after a mouthful of cold, sweetened chava. "He admitted to part of what drove them here—a multi-year drought—but from what I was reading, that's just the bare beginning of the truth."

"Why?" Zorsha asked sharply. "I mean, I hope you're relying on something more than instinct. I'd like to know what. Forgive me for stating the obvious, but you can't afford to be wrong on this."

From the dumbfounded looks on Teo and Kasha's faces, they hadn't expected that speech from Zorsha any more than Felaras had.

She was startled, but pleased—because this sounded exactly like the kind of questions she used to confront *her* Master with. It was beginning to look like her choice of Zorsha as her successor was the right one. Since this mess began, Teo was faltering every time she asked him to assert himself. Zorsha was rising to the challenge of the situation, or so it was beginning to look.

"Well, I'm a good deal older than this Jegrai—he's about your age, Zorsha—and while he may be very good at hiding the fact that he's not telling the whole truth from people his own age, he hasn't had my experience in prying information out of what *isn't* said. I've been dealing with the Order and with envoys for a good few years now. And think about it—it's me who deals with the Traders, and a more close-mouthed lot you're never going to find. I end up reading more off them than they ever tell me."

Teo chuckled, and even Kasha smiled, but Zorsha still looked worried.

Felaras decided to elaborate, to tell him how she was reading those she faced. "I asked him why they came. He mentioned the drought, then looked briefly away. Then he said, a little too casually, that other Clans may look westward for grazing lands. Now that's probably all true; but if they needed grazing land so badly, where's their other herds? All they've got with them are the horses. Teo? What should they have?"

He frowned in thought, and his heavy eyebrows came together to form a solid bar across his forehead. Now that it was just the four of them, he seemed to have regained his confidence. "They should have goats, sheep," he said, finally. "Or maybe—the chronicles talk about some other kind of animal, called a *yaeka*. There was a sketch, but it's hard to describe. I suppose a hairy sort of cow is the closest I could come. Something like an aurochs. Those should have been able to keep up with horse-herds, unless they were really forcing the pace."

"And all any of my scouts saw was horses," Felaras persisted. "All of the tents were very small, none of the big ones Teo's chronicles described. What does that tell you, Seeker?"

It was Zorsha's turn to wrinkle his brow in thought. "Well, my first guess would be that maybe they didn't come this direction voluntarily. They ended up leaving behind everything that slowed them down. They were driven? Maybe by a bigger Clan?"

"That would be my guess," she said, settling back into her chair, and very pleased that a non-Watcher had deduced the same conclusion she'd come to. It was even more gratifying that her choice of successor had done so as quickly as he had. It meant that he was able to see things as a Watcher would. "Now, unless I misread him, he also made a genuine offer of alliance against the poaching of other Clans. Which would do what?"

"Confirm your guess," Zorsha replied positively, looking much less worried. "So what did you tell him?"

"That we'd have formal talks in three days—and that I wanted his whole Clan to move to the bottom of the mountain, where we could keep an eye on them."

"And he agreed?" At her nod, he raised an eyebrow. "Great good gods, he has to be thinking he's moving them within *our* striking distance. Sounds to me like he's serious."

"I think so. I also think we could do worse than have an alliance with these nomads. If nothing else, I suspect they have a fair amount they could teach us. And there's a lot more advantages—and I'd like you to see if you can come up with some on your own, because I'm going to count on your bright young minds during this Convocation tonight. Because now that you've seen what I've seen, and concluded we ought to talk with these nomads, the really hard part is going to begin." She grinned crookedly. "And that is to convince your fellows of the Order that we're right."

This was the first time she'd ever held a Convocation after sunset. If anything, it was less pleasant. By night the hall felt even more like a bowl than by day. The only strong lights were lanterns placed in a little circle around the podium. Felaras could see nothing of the others with her eyes so dazzled by the light—although they could see every move she made. And she was uncomfortably aware that, despite the babble of voices all around her, she was the focus of all eyes. When she held up her hand for silence and got it, immediately, it only confirmed her feeling.

"All right," she said into the darkness, wishing she could see the faces of those that surrounded her, instead of nothing but vague shapes that didn't even tell her what sex they were, much less their identity. "The nomads have found us. We showed them what we can do. I arranged a three-day truce with them, and got them to move down to the bottom of the mountain where we can keep a tight eye on them. You all know that—now I want to hear what you think of it."

The babble began again, and began rising toward an uncontrolled roar until she silenced them with a grimace and a wave of her hand. "Ladies and gentlemen, you aren't children in the schoolyard! Let's have some order here! Thaydore—what's your say?"

From out of the dark to her right came Thaydore's soft reply—which she could have recited with him, word for word. She knew what he would say, and so did just about everyone else in the Order. She'd called on him just so as to have a place to start, and to let the others begin choosing their own words.

"Our knowledge must be used to serve all mankind," he said, with as much force as Thaydore ever said anything. "That means East as well as West, horse-nomads as well as those who dwell in Ancas or Yazkirn. We must open our gates and our books to these folk, and teach them—"

"The Order has nó place in the material world!" shrilled a female Felaras couldn't identify (though she suspected Archivist Brendis, a signs-and-portents type). "The material world must not pass—"

Someone else interrupted her, a male voice, but trembling and high; it sounded like Regas, but in the dark she couldn't be sure. "Exactly! There are some things 'all mankind' isn't ready to know! And it's our job to keep those things secret! We have no responsibility to teach anyone anything! Our purpose is to preserve and protect, not hand knowledge over to people who would only misuse it!"

Kitri flared up at that, her aged but strong, sharp voice carrying over the objections that followed that rather insular statement. "And just who's to decide when mankind is ready, hm? *You?* Great good gods, man, that makes you worse than those meaching priests back in Targheiden! Who the hell do you think you are? Hladyr's avatar?"

"A damned sight more sensible than you are, Kitri," growled one of the Seekers—and that deep bass could only belong to Jezeran. "Hladyr bless, what do you want us to do, hand out the formula for Sabirn-fire so these barbarians can burn down whole towns instead of just farmsteads? Shall we give them the knowledge of explosive powder too? Just imagine what they could do with that! What we know should be given to people worthy to have it, civilized people, people we know and can predict, the people of Ancas, of Yazkirn—not to a pack of unwashed, unlettered barbarians!"

Kitri's voice cut across the other objections—raised by those who did not happen to have been blessed with birth in either of those two lands. "People just like us, is that it?" Her voice dripped venom. "What noble, self-sacrificing sentiments! I suppose that's exactly what Duran should have thought. After all, everyone *knew* those Sabirn were worthless thieves and charlatans!" She laughed angrily. "And *of course* we all know that the gods check a person's pedigree before they assign him his eternal reward. We all know that only the worthy get the privilege of Ancas blood!"

Oh, that's *set the cat in the dove-cote*, Felaras thought, doing her best to conceal her amusement. It didn't help that Jezeran was almost pure Ancas and tended to flaunt the fact. Anybody who'd ever been snubbed by him had a chance to give him a piece of their mind at this moment, and there didn't seem to be anybody who wanted to pass that chance up. *If this situation wasn't so serious, I'd be willing to let this go on all night!*

She debated whether to exert her authority and break the argument up—but Zetren beat her to it.

"Fools!" he roared, like a spring-hungry bear. Silence fell, heavy and sudden. "You're damned fools, all of you! What do we owe any of those decadent bastards back there? Have any of them come to our aid? No!"

There was a certain grumbling of agreement from those who remembered the last Convocation, and Felaras' statement that she had asked for aid and gotten none.

"We should give these barbarians what they want," Zetren continued. "Open the Pass to them, let them through! We've been quiet long enough—it's time we took our own back, by the gods! These nomads can be our tool. We can let them through to overrun everything west of the Pass, let them wear themselves to nothing against Ancas, let Ancas bleed itself white against them. Then let us follow in and pick up the pieces of both sides, and become the power we were always meant to be!"

The absolute silence that followed that made Felaras' heart stop. *My great gods—they can't really believe that, can they? Oh gods—please, they can't agree with that—*

Then the storm of objections rose, even more cacophonous than the one following Jezeran's outrageous statements, and Felaras' faith in the good sense of her fellows was restored. And her heart started again.

Finally everyone seemed to shout themselves out. Felaras waited, hoping for someone, perhaps one of her three, to say what she dared not—that they should treat with the nomads as allies. It couldn't come from her; but it was a logical notion—and, strangely enough, something similar to Zetren's far more radical idea.

"You know, friends," Zorsha said quietly into the muttering, "despite the fact that Ancas and Yazkirn both claim this area, neither one rules here."

"Aye," replied Amberd, sounding thoughtful. "If anybody rules here, it's us. Quiet-like. The Vale folk come to *us* for judgements and the like, they look to us for protection."

"So why don't we make the reality official?" Zorsha asked. "Why don't we simply declare this area to be independent of both lands?"

"Because we haven't got a bloody army to back that claim up, young fool!" Watcher Kirnal snarled.

"Don't we?" Zorsha asked mildly. "Just what is it that's going to be camping below the Pass for the next three days? As motley as it seems to be, it's still an army, and a big enough one to have *us* shaking in our boots."

The silence was profound enough that Felaras could hear every member of the Order breathing. Or rather, could hear the ones breathing who weren't already holding their breath in startlement.

And Zorsha followed up on his advantage just as neatly as Felaras would have. "Ladies, gentlemen, we can ally with this Jegrai—we can use him. Yes, we can teach him and his people, but we can also use him. Set him up as the ruler of the Vale—gods know he's already in the position of ruler, he's Chief over as many people as live in the Vale and Fortress combined! So, let *him* protect the Vale—but under guidance! Give him the throne, but let us be the power behind it! And in that way, the Order remains out of the public eye, as it should be—but we also exercise a beneficial influence, as we must if we are going to remain true to Duran's plan!"

Good lad! Felaras thought with elation, as discussion— not argument—broke out all over the halls. *He's hit them* exactly *in the right place! Enough altruism to make Kitri and Thaydore happy, enough self-interest to wake up our baser selves—* As the babble increased, she thought, a little wryly, *I greatly fear he's better at it than I am!*

The discussion raged while the time-candle burned

down, but it was fairly well evident that the majority of the members favored Zorsha's proposal, for whatever reason.

Finally Felaras called them all to order again, when voices were growing hoarse and tempers growing thin, and bodies were crying for sleep.

"I'll call for a voice vote, since I can't bloody see to count your arms. All in favor of a treaty of alliance and a delegation to this nomad—"

The roar of "aye" shook the podium.

"Opposed?"

A thin but determined chorus of "nay"—the isolationist party was clearly outnumbered, but also obviously not shaken in their convictions.

"All right, let's get the formalities over. I'll conduct the initial treaty-making and leave a presence with this Jegrai to act as primary information-sources and go-betweens. Anyone have any objection to a delegation of—let's say, four? One Watcher, one Archivist; and two Seekers, one Hand and one Flame. Any nays?"

A little discussion, from the muttering out in the darkness; no objections.

Felaras sighed with relief. "All right; the Convocation is ended. Towerleader, Bookleader, Swordleader, meet with me after you get some sleep and some breakfast. Swordleader, you might send a scout out to the caves; tell the land-folk it looks like it's going to be safe for the next three days, and that we may have a permanent treaty with this lot after that."

"Master?" The voice was young; probably one of the novices. It shook a little. "Master, how are you going to pick who goes?"

"No novices, I promise that. Probably four folk with an equal mix of youth and experience. And we won't send anyone who doesn't want to go. If, on the other hand, you'd like to volunteer, tell your Leader. I'd rather have volunteers, if it comes to that." She looked out into the dark, hearing people already moving carefully along the benches, eager for their beds. "Any more questions? No? Then good night to all of you."

Kitri was the last to arrive, and Felaras closed the door of the study after her, thinking, *Thank you, oh gods, for Leaders I can work with*.

The study was a little crowded with eight people in it, and a bit stuffy; the group included Felaras and the Trinity, of course (as her personal aides they were privy to everything and very good at being invisible when the time came), and the three chapter Leaders.

"Kasha, open the window, would you?" she asked, as the three Leaders arranged themselves around the hastily brought-in table. The desk was shoved up against the back wall, the room's two chairs on either side of it. Kasha threaded her way through the furniture to obey the request, then returned to the rear of the room for further orders.

Kitri led the Archivists; Diermud had held that position when Felaras had first taken the Master's seat, but he'd thrown it gratefully into Kitri's lap when Felaras had hinted that it might be better for someone with more aptitude and inclination for worldly matters to have the Leader's badge. (Kitri's reaction had been hilarious. "Well," she'd said when Felaras handed her the badge of the open Book and the key to the Leader's study, "I appreciate the honor, but I thought we'd outlawed slavery here. . . .")

She was tall—taller than any man in the Order saving only Zetren. She was so thin that she kept a fire going in her study most of the year, for she felt the cold badly. She had large, spidery hands that could copy a text, make an inkbrush, or play a zither with equal dexterity. Her long grey hair would hang down below her knees if she let it; generally she kept it piled up on the top of her head in an untidy bird's-nest of a knot,

stuck together with hairpins that she shed so constantly
that one of the duties of her novices was to collect them
and give them back to her at day's end. Deceptively
mild hazel eyes were partially hidden by a contraption
of wire and glass lenses—something Lisan of the Seekers had made to correct her failing eyesight—an inven-
tion so successful that a number of other members of
the Order sported them now, and not just the older
ones. She wore a long, loose tunic belted at the waist
over breeches, both faded blue in color; clothing nearly
identical in color and cut to every other piece in her
wardrobe. One of Kitri's idiosyncracies was that she
searched until she found something she liked, and there-
eafter never altered it. This was a trait that endeared
her to her novices, since it meant that they always
knew what she would want and when she would want it.

Unlike Thaydore, sitting next to her—who never really
knew exactly what he wanted when it came to his own
needs. On the other hand, he would be satisfied by
inexactitude in anything except his work, so it didn't
matter to him if the fruit juice was warm, the soup cold,
and his robe too short in the sleeves. He spoke for the
Tower, the Seekers; and was himself a Flame rather
than a Hand like Halun. He was nowhere near as old,
nor as crazed, as he looked. His wildly untamed shock
of hair had gone pure white in his twenties, and the
vague, slightly demented look in his eyes was due more
to preoccupation than anything else. He was supremely
indifferent to his own physical surroundings, as witness
his out-at-the-elbows, ink-stained robe, but he was implacable when it came to creating the best possible
environment for the scholars under his authority. And
there was one thing on which he and Kitri were in
complete agreement—that the purpose of the Order
was both discovery and education.

The one way in which they differed was on the point
that Thaydore would assume without ever really think-

ing about it that those who wished to be educated would come to *him*. Kitri, on the other hand, was perfectly willing to load up a horse with books and go crusading for pupils.

And probably coerce them into learning whether they liked it or not, Felaras thought wryly, casting a glance over to her.

But these two would be getting exactly what they wanted out of a treaty with the Vredai. Given that, they'd let Felaras have about anything else *she* wanted.

The final chapter Leader, Ardun of the Sword, was an old friend, and had been one of Felaras' first novices when she'd reached full Watcher status. Bald as an egg, short, and bandy-legged; he was, nevertheless, a man not even Zetren would willingly go against. He was the acknowledged expert in more forms of combat than Felaras cared to think about, for not only did the Order gather recruits from every corner of the civilized world, but one of the duties of the Sword was to actively seek out and master new martial arts. Most importantly, he was one of the *calmest* people she knew. This could be an asset in any meeting where Kitri was involved.

"All right, friends," Felaras said, when everyone had been seated around the table she'd set up, after cups of chava had been handed round by her aides. This done, the Trinity had settled unobtrusively on or around the desk at the back of the room. "Do we want to talk about the treaty first, or the delegation?"

"Let's get the delegation out of the way," Kitri replied, a hairpin clattering to the tabletop as she reached for her cup. "That's the easiest. I'd like your young Teo on it for Archivist; that gives you *and* me a direct eye on the proceedings, and he asked me last night if he thought you'd let him volunteer."

"Did he, now?" Felaras looked over her shoulder, and Teo blushed. "I have no objections at all, seeing as he's the closest we have to a knowledgeable authority on these people. Thaydore, do you have anyone in mind for Seekers?"

Thaydore coughed, and looked a little embarrassed. "Well . . . yes. And I hope you won't think I'm suggesting him because he's troublesome—"

"Great good gods—you mean *Halun* volunteered?" Ardun exclaimed, eyes widening with unconcealed glee. "How amazing!"

"Well . . . yes."

"Nice balance," Felaras observed, making no effort to conceal her cheer. "Teo for youth, Halun for experience —I'd say fine, personally."

Kitri spread her hands wide. "No objections here. How about for the Flame side of the Tower?"

"I thought Eriel? I admit she's rather—uh—mystical—"

Thaydore's expression as he pronounced that last word was something between exasperation and extreme distaste. Eriel's star-charts were miracles of exactitude, for which she had Thaydore's admiration, mathematician to mathematician. The trouble lay in her attempts to calculate formulae that would enable her to contact the "spiritual entities" she was certain were guiding the stars on their appointed tracks. No amount of gazing through Lisan's finest far-seeing tubes would convince her that she was viewing anything other than a kind of festival lantern held in the hand of one of these invisible creatures.

On the other hand, if Eriel had volunteered, it would satisfy the "signs-and-portents" faction, and might give her a much-needed dose of medicinal reality.

"Ardun?" Felaras asked.

He shrugged. "Better than some—and puts a female in the mix. I can't think of anybody I'd suggest as an alternative."

"Kitri?"

"No common sense, but I'd trust Teo to keep her out of trouble."

"All right, Eriel's in. Ardun, who for Sword?"

He grinned crookedly. "I know who I'd *like*—but she hasn't volunteered, and—" He craned his head around and grinned at Kasha, who began glowering, though she didn't seem inclined to say anything. "—don't get your hackles up, Sparrowhawk!—I was about to say that the Master needs you too much."

"That I do, and I'll not part with her. So who?"

"Remember a woman named Mai? Scouts, mostly."

"I think so; not pretty, not plain, sort of a face-shaped face. Very quiet. Very good at being a piece of the landscape."

"Or of the furniture. Aye, that's the one; she thought that talent of hers at being unnoticed might come in handy, and she's been one of the scouts out shadowing these folk. She's curious as hell about them, wants to see them up close. Sounded good to me, and I trust her."

"And as a scout she has to have a good memory," Kitri mused. "Sounds to me like a very good choice."

Thaydore nodded.

"Well, that's it, then. Halun, Teo, Mai and Eriel. Next business: what Jegrai is likely to want and what we're willing to trade him."

"Felaras, what trouble can he give *us?*" Thaydore wanted to know. "Granted, he knows where we are now, and I'm certain he saw a great deal he'd like to have in *his* hands, but he can hardly take it by force—"

"The boy may be young," Felaras said slowly, "but he isn't dense. He's going to be thinking about the positioning of this Fortress—he's going to realize eventually that the reason we didn't hit him with the fire-throwers is because we *couldn't*—and he's also going to realize that even wizards have to eat. He could make life very unpleasant for us if he wanted to, and I'm relatively certain he'll have figured this out by the time we meet with him to talk this treaty."

Thaydore chewed on his lower lip for a moment, then nodded, slowly. "So what are we likely to have that we want to put in his hands? Idealism aside, I really would not want to put the secret of the explosives in the hands of a nomad we know nothing about. Later, perhaps—but not at this bargaining session."

"Maps," said Ardun succinctly, and two of the other three heads at the table swiveled to look at him in surprise. "My bet is that if he has maps, they're the ones he got off traders; inaccurate, not terribly detailed, not reliable—traders are *known* for putting mistakes in their maps. Certainly not reliable for a military campaign, which, if he was chased here, he may be planning on facing. And I would bet that every 'map' of the territory he's come through is in his head, not on paper. Whereas we know every gopher hole from here to Targheiden, and halfway into Azgun."

"Good. I can think of things he likely doesn't have that could be useful; springs, ballistics, western forging and smelting technique, the transverse cog." She thought back to her brief confrontation with Jegrai. "He asked if we did healing, and his face lit up for a minute when I said yes. There's things under that category I think both sides of this negotiation would like to see."

"There's a great deal he could probably offer us—" Kitri said slowly, drawing little pictures on the table-top with her fingertip.

"Oh, agreed. I'd like to be able to stop importing all our wine, for one, and I'll bet he doesn't have a blamed Vintner's Guild keeping wine-making a secret! We've got some medicines and techniques I'm sure he would want badly if he knew about them—and I'd bet it's going to be vice versa."

"About explosives—should we even let him know it isn't magic?" Ardun asked.

"Morally I'm against *not* giving it to him," Thaydore said doubtfully, "but practically speaking—great good gods, I wouldn't put a loaded fire-thrower in the hands of a novice—"

"But keeping him from that information is perilous close to betraying our whole philosophy," Kitri snapped. "Certainly, letting him think it's magic *is* a betrayal of that philosophy!"

"Steady on, Kitri," Ardun replied calmly. "Nobody's suggesting any such thing. At least not in the long run. We're only talking short run here."

Kitri took a deep breath and subsided, nodding a reluctant agreement.

"The question may be out of our hands," Felaras said with equal reluctance. "I told you, my impression is of a very sharp young man. As he keeps the peace over the next few weeks, the land-folk may well come in and talk to him. He'll find out sooner or later that it isn't magic. I think the question is going to be how long we can hold out against his desire for it."

"As long as he doesn't *need* it. . . . " Kitri said slowly.

"Good point," Felaras replied, relieved. "We can always claim our gods would be very angry at us if we gave the secret away when there was no need to use it. Good; that should stall him until we think he's ready for it. Now, think hard; we should be making some demands too—in fact, a lot of them, or he's going to reckon us for weaklings. What do we ask for?"

"You mentioned wine-making. All that herb lore and medicinal lore," Kitri responded. "I know Vider will want that."

"These people are experts in making things portable," Thaydore put in. "We may need that knowledge some day again, and it's beyond price."

"Their entire martial tradition. I *want* that, Felaras," Ardun's face was determined. "Their tactics alone—under the right circumstances, those strike-and-run maneuvers with horse-archers could be absolutely devastating! Can you imagine them up against an Ancas shield-wall? And weapons construction. The scouts say those little bows of theirs are powerful out of all proportion to their size—"

"Enough, Ardun—you're preaching to the converted," Felaras said with a laugh.

"What Zorsha said last night," Kitri began after a moment of silence. "Was that something of what you had in mind?"

"You mean about giving this boy something more than a set of specifics? Really educating him, making him into the kind of enlightened ruler we've all prayed for and never yet seen?"

Kitri nodded, and sipped at her cooling chava.

"Some. Some was his. I stand behind it all. I think it's a damned good idea, and I'd like to see us try it; I think this young man may be bright enough to think for himself, but willing to learn from us. This is going to sound like heresy, I know, but we don't have to remain bound by Duran's strictures—we can change, we can evolve. There is no reason why we couldn't become the guiding hand behind the throne—"

"That's dangerous—" Thaydore said, unexpectedly. "That's a temptation to control—I don't know, it's perilous, perilous. One could have absolute control there, and isn't that why we divided the rule among all three chapters of the Order in the first place? To avoid absolute control?"

"I haven't worked it all out yet, Thaydore," she admitted. "I truly haven't. This is something that is going to take a great deal of thought, never doubt that I hadn't realized this. The decisions we make on it are going to involve all four of us. I can't and I *won't* make decisions that will bind the whole Order all by myself."

All three of the Leaders nodded—Ardun with a wry smile, Kitri and Thaydore with relief.

"All right, then, let's deal with the immediate future," she said briskly. "Teo, get your materials out."

She raised her eyebrows at them. "Let's get exactly what we want, and exactly what we're prepared to lay on the table, down in writing. So there won't be any questions by anyone."

Least of all, she thought wryly, *from Halun*.

Chapter Five

Jegrai was dazed; at his easy escape out of the hands
of the wizards, at the near-miracle of a truce, at the
thought that the wizards might, indeed, be of the same
brotherhood as the Holy Vedani, and therefore to be
trusted as he had trusted no one but his four councilors
since he had become Khene.

Dead men cannot speak, the strange old woman had
said. And *We seek knowledge.*

He hoped, and feared to hope. He feared and wondered if his fear was valid or foolish. He scarcely knew
where he was going as he walked away from the woman,
only realized after several moments that he was back
among his riders and they were besieging him with
questions.

He cut their babble short. "We have sworn truce for
three days," he said curtly, handing the truce-staff back
to Abodai and mounting his spent gelding. "After that
we talk greater truce. Perhaps more; it may be that
these folk are of the same brotherhood as the Holy
Vedani. All that is for myself and my advisors to
decide."

"And the cost to us?" Abodai asked shrewdly.

He looked over his shoulder at the tracker, the oldest man in the party. Was that a challenge?

No, he decided. It was just Abodai, who had to know the track he was set on. "No raids during truce-time," he told them, looking from one fearful face to another. "And—we move the Clan."

They clamored to know to where.

And when he told them, their faces went as white as when the wizards had thrown the lightning at them.

It took them most of the afternoon to bring their tired mounts to the camp, and the wizard's mountain stood black against a bloody sunset when they finally reached that haven.

Jegrai had a great deal of time to think about what had happened during that slow progress. It occurred to him that the Vredai stood on the brink of either disaster or tremendous change. And *he* was Khene; ultimately it was up to him to lead them, whichever the outcome.

Wind Lords, he thought, cold in his gut as he looked back over his shoulder at the looming mass of the wizard's mountain. *I don't want this. I wasn't afraid of death at the hands of Khene Sen—but I fear those wizards, I fear that strong old woman and her lightning. And yet—my heart tells me they can be trusted. Fear. Trust. Which path, Wind Lords?*

But as he came to think about it, he began to wonder why the wizards hadn't used that lightning before this time. And the more he thought about it, the stranger it seemed. Until gradually a thought began to creep in—

Could it be they hadn't used it—because they *couldn't?*

Could it be that their weaponry had its limitations, even as the most powerful of bows had its range? Could that be why they had insisted on the Vredai moving to the base of their mountain?

And could it be—could it possibly be—that they had not slain the raiding party out of hand because the Vredai had something they wanted?

But what?

Information; knowledge, perhaps?

Or even, as the old woman had said, the strength of the Vredai fighters?

Could it be that these truce-talks would not be so one-sided as they first appeared?

And could Jegrai even begin to hold his own in such talks against a canny, clever old wizard-woman?

The prospect of trying to do so was nearly as frightening as his first impression of godlike powers.

When they reached the camp in the crimson sunset, Jegrai sat in his saddle and stared at the wizard's peak long after the others had dismounted and had led their mounts away. The lore of the Wind Lords said that a red sky at day's end was a portent of change; Jegrai found himself only hoping that the scarlet of the sunset did not betoken an omen of spilled blood to come.

". . . so, now you know all."

Jegrai was as weary as he'd ever been in his life, but he had called this council together as soon as he reached camp. By now his raiders were spreading the news of what had occurred, for he had not forbidden it. He did not know if that had been wise, but he did know that trying to keep this a secret would be like trying to stop a plains fire in a high wind. It would have to burn itself out.

He took the cup of good spring water Aravay offered him with a nod of gratitude, and waited to hear what his advisors had to say.

"A woman—" Shenshu said doubtfully. "A *woman* is Khene to these wizards? It hardly seems likely."

"These are wizards," Vaichen reminded her. "Magic power does not depend upon strength of arm, eh, Shaman? So the strongest could be a woman. Certainly the cleverest often is!"

The Shaman only gave him a shrug of the shoulders

and a wry look. "I see no reason why a woman could not be Khene to these people. Wizards need follow no laws but their own. They may not even pass the office by kin-right."

"She had the presence of Khene; I could not doubt her." Jegrai sighed tiredly. "To tell the truth, she had the presence of Khene, the strength of Ghekhen, and the shrewdness of Shaman. It comes to me that if she had bent her mind against me with full will, I would have held few secrets from her, for all that we shared only Trade-tongue."

The Shaman hissed softly, but when Jegrai looked over to him, his face in the flickering lamplight bore only a deep thoughtfulness.

"How say you, Northwind?" he asked.

"Sa-sa. I would see this woman. You say part of the truce is that we must move the Clan to the foot of their mountain?"

Jegrai nodded. "It may be that they cannot reach us with their lightning, but I do not wish to risk Vredai lives on that gamble. Shaman—warlord—I want to please these wizards. I want alliance with them! I want some of what they hold! Is that so wrong? Is it a fool's wish to think we might have it, if we are careful enough?"

"I think not," Vaichen replied, after a silence broken only by the noises of a restless and uneasy camp beyond the walls of the tent. "Some would call me coward—but I see no profit to any in opposing these wizards, and much, much good that may come of treating with them."

Shenshu nodded vigorously. "You know my feelings. There has been enough death."

Aravay looked to be deep in thought, and took a long time to answer that question. "It may be," she replied at last, "that there is a certain deception on both sides."

Jegrai bit at a ragged thumbnail. "I had thought of that," he said. "It came to me that both of us may be setting up empty tents and dragging brush behind the scouts. It came to me that although they hold the pass and live in stone walls, it would be easy to isolate them. It came to me that perhaps they cannot send lightning to strike what they cannot see. But it also came to me that their words are very like that of the Holy Vedani, and it were folly to throw away the chance at such wisdom as *that* one held. I truly wish to trust them; I wish to believe in their honor."

The Shaman nodded vigorously, and Shenshu nearly bobbed her head from her shoulders. "If this woman is indeed Khene, then it means there are other wise women among them. There are no secrets when wise women trade learning, Khene. I burn to speak with the wise women of these people, I thirst for what they can tell to me and my healers. And doubtless there is that we can teach to them; it is ever so when healer speaks to healer."

"In many ways, Khene, we have no choice," the Shaman said at last. "If we were to fling this gift of the Wind Lords back into their faces, they may *truly* turn their eyes from us."

"Is that how you read this, Shaman?" Jegrai said, hope making him tremble inside, although he would not betray such weakness even to these trusted councilors. "That this is indeed the way set for us by the Wind Lords?"

"I can see no other reason for these things, at this time, and this place," Northwind said positively.

"Very well. Then I, and you, my councilors, will meet with these wizards in three days' time. Tell the people that it is my will that we move to the new camp-place at dawn. We will know something of these people by the place they give us, I think."

And Wind Lords, Jegrai prayed, as his advisors rose from their places at his hearth and slipped from his tent, each wrapped in thought, *Wind Lords, if ever you have heeded me, let me be right in this. . . .*

*   *   *

The Vredai murmured, the Vredai looked fearfully over their shoulders, but the Vredai obeyed their Khene. In the pale grey light of early dawn they were packing up their belongings and their tents; by the time the sun showed a bright rim over the eastern horizon, they were on the move. They ordered themselves in a compact file that filled the road and spilled over it on both sides, but there were no laggards. Vredai with a tendency to lag behind had been buried many leagues and moons ago on their backtrail.

Halfway across the valley, one of the outriders came pounding back to Jegrai and his advisors with word that there was a strange man waiting for them on the road ahead.

"What manner of man?" Jegrai asked the sweating, wide-eyed outrider.

"A young man, Khene; he speaks Trade-tongue and said he was come from the wizards to guide us." The young warrior wiped at his forehead with his sleeve, leaving a smear in the dust that covered his face. "Truly, he must be; he is a man as tall as the mountain, and his horse as tall as two mountains!"

Privately Jegrai thought that the outrider's fear had inflated the stranger, but when they came close enough to see the calm, patient figure waiting in the middle of the road, he thought better of his scout. The man *was* huge; standing, he would best Jegrai by a head, and Jegrai was reckoned the tallest of all his folk. And his horse was proportionately large. Behind him, Jegrai could hear the mutters of wonder and fear at the sight of such a prodigy. To send out a giant to guide them seemed unlikely. But to guard them—that seemed likelier.

Until Jegrai came close enough to see the man's face.

It was not a handsome face; very craggy, as rough as the side of one of these mountains about them. But it was a good face, and in many ways, a gentle face, the face of a man who knows that he is strong and tempers that strength so as not to overpower others. Brown of hair, of eyes, of skin and beard, of clothing, even—he could have been the personification of one of the Earth Spirits the Suno called upon, save that he showed none of the fierce harshness of one of those bloodthirsty godlets. His flat nose gave him a little of the look of one of them, and the shy smile on his face told Jegrai that it was very likely that he and this stranger were of an age.

"You are the Khene?" the strange man said when they were within speaking distance. His voice was deep, and held a note of diffidence. At Jegrai's nod, he continued, pronouncing his words with great care. "My name is Teokane; I am sent from Master Felaras to show you the way to a place of water and good grazing. The Master wishes also to know if your people have provisioning for the next four days."

"We will do well enough," Jegrai replied, carefully.

The young man blinked, and looked a bit doubtfully back at the thick column of Vredai behind the Khene. Jegrai's outriders gathered in a little closer, and there was some quiet loosening of blades in sheaths.

"I am sent to tell you that if there is any need, you must tell me of it," Teokane persisted. "The Master holds herself your host in this—she offers to you guest-right for the time until we speak together."

Jegrai felt as if the wizards' lightning had struck him directly, and from the dropped jaws about him, the others who had heard were no less thunderstruck.

"This is no trick?" he managed, recovering long before the rest did. "You mean by this *our* notion of guest-right?"

The young man nodded, almost desperately, and nudged his horse forward a little. "I am to offer you bread and salt, Khene Jegrai. More, I am to offer you bread, salt—" he paused significantly "—and water from the well of our home-place."

The world dropped out from underneath Jegrai's saddle for a moment. To offer bread and salt was a guarantee of safety—but to offer the water was a pledge of life for life. Not even Sen had dared to violate that bond; he had once shared Talchai's water with Jegrai's father, and had been forced to wait until the Khene was dead before moving against the Vredai.

This was more than unexpected—it was impossible. Impossible that the wizards should know this pledge of Jegrai's people. Twice impossible that they should offer it.

"You know what this means?" he croaked harshly, determined to try this young man, even though he heard the Shaman gasp in dismay at his rudeness and audacity even as he said the words.

Three times impossible, for the young man nodded. "That we are bound from harming one another if you accept the pledge, Khene. Even if the talk comes to nothing, we shall not send the lightning against you. But you will be equally bound."

Shock on shock; and Jegrai almost chuckled as he realized the young man called Teokane was right. If he accepted the water, he bought safety for the entire Clan—but he also bound the Clan from further depredations, not only in this valley, but for however far the wizards claimed territory.

Teokane fumbled out a packet from his saddlebag; unwrapping it, he revealed a small brown loaf of bread, a little pile of salt in a separate wrapping, and a flask that presumably held the water.

"I am to offer, I am to stand for my people," Teokane said formally. "Khene Jegrai, do you accept for yours?"

"And if I do not?" he asked, startling a further gasp from the Shaman.

"Then I guide you nevertheless, and the truce holds

until we talk, and thereafter as your gods and ours decree."

I like this man, Jegrai decided suddenly. *I like him. I trust him.* And, with a ferocity that surprised him in a day of surprises, *I want this man for my friend.*

He looked up into those frank brown eyes, and thought, perhaps, he detected some of the same sentiments there.

"Friend of the Vredai," he replied, feeling the muscles of his face stretch in an unaccustomed smile, "I do accept."

"It's a gamble," Teo'd said, when Felaras had finished reading the chronicle herself. "We don't know how accurate this is. We don't even know if we're facing a Clan of the same type as this one in the chronicle—"

"It's entirely possible their customs have changed," Felaras said into the silence when he left his thought unfinished.

He nodded helplessly.

"On the other hand," she continued, "everything else has held up so far—and to our benefit. If we take the gamble and it pays off, we've guaranteed not only our safety, but that of the Vale folk. What do we stand to lose besides face?"

"Felares, with these people, loss of face could be a catastrophe."

"Teo, look at me."

He found it very hard to brave those penetrating hazel eyes, but he lifted his head and met them as squarely as he could.

"Teokane, knowing everything we have at stake here, do you think it's worth the risk to try this bread, salt and water ceremony on these nomads?" Her voice was level, her face without expression. Teo swallowed, and nodded.

"I do not dare to leave the Fortress; the Order would

have my head for it at this point. They're livid enough
about the truce-staff business. Of the three whom I
trust, you are the best at reading people. On your
honor as an Archivist of the Book, on your Oath to the
Order, do you think you'd be able to read this young
man well enough to know if this wasn't going to work
before we found out the hard way?"

Oh gods—he closed his eyes, tried to shut out his
fear, his feeling of uncertainty, and tried to weigh and
measure himself. *It all rests on my being able to do
what she does without thinking. Oh gods. I haven't her
years, I haven't her experience—but—*

"Yes," he heard himself saying. "Yes. I can."

He opened his eyes; Felaras was smiling faintly, and
nodding. "Well, as it happens, I think so too. Get
yourself down to the kitchen; pick up whatever you
need down there. I'll have your horse readied for you."

They differed in size, in language, in every way—
except the ones that mattered, Teo thought a little
dazedly. He *liked* this Jegrai, with the kind of liking
that came all too rarely to him. It was almost as if they
had been old friends for years without knowing it. They
rode side by side in the warm spring sun, Teo towering
over Jegrai, and neither of them much noticing the
fact—except that once Jegrai remarked with a laugh
that he would be pleased if Teo would always ride at his
side—for shade! They chattered away at each other like
adolescents, learning each other's language, Teo finding
with a shock of pure delight that Jegrai was as quick at
picking up a tongue as he was.

And they shared so many things; Jegrai even had a
keen appreciation of the beauties of the Vale that was so
like Teo's own that he found himself pointing out this
twisted, blossom-covered tree, or that boulder-covered,
evergreen-topped hillock, knowing that Jegrai's eyes

would widen with delight the way Teo's must have the first time he'd seen it.

And the Khene's flat-footed surprise at seeing the campsite Teo and Felaras had chosen was well worth the long, dusty ride.

It was a lovely little side canyon, well shaded by clusters of trees, with grass that was knee-high even this early in the season, and watered by its own clear spring. The Order used it for grazing their horse-herd in the summer, but the herd had other pastures. There was no other place so well suited to the needs of the nomads.

And the steep sides of the canyon should reassure them that the Order was not going to attack them in the night. They would feel reassured that nothing *human* was going to scale up those walls. A few of the Watchers—a very few—could have climbed down from the greater heights above, but Jegrai wouldn't know that. And no Watcher was going to be a threat to them while Felaras was Master, anyway—not unless *they* broke truce.

"By the Wind Lords," Jegrai breathed, as the outriders gathered at the mouth of the place and gaped in awe. "She is generous, your Khene. Had I this place in my keeping, I would think twice on giving it over to strangers. With five men I could hold off every Clan on the plains." He looked skyward for a moment, then shrewdly back down at Teo. "And your wizards cannot overlook this place."

Teo shrugged, mouth twitching. *So he's already figured we can't bombard without being close to the walls, hm? Felaras will be interested to hear that, seeing as it bears out her assessment of him.*

But he pointed out, "We have shared bread, salt, and water, Khene. What have we to fear from you? What have you to fear from us? The only questions lying

between us now are how far we are willing to aid each
other."

"Sa-sa," Jegrai agreed. He stood up in his stirrups
and waved to the people crowded behind him, even as
he nudged his own horse aside so that they could pass.
He shouted something in his own tongue that was
answered by a weary cheer, and the dust-covered nomads began pouring through the mouth of the valley in
a tired but increasingly cheerful stream.

There seemed to be no end to them, and the noise
was incredible. As were the people themselves. Children that Teo thought hardly old enough to walk sat
atop their own sturdy ponies and managed them as well
as most Seekers or Archivists (Watchers didn't count,
not to Teo's mind. They were riders equal to the adult
Vredai fighters). Women held smaller children balanced
on the saddle-pads before them, and frequently rode
with wrapped babies in a kind of pack on their back.
The chatter of the children as they passed Teo and
looked up at him in fascination made him grin like a
fool.

But then the noise faded to almost nothing—and Teo
saw the living cost of their flight.

Gods—oh gods, I was right. They were *driven here.*

That was his first thought. His second was pure shock,
a blow to the gut. He was seeing things he had only
read about—and they were horrible. Men with one
eye, or one arm, or half crippled. Some younger than
he was. And not just men. There were young women—
armed and with Kasha's dangerous grace, but with a
hollow look in their eyes that said they had faced terrible things the like of which Kasha had only seen in
chronicles.

*We—we've been so sheltered. The only person I ever
saw die was another novice, in a fall. I've never seen
wounds like this, inflicted in war, in anger.* He couldn't
look away, somehow. *We've been so sheltered. . . .*

And near the end, a horse-litter, with a plump, middle-aged woman riding beside it. It was at this point that Jegrai's face lost all signs of pleasure—that it went shadowed, and brooding. He nudged at his horse with his heels and threaded his way through the last of the riders toward the litter; and, moved by some impulse he didn't understand, Teo went with him.

Jegrai spoke briefly with the woman as she stopped for him; Teo looked down at the litter. It held a boy—not yet a young man, and by the look of him, not likely to reach that state without some help. His face was greyish, the color of someone with a bad head injury, and his head was wrapped and padded. He was bandaged in several places, and though the bandages were clean, they were stained with blood and other fluids.

Teo's heart lurched, and he spoke on impulse. "Khene Jegrai—who?"

Jegrai touched the boy's forehead before answering. "My cousin. Yuchai. The night of the great storm he was riding guard; his horse shied and went into a pit-trap." He sighed. "He grows no worse, but he grows no better, either. He has not woken except to rave since he took the fall. He has taken an injury to his head, he burns with fever, his wounds do not heal, and we can do nothing."

"But—" the words burst from him; he couldn't have stopped them if he tried. "My brother, why aren't you giving medicine for the fever? Why have you not seen to his head? Why do you let him lie in pain?"

The light in Jegrai's eyes was as bright and sudden as the lightning. "*You* can do all this?" he cried.

"Not I, but those of our Order can—and by the gods, by the brotherhood we swore, we will if you'll trust us with him!"

Jegrai swiveled in his saddle. He reached out like a striking snake and clasped Teo's wrist with a steel hand. "You will swear this by the bond of water?"

The hope and fear in his face were painful to see. Teo did not pull away; instead he clasped his free hand over Jegrai's. "I will swear this on my own blood," he said tightly. "Give me but long enough to ride to the top of the mountain and back, and what we can do, my brother, we *shall* do."

"A head injury, you say?" asked Boitan, carefully packing a traveling basket with herbs, clean bandages, and boiled scalpels. "Did you see it?"

"No, sir," Teo replied, packing a second basket with the traveling surgery lantern and other oddments Boitan laid out. The cool of the rock-walled infirmary was pleasant after the wild ride up the mountain. "The boy's head was bandaged—all I can tell you is that it didn't seem to be the temple. And although they had his wounds bandaged up, I would guess that they don't suture wounds, that they just use pressure bandages and hope the flesh heals. From what little I know, it looked like they'd wrapped him awfully tight, and he was leaking fluid."

"Probably a depressed skull fracture, by the symptoms," the physician muttered, packing something that gave off a pungent odor when he squeezed the packet to fit it in. "And if that's how they're dealing with wounding—*you* know that half the time pressure bandages do as much harm as good, cutting off the blood and letting the tissue rot. I'll probably have to open him up and cut out dead tissue. I hope to hell they don't have any taboos about surgery, or you and I may be decorating stakes down there. There. That's it."

"I've already gotten fresh horses ready."

"Good man. Damn good thing I'm a rider." Boitan smiled crookedly; Teo returned it. The absent Vider was *not* a rider; rather than the fast horses Teo had called for they'd have been taking ambling old cobs—

and would have probably reached the nomad camp well after midnight.

"Tell you the truth, sir," Teo replied, slinging one of Boitan's two baskets over one shoulder, and heading past the bench to the door. "If Vider had been here I would have—uh—not been able to find him. Besides, you're a better surgeon."

Boitan followed on his heels. "I'd be a happier physician if we just had some way of keeping incisions from infecting. Duran had it—but his notes are so vague, as if he expected the method to be common knowledge." Boitan sighed, and hitched his basket a little higher on his shoulder. "Given that, there's not a lot I can do—"

"It's going to work out all right, sir, I just know it is," Teo said fiercely. The physician gave him a strange, sideways look, then shrugged. "Sir—" he ventured again, just as they reached the door to the courtyard, "This is the one opportunity we have to show them that they can trust us to keep our word. To show them that they can trust us, period."

"Ah." Boitan paused by the closed door. "I wondered if you'd seen that."

"Yes, sir, I did. This is our testing, I think. If you do everything you can—well—I don't think we'll fail it."

Boitan smiled thinly and reached for the door-handle. "I could wish," he said, as they stepped out into the blue dusk, "that I had your faith."

It was fully dark and the stars were blossoming overhead by the time they reached the canyon; Jegrai himself was waiting for them at the entrance to the canyon, looking much gaunter than he had this afternoon by the light of the torches held by the two men standing sentry there. He led the way to a round, white tent that appeared to be made of felt; the flaps were standing open to the warm night, and the sides were tucked up a little to permit a breeze to come through at the the level of the floor. Teo had expected the "floor" of the tent to be bare dirt, or flattened grass at best, but the tent was carpeted with what seemed to be several layers of thick rugs.

The boy was on a pallet near one side; the middle-aged dusky woman knelt beside him, but moved deferentially away when they entered. There was no one else in the tent, and only one lantern hung from the centerpole. Boitan took one look at the amount of light within and shook his head. "We'll have to do better than this, Teo, or I won't be able to see my own hands. Tell them to bring me some water, would you? Two buckets full, at least."

With that he began rummaging in the basket Teo had brought, bringing out a wooden frame with leather slings on it, four hollow glass globes, and an oil lamp. Teo asked for the water as Boitan began setting up the cube-shaped frame, putting the oil lamp in the middle and the four balls in their slings on all four sides of it. When the water came—within a few breaths of Teo's asking—he filled the balls with it, and lit the lamp.

There were sighs of wonder all around the tent as the water-filled balls picked up and magnified the light from the flame. Boitan nodded with satisfaction, set the lamp on its collapsible stand beside him, and pulled out a metal bowl, filling it with water. There was already a small fire in a kind of pot or brazier burning over at one side. Boitan nodded again and set the water there to heat. He dropped some herbs in it, washed his hands in one of the other buckets, and turned to his patient.

"Now, let's see about this boy."

The middle-aged woman inched forward on her knees and said something. Jegrai translated. "This is Shenshu; she is our chief healer and one of my advisors. She wishes to watch, and help if need be."

Boitan, who also spoke Trade-tongue, gave the woman a careful looking over. He lifted one eyebrow at Teo, who replied to the unspoken query softly. "Vider is also not as—ah—flexible as you are, sir."

"If laughing weren't so out of place at the moment—" He turned, bowed slightly, and gave the woman a real smile. "From what I can see you haven't done at all badly, lady," he said to her, directly, as if she could understand him. "I'll be able to use a pair of hands used to this sort of thing, if you think you can follow my pantomime. Teo, I fear, lacks the stomach to help me except in an emergency."

"Pan-to-mime?" Jegrai said, puzzled.

"Hand signals," Teo filled in hastily, and Jegrai translated in a burst of speech too quick for Teo to follow any of it. The woman Shenshu nodded, and scooted over to wedge herself between the boy's pallet and the tent wall, out of Boitan's light.

"Let's get the worst over first," Boitan said, unwrapping the boy's head and not looking up. "Explain to them, Teo. Then tell them how I'm going to open up the wounds again and cut the bad tissue out—maybe scrape bone if I have to."

Right. Explain to them that this stranger is about to cut open the head of the Khene's cousin, then mutilate the rest of his wounds. Thanks, sir. Teo took a long, deep breath, and launched into it.

At the description of how Boitan planned to raise the bit of broken skull off the brain, Jegrai looked as if he was repressing revulsion or horror; Teo couldn't read the woman. The description of cleaning out the wounds seemed to sit better; the woman exclaimed sharply once, but this time her expression was plainly one of "Why didn't *I* think of that?" There were many questions from the woman, some of which baffled Jegrai's ability at translation, for he could only shrug after failing to find the correct words.

Teo did his best to answer them. It was a tense moment, although Boitan, carefully examining the purpled, pulpy place on the boy's head, seemed to be able to ignore the tension.

Evidently his best was good enough.

"Wind Lords," Jegrai sighed, finally. "If you do this, Yuchai may die, but if you do not, he certainly will die. Shenshu says that she is satisfied you mean no harm and perhaps know what you do—"

"He's done this before, about half a dozen times that I know of," Teo said tentatively.

Jegrai shrugged. "Gods guide him, then."

At this point Teo couldn't watch. He really didn't want to stay in the tent, but Boitan needed his command of Trade-tongue. So he compromised, and hoped he could control his stomach. He turned his back on the physician, the healer, and their patient, and sat in the open tent-flap, resolutely ignoring the moans of the boy, and Boitan's murmurs.

The camp beyond was mostly dark; a few flickers of fires in carefully watched fire-pits, and the two tiny sparks of the torches at the mouth of the valley, but otherwise the camp might have been deserted. Teo looked up at the bright stars overhead and reflected that, given how weary the Vredai had looked, the quiet wasn't surprising. They were trusting the water-pledge, and taking what was probably the first unguarded rest they'd had in a very long time. For a moment he had to hold back tears of pity. All those bright-eyed children— those vacant and haunted eyes of their parents and older siblings. It wasn't fair. . . .

Boitan spoke up, interrupting his thoughts. He sounded a little more optimistic. "Well, the worst is over—the fracture wasn't bad, Teo. This boy's gods were surely looking after him."

A nasty stench wafted by, telling Teo that Boitan was now cleaning the boy's wounds out. He gagged, and held his stomach under control only because there was nothing in it at the moment but water.

There was a whisper of movement and a presence at his elbow. Teo noted the same thing Felaras had—Jegrai was as cleanly as anyone in the Order. He smelled at the moment only faintly of horse and more strongly of herbs. Some time before they'd arrived he must have taken time to bathe. *These are no barbarians, no matter what some of the others think. Nobody who keeps themselves and their camp as clean as these folk do is a barbarian.*

"I—cannot watch either," Jegrai whispered, his voice shaking. "Strange, is it not? I, who have faced battle many times, have faced death and seen it pass me to strike one at my very side, am a-quiver, and I cannot bear to watch the healers at their work. I had to see what they did with Yuchai's broken head, but now—"

He made a little choking sound.

"—my stomach rebels. And my courage flees at the sight of all those little knives at work."

"Boitan is very good," Teo ventured. "He—the only thing that has ever defeated him is when—uh—rot comes back after he has cleaned wounds, or when it comes into the cuts he made."

Jegrai's head jerked around, his face registering a look of surprise. "What, you do not have the powder-of-mold?"

"The what?"

"The powder-of-mold, that we put on wounds—do so and they do not rot."

Teo kept himself from jumping up only by a powerful exertion of will. If he startled Boitan—but this was something the physician needed to know, and now.

He raised his voice and forced himself to speak calmly. "Boitan, the Khene tells me these people have something that prevents infection."

There was a long moment of silence behind him. Then Boitan spoke, though not in Trade-tongue; he was too preoccupied. "Teo, it is a very good thing that I am not Vider, or this boy would have a new wound, and I would have a deal of explaining to do. They have something that prevents infection. Do they also have the elixir of immortality? No, forget I said that; I believe you. The crippled men you described couldn't have survived without something like that. Would the woman happen to have any of this god-given stuff here in the tent?"

Teo translated, but Jegrai did not even have to ask. "Of course!" he said in astonishment. "How not?"

"Then I trust when I am finished here, this good lady will instruct *me*, please?" said Boitan, an edge of pleading in his voice. Behind them, the woman actually chuckled.

After that, Teo and Jegrai watched the stars, and the silent camp, for what seemed to be an eternity, trying to ignore the sounds behind them when Boitan did scrape at bone. It was one of the longest nights Teo had ever spent and he was amazed when light showed in the east, and it proved to be the moon, not the sun.

At last Boitan gave a grunt of satisfaction, and the woman spoke Jegrai's name. Jegrai let out a sigh of relief as she chattered at him, and his shoulders slumped. "Never, never will I regret pledging to you, my friend," he murmured, almost to himself. "Shenshu says that Yuchai will undoubtedly live, that he looks better already. And—"

There was more than a hint of rueful self-mockery in his voice.

"—that it is 'safe to look now.' "

Teo craned his head over his shoulder as Jegrai inched back into the tent. The boy *did* look better; there was color in his face that hadn't been there before. Even as he watched, the boy's eyes opened and he spoke, dazedly. The healer Shenshu grinned and said something in a voice too soft for Teo to hear anything but a murmur. The boy didn't much seem to notice the presence of the two strangers, but Shenshu and Jegrai he recognized, and seemed comforted.

"Hah!" Boitan snatched at the bowl of stewing herbs and decanted some into a wooden cup, handing it to the woman. She took it, as he mimed drinking, and propped the boy up enough to help him sip at it. She managed to get more of it in him than on him before his eyes closed again.

"That was for fever and for pain," Boitan told her as Jegrai translated. "Willow bark and poppy gum. You saw me make it up; I'll leave some with you. Give it to him whenever he wakes for the first three days; after that, be careful—the poppy gum calls up a craving for it." The woman nodded at that, and mimed frantic scrambling after the bowl. Boitan smiled, a bit grimly. "Exactly. We don't want that to happen. Be very careful with it. Now, tell me why it is that wounds rot."

The woman listened to Jegrai, frowning slightly, then began speaking—but this time slowly. "It is—she says—poison. Poison in dirt, on hands that might have touched something rotten, on knives, on arrow-points. On the teeth of animals. It makes raw flesh rot. Powder-of-mold is the antidote."

"Mold?" Boitan's eyebrows shot up. "You mean, like bread-mold? Forgive me, lady, but that's an old wives' tale."

Jegrai translated, and Shenshu laughed. "She says, is she not an old wife? But she says also, look to our fighters, all the scars they bear. That speaks for the truth of the tale."

"Then why did this boy—"

"Ah, that I can tell you," Jegrai interrupted. "Yuchai was hurt when we had very little of the powder left, enough to keep the rot from killing him, but not enough to prevent it from coming. We did not know what to do then—boils I have seen lanced and drained, but never deep wounds. Never have I heard of this—to open a wound again and cut and cleanse—and then to sew it like a garment! It is a great wonder to me. To Shenshu, also. And the lifting of the bit of bone from the brain—I would not have had the courage."

The woman spoke.

Jegrai laughed, and reached over to stroke his cousin's forehead. The boy was sleeping peacefully, and Teo felt his heart lift to see it. "That is an even greater wonder to Shenshu also, and she begs that you will teach her—even if you are not a woman, you are wise, she says. So she will forgive you not being a woman!"

The tent filled with the wondrous sound of soft, but heartfelt, laughter.

Chapter Six

Yuchai finally woke—really woke up, and not simply moved from a fevered dream into a dreaming fever. His dreams had been full of pain and terrible ghosts: Vampire Heads, Cat Women, Snow Demons, and Blood Stones. They had taken turns tormenting him—and even the bravest warrior could be forgiven his fear of facing such an appalling array of supernatural torturers. Once or twice he shook free of them, and opened dry and burning eyes to see familiar faces full of dismay and concern about him. It was then that he would realize, dimly, that his pain was due not to the claws of the Cat Women, or even the Blood Stones sucking his soul out of his head—it was from all the hurts he had taken when his poor horse shied into that pit.

But always he had dropped back into his fever dreams, and each time he did it was to fall into the hands of his torturers a little weaker than the last time. A little less able to break free.

Then a dream of great strangeness: it had felt like those times of almost-awakening, except that there had been only one familiar face—Shenshu's. And two strangers: a man with the pale face of a spirit, and a giant.

Then a bitter-tasting drink, and finally peace, and sleep with no dreams.

He opened his eyes carefully, to find he was in his cousin Jegrai's tent. Sunlight that filtered through the walls made white felt glow warmly, but the air was cool, and smelled of grass and fresh water. And the camp-sounds were peaceful, as they had not been for more than a year.

This could not be their previous campsite, which had smelled only of horses and dust, always. And he could hear the cheerful gurgle of a spring or brook nearby, and that was not the sound of the great river they had crossed, either.

He hurt—but it wasn't like before. His head hurt, but he could think again, and the pain was localized and not nearly as bad as it had been.

He didn't want to move, much, especially not his head; but he could see what he really wanted to see without moving. His cousin, the great Khene of the Vredai, dozed beside Yuchai's bed, propped up by his saddle, and within touching distance.

Jegrai had taken charge of him. The thought startled a little croak out of his throat.

Jegrai came awake immediately, as any warrior would—but he smiled when he saw Yuchai's amazed eyes on him, a smile with no hint that the Khene considered his injured cousin to be any kind of burden on him.

Yuchai nearly wept with relief, and was immediately ashamed of such a maidenly reaction.

"There are too many in your father's tent for you to be undisturbed, and only me in mine—so I carried you off here, where you might heal in peace. So, young warrior, have you seen enough of battle to suffice you?" Jegrai said teasingly as he stretched limbs that must have been cramped, from the way he winced.

"I have seen nothing of battle, Khene," Yuchai whispered. "All I saw was a storm—"

"Wind Lords willing, that is all you will ever see, cousin," Jegrai replied, his face darkening. "Yuchai, little cousin, will you *now* content yourself with your father's path? I know you have it in you to be a Singer, and a great one."

"How can I think of the path of the Singer when half of the warriors who once followed our banner are *dead*, Khene?" Yuchai croaked. "Vredai needs fighters, not tellers of tales and keepers of lore!"

Jegrai shook his head. "We have said this before, you and I. I know all your arguments, as you know mine. Wind Lords willing, there will be no more of fighting for some time. There has been much afoot since you were hurt. But—all that is new in your case is that at the moment you can neither sing nor fight—though the *chagun* healer says that you will heal well enough to fight again, and Shenshu agrees with him." Jegrai picked up a bowl from the little flat table beside the fire-pot in the center of the tent, and stared moodily at its contents. "I could almost wish you crippled, little cousin. You have too fine a mind to waste . . . ah, enough. Drink this. This time it will not put you to sleep."

"This time?" Yuchai said, wonderingly. "*Chagun* healer?"

He remembered something more of that last dream. The man with his thin, pale face and gentle hands who brought both agony and soothing. The brown giant who filled the tent, nearly. He'd thought them visions.

"Whenever you woke I have been giving you of this to make you sleep again," Jegrai said. "It is from the healer-with-the-knife. But he said to leave off part of it, else it would make you crave for it."

"Cousin," Yuchai said wonderingly, "Where—*hai-kala*, in the name of the Wind Lords, where are we gotten to? This is not our last camp—I hear water—and the strangers you spoke of—"

"We have," Jegrai told him with a smothered twinkle in his eyes, "come to an unusual place, by the grace of the Wind Lords. Almost it could be the lands of blessed spirits. We have been granted water-pledge by wizards who hold lightning in their hands. One of them came himself from their home in the clouds to heal you with his own hands."

"That sounds like a tale to me, cousin," Yuchai said skeptically, sipping at the bitter brew of herbs Jegrai had handed him. As son of the Clan Singer he had a sure instinct for bald truth, the gilding of truth, and the warping of it.

Jegrai chuckled. "It *is* a tale. A tale a good many of the Vredai believe, but still only a tale. The 'wizards' are only men and women, I think; and though they have much wisdom, still, they can learn much of us. And if they are to be believed, this is their wish, to learn. The lightning I *have* seen, with my own eyes. Aya, it is powerful and fearful, but if men made it, other men can learn the use of it. The place in the clouds is a tall stone building up on the mountain pass on the western side of the valley."

Yuchai managed a feeble grin. "That sounds like less of a tale, though it is wonder enough."

"There is more wonder. One of the wizards did come to heal you, for no other reason than that another asked it of him, and both are good men. He gave us of these herbs that kept you in a healing sleep and took your pain, and as I said, he also told us that after three days you would begin to crave them and that we should use them more sparingly. The Shaman thinks you are brave enough to do without except when you must sleep of nights, and I agree."

If Jegrai thought him brave enough to bear pain,

then he would bear it until it tore him to ribbons before he complained. "I can bear it, cousin."

"I—I think I would like to ask another thing of you," Jegrai said after a moment of heavy silence, all the laughter gone from his face. "No—do not agree without thinking, and hear me out. We are under a three-day truce with the wizards. I go to speak with them before long, this very day, in the matter of—perhaps—an alliance. I think that there will be an exchange of hostages. Shenshu would go; she is wild to learn of this healing-with-knives. With her, Losha, equally wild to see new herbs and their uses, and to see the craftwork of these wizards. Shaman Demonsbane is to be the third. Shaman Northwind will be sometimes here, sometimes there if they permit; I think perhaps he and the woman-Khene of the wizards are two of the same mind. But I think that there should be a fourth to go." He paused. "Someone whose life they well know I value."

Yuchai blinked, and licked his lips. "M-me?"

"How better to hold my loyalty than to hold one who cannot escape them should I determine to betray them? And how better to prove my intentions than to offer that same person?"

Yuchai shivered. To be left alone, among wizards, trapped by a wounded body in a great hulking stone prison . . .

How better to serve his adored cousin, his Khene?

"Hear me, Yuchai—there may be something more here than being a hostage. The others speak of going to learn, so why not you also? You say you would be a warrior for the Vredai—would you wield your mind for me instead of a sword? Would you learn to cast lightning instead of shooting a bow?"

That possibility had not occurred to him.

"But I will not force you," Jegrai continued. "Though you would serve me and Vredai there as no one else could. You—little cousin, you are the only one of Vredai other than the healers and the Shamans—and your father, whom I do *not* trust, as you know—with the quickness of mind to learn these things for me. You know Trade-tongue. You are the only one at all who would do this out of love for me and for the learning. You are the only one except perhaps Shenshu and Northwind who would see things clearly, and with no baggage of omens and portents attached."

"I would?" Yuchai said, bewildered. "Why do you say these things?"

"Because, little cousin, you ask too many uncomfortable questions," Jegrai replied, grinning. "You accept too many inconvenient answers, provided they be truthful. You are, in short, too much like me. I have another reason for wanting you in the hands of the wizards, and it is an entirely selfish one. I want you entirely whole again, little cousin, as strong and limber as before, and with both Shenshu and the healer-with-knives within the fortress walls, if such a thing can be, it will be."

Yuchai did not really need to think upon the matter long. Jegrai wanted this: well, Jegrai would have it.

Although—when he thought a moment longer, the notion of all the new things to see, to learn—that alone would likely have been as much a temptation as Jegrai's need.

"I will go gladly, cousin," he said softly.

The Khene sighed. "You may come to regret your decision before the day is over," he replied, "and your father will want my head upon a stake before his tent. But I thank you, Yuchai. You buy me more than you know."

It had been Felaras' decision to make the nomads come to her choice of ground, so they met in a pavilion set up by the side of the road within sight of the Fortress. The Order had used this pavilion at harvest festivals in the Vale; it held fifty people and tables for

all of them, and was more than large enough for the two
delegations and the single bargaining table.

They lined up on either side of it, her group, then
the nomads. She'd wondered about chairs, the table,
but the nomads seemed reasonably acquainted with
such furnishings. The nomad chief Jegrai—even hand-
somer now that he was clean and rested—had brought
with him only seven other folk (and Eriel had babbled
about auspicious numbers), so she had ordered the
same. The four of the delegation, and Zorsha, Kasha,
and Boitan.

Kasha, because Felaras was going to be luck-wishing
this colloquy with all her strength, and she wanted
someone ready to deflect any ill-wishes. It was a pity
Kasha wasn't as expert at this as Felaras was; she could
deflect, but she didn't yet have the level of fine control
needed to send an ill-wish right back in the teeth of the
sender. But this time, deflection should be enough.

Boitan was here, because one of those with Jegrai
was the injured boy, in a horse-litter. The boy was
half-asleep over on a cot that had been brought at some
haste from the Fortress, and set up at the side of the
pavilion. Before long he should be completely asleep,
as he'd been well dosed with poppy-gum. That was on
Boitan's orders, after one look at his strained, white
face. And, without prompting, Boitan had silently put
himself at the boy's side rather than make an unmatched
number at the table.

That was a likely ally she'd overlooked. Vider was
hers, but inflexible and very cautious—he'd take to new
ways only if others tried them first. But Boitan—quiet,
unsmiling, but always ready to try something new and
different—this was the one to learn whatever the nomad healers could teach, and giving him that opportunity might well make him hers. A lot like Duran, from
what Felaras could judge of that near-legend. *Boitan is
definitely one to cultivate, a word of thanks and putting*

*him in charge of dealing with the nomad healers will go
a long way in that direction.*

There had been relief in all the nomads' faces when
they'd seen Boitan was one of those in the Order's
party, and more relief when he'd taken charge of the
boy as if it were a given.

That boy—Felaras fancied she knew what was coming; it made very sound sense in many ways for the boy
to become a hostage. It was no secret to anyone how
much the nomad leader valued his young cousin. There
was this—he would certainly get the best care of *both*
worlds up here.

And there was the other aspect—he certainly wouldn't
be able to escape if Jegrai turned his coat, so that made
sense too. It virtually assured her of Jegrai's sworn
word.

*Lords of light and darkness—that says a lot of nasty
things about the folk these nomads have been dealing
with of late. If I were a betting woman, I would bet
that the last leader he talked truce with would have
demanded the boy. Not exactly used to dealing with
anyone reasonable; wonder if they'd know a potential
friend now if they saw him? But if the boy is anything
like his cousin . . . hm.* Felaras took her seat on her
side of the bargaining table, keeping one part of her
mind on the boy, the other on analyzing the Khene's
expressions. *A sharp mind generally hungers after learning. I wonder if we could gain ourselves an in-camp
advocate with the Khene's ear just by teaching him as if
he was one of ours. It's certainly worth a try.*

She'd have preferred having the boy awake, so as to
get the interactions between him and the Khene, but
. . . no. The boy had endured the pain of the journey
up the side of the mountain, but he did not have to
continue to endure pain while his elders made noise at
each other. She would have ordered that poppy-drink
herself if Boitan hadn't anticipated her.

Let him sleep, Felaras thought. *It's not as though knowing what's in his head is going to make any real difference at this stage. We'll be turning his world inside out soon enough.*

So while the boy drowsed, oblivious, on the side of the pavilion, his elders drank wine and made diplomatic sounds at each other.

Jegrai was amazingly good at it for a "barbarian." Better than most of the folk in the Order.

Felaras was good at it, but wished she wasn't. Polite noise, pretty compliments, all the rest of that diplomatic rot; Felaras mouthed it and loathed it even as she mouthed it. She was prepared to continue it indefinitely.

And then a glance at Khene Jegrai when his face was momentarily unguarded made her decide that enough was enough. That combination of tension and boredom was nearly identical to the emotions she was keeping hidden.

"All right," she said abruptly, putting her half-empty goblet down on the table. "You've danced your dance, I've danced mine. You want peace with us, we're willing. What are you prepared to give us for it?"

Jegrai's eyes widened a little. "That would depend on what you demanded," he said, his syntax having much improved after a three-day period spent in chattering with Teo. "I may tell you what we are prepared to offer. Hostages—and hostages willing to tell you of the lands we have traveled through, of our ways, of our fashion of healing and other crafts."

She nodded; this was exactly as she'd expected. "How many?"

"Four. The Second Shaman of Vredai, Demonsbane—"

A young man with very old eyes (sitting at the left hand of the wierdly-bedecked ancient Felaras knew was the First Shaman, Northwind), nodded at her, and smiled faintly.

"—the First Healer of Vredai, Shenshu—"

Felaras had liked this one immediately, and not the least because of Boitan's descriptions of cleverness and competence. Shenshu twinkled as her name was spoken; there was no fear in her of what she was going to.

"—Losha, who studies plants and all their uses, not just of healing, and who teaches some of the other crafts, including that of weaponry—"

Another intriguingly handsome man, not so young as Jegrai and not quite so handsome, but in the same mold.

"—and—"

"And?" she prompted.

Jegrai simply looked over at the sleeping boy. "—Yuchai. I would have you to know that he is my heir until I breed those of my own body."

"Is it your wish, Khene, that this be more than an exchange of hostages?" Felaras asked carefully. "I am empowered to allow you the indefinite use of the place where you are now camped, and provisions, if you would help us to guard the Vale from wild beasts and . . . the like. But we could also offer you more than this. Would you have an exchange of something far more precious than hostages? Of knowledge? If we engage to teach those you leave with us and to learn from them, will you pledge likewise?"

Again Jegrai's eye widened in surprise. "That—you freely offer this?"

"Freely offered," Felaras nodded. "There is nothing more important in our eyes."

He drew in a long breath. "We will so pledge."

"Then here is my *envoy*," she said, stressing the fact that she had not used the word *hostage*. "Four in exchange for four. Teo you already know. This is Halun, one of our finest artificer-scholars. Mai, wise in many things, including the arts of warfare. And Eriel, who searches for the ways by which we may understand the world. As much as you show to them, so they will teach you." She smiled at the young Khene, who was showing signs of the odd little light in his eyes that the best of the novices got when they discovered that they were going to be learning, and not just playing servant to their mentors. "I would take it well, Khene Jegrai, were you to keep Teo at your hand, yourself. There is much you could share with one another."

Jegrai and Teo exchanged a look bordering on the conspiratorial, and Teo began to grin.

"Master of the Order," Jegrai said formally, under far better control than Teo, "it is well. My people came prepared to stay."

"And mine to leave," she told him. "Let there be truce between our peoples, then."

"As long as the grass shall grow," he said, making it sound like a vow. "And, Wind Lords permitting, let this be the opening to something more than truce."

"Hladyr grant," she said fervently, and stood up from the bargaining table. She nodded briefly at Kasha and Zorsha, who made their unhurried way to the side of the pavilion, and picked up the boy Yuchai, cot and all, without waking him. She nodded again to Boitan, who gathered up the other three the way a kridee gathered her chicks, and with as little fuss.

"Do not fear, Khene Jegrai," she said, reacting to his look of worry. "We shall care for him as one born of us. Kasha, for the duration, the boy's a novice; equal shares with you and Zorsha until he proves out where his interests lie."

"Yes, Master Felaras," Kasha murmured, after casting her a single startled glance.

They headed for the pavilion entrance, following Boitan and the rest of the "hostages." She prepared to go after, but Jegrai cleared his throat urgently.

"Master Felaras, there is a favor . . ."

"Ask."

"Shaman Northwind would come and go here—if that is permitted."

Felaras thought about that; it was obvious to a child that the old man could carry messages back and forth. Then again, they were asking openly. This wasn't exactly clandestine.

She looked out of the corner of her eye at the bizarre old man—who caught her eye, grinned, and winked.

By the gods, I like this old goat! she thought with amusement. *Why the hell not?*

"Why not?" she said aloud. "Surely your envoys will wish to send words to their families from time to time. He is welcome in our home—*if*—" she said with sudden wild inspiration "—I will be welcome from time to time in yours."

The young Khene was plainly not expecting that response. She watched him grope for an answer, and the Shaman forestalled him by answering her smoothly.

"How not?" he said in passable Trade-tongue. "One wizard should always find a welcome in the home of another. It is plain to me that you and I have much we should speak of together; now, if we may." He gave her a long look, and continued, with emphasis, "Is it not always so when folk share . . . knowledge?"

She felt just a hint of a tickle at the back of her neck, the pleasant little sensation that meant someone was luck-wishing (not ill-wishing) her, and looked at the Shaman with wild surmise. *By the gods, he's not mouthing platitudes, and he's not making boasts! He's a real wizard—and he's got me pegged as having the power too! He must have felt the luck-wishing I was doing, and—*

She glanced at Kasha, disappearing with the boy.

As if in answer to her thought, he followed the glance, then winked again, slowly.

—by the gods, he felt Kasha's deflection shield, too! This is going to be a very interesting conversation.

"It isn't so as often as I'd like, Shaman Northwind," she replied courteously, gathering her scattered and ambulatory wits again. "Pray, come with me. If you will excuse us, Khene, I think Shaman Northwind and I indeed have a very great deal to discuss."

"Where should we put our new novice?" Zorsha asked Kasha's back with a half grin as he balanced his end of the cot over a rough place in the road. A rough place that was a legacy of those little efforts of Felaras's at impressing the nomads. "I've never had a novice before—only a puppy. I don't suppose we'll have to housebreak him, will we?"

Sunlight on the top of Kasha's head gave her hair reddish highlights that looked very nice against the dark brown of her tunic. "I think we'd better put him somewhere he's not likely to be frightened when he wakes up. Some place as open as possible. With a window." Her voice had gone flat the way it always did when she was thinking. "Hm. You know, there's the Master's Folly."

"There is, and probably the best bet if what you want is 'open,'" Zorsha agreed. "I just hope he doesn't get just as frightened when he sees how high up he is. He's just lucky it's spring, though, or we'd have to shovel a path from his bed to the door every morning."

"Oh, it isn't *that* bad. I stayed there when the Master had pneumonia. I'll grant you it's cold and drafty in winter, but I've been in worse inns. And it should keep him from feeling like he's buried under a pile of stone."

"I'll give you that. It also puts him right next door to Felaras, which is no bad thing. . . ."

Kasha gave him a sharp look over her shoulder. "Are you thinking what I'm thinking?"

"If you're thinking that there are some folk who, for all their learning, would take a certain enjoyment in tormenting an injured and helpless barbarian boy—"

"That's what I'm thinking, all right." The expression on her face as she turned away again was of someone who had tasted something sour. "Easy on, threshold—and dragon—ahead."

As they neared the white stone wall and the dark, arched hole of the outer gate, Zorsha craned his head around a little and could see Boitan waiting for them.

"Stop a bit, children." Boitan's voice was unusually gentle; when they paused, he put his wrist against the boy's forehead, then pried up one of the boy's eyelids and smiled at what he read there. Zorsha nearly dropped his end of the cot; Boitan *never* smiled!

"No fever, no sign of permanent brain injury, and healing faster than any of *you* ever had the grace to do," the physician said with satisfaction. "The boy's a credit to his physicians. Where are you putting him? Novices usually go in the room next to their mentor, and you can hardly split him in two."

Zorsha actually had a solution to that—involving sharing a room, and presumably, a bed—but one look at Kasha's face convinced him that it would not be politic to voice that solution.

"Well, Kasha thought he might be frightened if he was too closed in, so we thought maybe we'd put him in the Master's Folly," he said instead.

Boitan considered this for a moment, then nodded. "If we did that, then Shenshu could take the room next to that; it's empty since I don't know when. That would put him between Felaras and his own healer. I'll meet you there, all right? The herbalist has the boy's things with her, so we'll bring them. It seems the Master has given me the duty of getting the adults settled in, and I thought since I don't currently have a novice I could pack that herbalist and the Shaman together in my novice's room."

Zorsha raised an eyebrow at that, and the look Boitan gave him said that the physician had also considered the possible unfriendly actions of his fellows, and had decided to deal with them before they happened.

"Fine," he replied, as the expectant silence on Boitan's part seemed to indicate that the physician was waiting for his approval. "I doubt Felaras will disagree with you. Now if you don't mind, this boy is not getting any lighter, nor the staircase shorter."

Boitan stepped gracefully out of the way, and Zorsha could see that the other three nomads had been—not concealed, not exactly, but certainly arranged so as not to be terribly visible—behind him.

There were plenty of curious gawkers on the way to the room they'd chosen for the boy. A few even looked sympathetic, and those few included Kitri and Ardun.

Which should make anybody think twice about trying anything, Zorsha thought.

Kitri even walked with them down the corridor once they told her where they were taking him. "Poor little lad. Gods, at an age where our youngsters are just thinking about their final choice of mentor, this child was out fighting wars. It doesn't bear thinking about."

"I think the Master has some notion of sparing this one that fate, Leader," Kasha said without turning her head. "She assigned both me and Zorsha as the boy's mentors, and she means it. She said to that Clan Chief of theirs that he was to be treated like one of our own, and told Zorsha and me to teach him until his real aptitudes show up."

Kitri looked like a cat who has just been presented with a particularly delicious cheese-rind. Surprised, then smug, then extremely acquisitive.

"Now, now, lady," Zorsha admonished her, laughing. "Felaras gave him to *us*. If you want any little nomads to drag into education, you'll have to go find your own!"

"Go on with you—" she objected, then smiled sheepishly. "That obvious, was I?"

"Leader, I could have predicted the expression on your face," Kasha giggled. "We know you."

Kitri chose that moment to get ahead of them and open the door to the boy's new room. "Well . . . if he shows any signs of aptitude as a pure scholar—"

"We'll let you know," Zorsha promised, and they stepped through the door and gratefully put their burden down.

The room called "the Master's Folly" had once been the large and airy bedchamber reserved for the Master's use. Then some unnamed Master had decided that it wasn't quite airy enough, or else decided that he or she wanted an unobstructed view of the northern mountains. The tales said both, and whoever had been chronicler at the time had tactfully "forgotten" to memorialize this particular piece of bad judgement. Whatever the reason was, that past Master had ordered the north wall of the chamber knocked out and made almost entirely window.

So it was done; the Hands being what they were, metal supports were crafted that took the place of the absent wall, the stone was removed piece by careful piece, and it was accomplished without fanfare or fuss, right down to heavy shutters to be closed against the worst weather. The view was virtually unobstructed, and the Fortress retained its structural integrity at that point.

The Master was pleased through spring, through summer; then came the fall.

The shutters were so heavy and so hard to get in place that when the first autumn rainstorm moved in, the entire contents of the room were soaked before those shutters could be closed.

But that was not the worst.

Winter brought the usual snow and icy cold—and the Master learned that shutters do not take the place of a solid stone wall the night of the first real blizzard.

The Master, so it was said, had to abandon the room that night. And in the morning the snow that had been driven in through the cracks and seams of the shutters had to be shoveled out.

The Master moved out of the room that very day, into the novice's room. And no Master had used it since.

Kasha was already putting the shutters aside, letting in light, a playful little breeze, and the most spectacular view obtainable short of standing on top of the walls or the roof.

"Should we get him into bed, do you think?" Zorsha asked, looking down at the boy and wishing vaguely that he could do something to make him get well faster. *Poor little fellow. I think I'm going to like him.*

Kasha shook her head. "No, I don't think we should. The bedding hasn't been changed or aired in ages, for one thing. For another, if he wakes up and finds himself in one of our beds, it might confuse or frighten him. That cot will do for now." She pulled back the coverlet on the bed, and wrinkled her nose at the musty odor. "Hladyr knows there's enough room in here for three beds and twenty cots without crowding anything."

The room did seem rather empty, with only the bed and a wardrobe and a couple of chests. They'd set the cot down against the eastern wall, between the two chests. It seemed as good a place as any to leave the boy. Kasha stood at the enormous window, looking out on the mountains.

The boy was still quite thoroughly asleep. And Zorsha was effectively alone with Kasha—as he had not been for months.

His throat tightened. *Say something, anything. Now, before the moment gets away. Teo's going out of the Fortress, and now, if ever, is going to be your chance.*

"Kasha," he said softly. "I'd like to talk about us. And Teo—"

"Don't say it," she replied tightly, staying exactly as she was. There was controlled anger in her voice, and he knew he'd made a mistake. "He's not going out of reach. He's only down at the base of the mountain. No matter what you think, nothing's changed."

"Except—" He groped for words, desperately. *As long as I've put my foot in it, I might as well put it in good. Besides, what do I have to lose? She's already pledged that she'll never break the Trinity.* "Things might change. I just want to know . . . if they do change for Teo, could—could they change for us, too?"

"Zorsha, things could change for you, too. Did that ever occur to you?" she asked sharply. "A hundred things could change. The point is that one of the two of you is going to have to make a decision, if you want a change in the relationship between the three of us. It won't be me. I won't change things. And you and Teo are too good friends to pick a fight—especially when you know both the winner and the loser would lose. You won't force me into making a choice between you. You know that, you know that very well."

He looked down at his feet. His chest felt tight, his throat choked—

—and yet, there was a little relief there too. Relief that the change wouldn't be coming; not yet, anyway. *I want Kasha—but not at the cost of losing Teo. There's changes enough right now. Maybe Teo will fall in love with a little almond-eyed archer-girl down there, and the problem will solve itself. If there's got to be a change, I'd like it to be for the Trinity to turn into a Quartet.*

"Sorry," he said to his feet. "I—never mind."

"Besides," she said briskly, turning away from the window. "You are going to have some more pressing problems on your hands when this boy wakes up. I believe you asked about housebreaking?"

If he hadn't heard the anger in her voice a moment before, he'd never have known she'd been close to the point of rage at him. Certainly the expression of wry humor she wore now wouldn't have told him.

"Housebreaking?" he said stupidly. "What on . . . oh." The back of his neck and his ears grew hot—hotter still when her wry expression broadened into one of pure, malicious enjoyment.

"Exactly," she said. "You are dealing with a young man who likely never saw a privy in his life, much less one of ours. And I think he would be most profoundly embarrassed if I tried to show him. This is assuming he's healed up enough to take the walk across the room—if he isn't, you'll have to show him how to use the chamber pot."

She was grinning fiendishly, and he had the distinct feeling that she was enjoying his embarrassment. "I can't say that I envy you—and I hope he speaks Trade-tongue."

"But—" he began, feeling no little panicked, when Boitan and the nomad healer came bustling in like they had been blown in the door by a gust of the boisterous breeze.

"Well! Here—" Boitan began, then looked at the two of them sharply. "Am I interrupting anything?"

And to think I volunteered for this, Halun mused ruefully, surveying his accommodations. He had been allotted the felt tent of a now-deceased unmarried warrior; it was scarcely the size of his laboratory storage closet. And no furniture except a pallet and a couple of low tables with folding legs.

He was very glad he'd yielded to impulse and exchanged his long robes for more utilitarian tunics and breeches. Sitting cross-legged on the tent floor in a robe would have been nearly impossible.

The Khene and Teo had shown him how to raise the sides of the tent a little to allow cool air to flow in, and had shown him the sanitary arrangements. . . .

Or lack of them. Bathing in the brook, and eliminating in slit-trenches. He shuddered. It was one thing to be living like this during the haying holidays when one was a novice, and quite another when one was on the down side of fifty.

It was a good thing he'd brought his own bedding. Granted, what they'd given him seemed clean enough, but still—furs, sheepskins tanned with the wool still on, and undyed wool blankets still oily with lanolin—it all seemed the perfect haven for fleas and other less savory things.

He'd used it all to augment the thin pallet, which was of clean cotton. Furs and sheepskins and all going *beneath* the pallet. *Sleeping on the ground. My bones are going to wonder what my head has done to them.*

He wondered if he was being a fool.

Tonight he was to meet with the father of that injured boy. Teo had said that the man's title translated as "Clan Singer" but that what he actually did seemed to be to act as a combination of Archivist and chronicler. Since the man was the only person in the entire Clan to speak Trade-tongue fluently, he was the logical choice as Halun's "guide" in this place.

No, I'm not being a fool. There's too much to learn here. I couldn't trust anyone else in the Hand to get it right except Zorsha, and he will go only where Felaras wants him to go. The writing's in the scroll there for all to read. She's made up her mind—it's very likely that Teo will not be her successor. Somehow I doubt that'll break his heart. But that's why he's down here with the Khene, instead of up there at the Fortress, learning to be Master.

Halun already had a hundred questions; the construction of the nomads' bows, for instance. He could understand the patchwork construction. These folk came from a nearly treeless plain, after all. But when he'd had one of the bows in his hands, he'd been amazed at the flawless mating of materials, and even more surprised at the strength of the tiny bow. Some of the materials had not been wood; there were bone plates, but some of the rest of the laminates hadn't been immediately identifiable. He wanted to know what they were, how they were put together to obtain that incredible strength and toughness.

Then there had been some body armor he'd seen, like boiled-leather scale, but made of horn or similar substance. It looked tough, yet lightweight; an immense improvement over both the Yazkirn boiled-leather and the Ancas metal plate-mail.

In fact, the uses these people put leather to, and wood, replacing pottery—*which would be broken the first time they packed up and moved,* he reflected— was amazing. He'd seen leather made absolutely waterproof, virtually flame-proof, soft as fabric and as hard and tough as horn. And always the question of how they had done this nagged at him.

Their smiths, however, were not up to even the standards of the Ancas, much less the things the Order could do. Their swords and knives were mostly bronze, with a few that were obviously family heirlooms of inferior steel.

Halun supposed with a sigh that he would be expected to teach them *that.*

At least Felaras isn't fool enough to give them the secrets of explosives, he thought soberly, trying to find a way to sit comfortably on the floor of the tent. *Hladyr bless—I can just see it now—the slaughter these people would wreak if they had mortars and mines. Even walled cities wouldn't be safe. These barbarians would*

*send the world floating into oblivion in its own blood,
and the blame would be all ours.*

He opened his writing chest and took out his notes
on the language, hoping to be a little more fluent by
evening. There were some concepts that simply didn't
translate well into Trade-tongue. But his mind kept
circling in on Felaras, this near-alliance of hers, and his
own ambitions.

*Zorsha wasn't haring off on a tangent at the Convo-
cation,* he thought after a bit. *That was not a bad idea;
allying with these barbarians, then declaring the Vale
an independent entity. Knowing we had cavalry to en-
force our sovereignty, not even Yazkirn or Ancas would
dispute it. Gods above and below—no more taxes sent
off to those crowned fools! Hm . . . we've gotten the
nomads tied in closely enough with us so that we could
use them—we could control not only the Vale, but the
entire region.*

He took that line of reasoning one step further. *If we
were to educate whoever is Khene just enough so that
he depended on what we could manufacture for him
and came to rely on us for our advice, but realized that
without us the things he had come to depend on would
no longer be appearing—we could be the real power
behind the throne. Whoever was Master could dictate
and the Khene would obey.*

He sighed, and finally stretched himself full length
on the pallet. *Felaras would never agree to that; never.
A fool, a fool, we have a fool for our Master. The first
chance we've ever seen to come back into civilized lands
with a power-base of our own, and she'll throw that
chance away because she refuses to use people.*

He ground his teeth together in frustration. *Damn it
all, I should be Master here! I know how to use these
barbarian children, and do so in such a way that they
would never know they were being used. If only Felaras
would have the grace to die, or become ill! Damned*

*woman was always too damned healthy. Not even pneu-
monia at the height of snow-season killed her! She's
maneuvered so that virtually everyone in the Order is
going to be supporting her on this alliance, so there's
no way I'm going to get her unseated. And with whoever it is protecting her, I can't even ill-wish her.*

He'd tried, especially during the truce-talk. Nothing
had happened; the ill-wish had just bounced. Where it
had gone, Halun had no real idea, although he'd had a
suspicion. Dosti, and Dosti's novice Urval, had had a
spectacularly bad day. On every loom they tried to
string, either the warp threads had tangled, or they'd
broken. The cats had gotten into the punched cards for
the pattern-looms, and had made a few holes of their
own, which meant Urval would have to re-punch all
those cards again from the archived patterns. When
they decided to turn their hands to just plain weaving
for the Order, it turned out that the only yarn they had
in sufficient quantities to make anything in the way of
garment-lengths was dyed in particularly hideous, muddy
shades of green, yellow, and dun. Checking the rec-
ords, they discovered that those stored skeins had been
dyed in muted, but pleasant, usable colors—but prox-
imity to the bleaching vats had leeched the color out of
the yarn-skeins, turning them ugly. They would all
have to be re-dyed. And just moments before Halun
had given up his ill-wishing, Urval had fallen into a
(thankfully cool) vat of ochre dye. He now was ochre,
brightly ochre, from top to toe. He looked like a bad
case of liver disease, and it wouldn't wash off, it would
have to wear off.

If only Felaras had some truly virulent enemy. . . .

Then the thought occurred that made him sit straight
up.

*After that business on the walls—she does. I would
be willing to bet my life that Zetren is so unbalanced
now that he'd be child's play to tip! He never was all*

*that well wrapped to begin with, and he holds a grudge
like a badger holds its brock. I can't ill-wish her directly, but I can certainly work on Zetren. . . .*

He contemplated the best way to set the mind-spell.
*I'll have to aim this at Zetren rather than her—but—
the worst thing Zetren could do at this point would be
to start taking this thing from a grudge to an open
vendetta. That would destroy him, because no matter
how it came out, he'd be cast out of the Order. Yes.
Yes. At the very worst, she'll be distracted and unable
to give her whole attention to what's going on down
here, which will give me a free hand to work. And at
the best—*

He found himself smiling.

*At the best—the Order will require a new Master.
And with neither boy trained or seasoned enough to
take it—I become the only logical candidate.*

Yes, indeed.

Chapter Seven

Kasha leaned forward in her chair and shook her head in pure wonder. "You're *how* old?" she asked the nomad boy.

"Fourteen," Yuchai replied in nearly unaccented Trade-tongue, feeling worried. "Am I—am I learning too slowly?" He clutched his Ancas primer so hard his knuckles were white. Trade-tongue was very like the speech of Ancas, and he was making—he thought—reasonable progress in learning that language. But this business of equating sounds with marks on a page was very new to him. The idea that words could be saved, forever and ever, unchanged, had excited him so much he resented every moment not spent in learning how to decipher those marks.

"Gods above and below," Kasha laughed, her eyes crinkling at the corners. "Too slowly? Anything but that! You're learning as quickly as a very young child—and that's supposed to be impossible for a boy your age. You already speak Trade-tongue as well as I do, and you're learning Ancas as fast as I can pour it into you."

Yuchai relaxed, and sagged back into the pillows that had been piled behind him so that he could sit up. "It is that I have very little else to do except learn, *gadjeia* Kasha," he said. "And I—have pleasure in this learning. Besides, I certainly cannot practice the warrior arts from a bed."

Kasha snorted and made a sour face. "If I have my way you won't be practicing the 'warrior arts' at all, young man. You've too good a mind. I'd cripple you myself before I'd see you die by the hand of some stupid ox who happens to outweigh you by three times."

Yuchai felt a strange apprehension at her words. For so long he had wanted to be a great warrior like Jegrai— and yet the great warrior he admired would have been happier if he'd never touched a weapon. And now this fighting-woman who said the same thing; she was *very* good—he'd watched her at practice from his huge window, for besides the mountains you could look right down into the courtyard of the Sword-folk, if you stood—or in his case, sat—close to the edge. Would she do such a thing? To keep him a scholar—scholars were forbidden weapons. Was that her purpose, to see that he did not violate that law? He licked his dry lips. "That—that is similar to what Khene Jegrai tells me," he ventured. "But, forgive me, honored teacher, but Vredai needs warriors. Vredai does not need a man who is neither feeble nor crippled, yet who cannot raise a blade in his own defense—"

"Yuchai, do you really enjoy fighting?" she asked, her face gone quiet and very serious.

"I—I—the moving, like dancing, doing it well—I like that," he temporized.

"I'm not talking about that," she said, frowning, "I'm talking about *fighting*. Killing, trying not to be killed. Do you find that . . . attractive? Some do; acts on them like wine. Nothing sinful about that, nothing wrong, just the way some people are made."

"No—I—I haven't seen much of fighting, but—they always set me to guarding the Clan heart, the children, you know? The fighting got that far, once or twice. I—the closer it got, the sicker I got." He hung his head, admitting his shame, the weakness he had confessed to no one but Shaman Northwind. "When I closed, the moment before, you know, I almost couldn't hold my sword for wanting to throw up. But—Vredai *has* a Singer. They don't need another fool that can't even defend himself."

He colored as he realized that he had just slandered his own father.

"Did I say you shouldn't know how to defend yourself?" Kasha demanded. "Have you ever once heard me say anything like that? I'm no fool, Yuchai—your people are warriors by their nature. Wherever you go, there's likely to be fighting. There's no harm in knowing weaponry—every member of the Order knows bow, at least. I'm just saying you don't belong on a battlefield, except in a case of last resort."

"Everyone—in the Order—knows weaponry?" Yuchai's thoughts went whirling as if they'd been caught in a dust-demon. "But—except for those of the Sword, are you all not as Singers? Is it not forbidden among you for Singers to touch a weapon?"

Kasha's mouth twisted as she labored to disentangle that last sentence. "No, it's not forbidden!" she exclaimed when she had the sense of it. "Great good gods, we'd have been slaughtered a dozen times over if we held that rule! If a novice from one of the other chapters wants to spend his free time learning Swordways, that's his business. We've actually had one or two Masters that could have been both Sword and either Book or Tower by earned skill-level if they'd chosen to ask for the Sword badge as well as their own."

"You—have?" He felt rather as if he'd fallen on his head again.

"I take it that it's very much forbidden among your people."

"One must choose," he replied carefully. "The Singer must never touch a weapon; the Wind Lords favor the wise, but—you know that among us the wise one is almost sacred? It is a terrible thing for a man to raise his hand against a scholar; the Wind Lords will surely curse him for it. So—for a wise one to bear a weapon, to fight with a weapon—that is taking dishonorable advantage."

It didn't take his tutor long to fathom the meaning of that. "Uh-huh," Kasha said, nodding. "Yes, I see what you mean. It's like a whole man taking on one with no legs. The opponent of a scholar in a fight has a choice between being dead and being cursed."

"Exactly so," Yuchai said with a sigh.

"Well, we don't have that particular restriction, and it doesn't look like the Wind Lords have cursed us yet." Kasha settled back in her bedside chair and put her hands behind her head. "My friend, if you want to go trade bruises with me or anyone else in Sword and you happen to have landed in Tower or Book, feel free to come to us in your spare time. We're always looking for new sparring partners, and I'll wager you could show us a few things new to us. And if you don't happen to tell the Wind Lords—" she grinned "—neither will I."

Yuchai felt his breath stick somewhere in his throat. It took him a moment to get it moving again. "I may?" he asked.

"You may. But not at the moment." Kasha pulled one hand out and wagged an admonishing finger at him. "At the moment you can barely hold up that book, and it takes Zorsha to get you to the privy."

He felt a blush crawling up his face.

"So at the moment, my friend, you'd best keep your attentions on that primer."

He gladly buried his nose in the book, hoping Kasha hadn't noticed his blushing.

*   *   *

"So, if the world is round, like a ball, why don't we fall off of it?" the boy asked. "And if it's spinning, why aren't we flung off of it?"

Zorsha grinned. At first he'd thought this notion of Felaras'—to teach a wild nomad boy—was going to be sheer torture for both of them.

It was turning out to be sheer pleasure. The boy drank in everything Zorsha could teach as thirsty ground drank spring rains. There was such a need in him to know—sometimes Zorsha could almost see him physically beating against the walls of his limitations of language and understanding. And every day those walls crumbled a little more; one day there would be nothing to stop him.

"Because," he said, answering the question with an example, "we *think*, Yuchai, that when something gets big enough, it attracts smaller things to it—the way this bit of amber picks up a feather after I rub it with the silk."

Zorsha took an amber bead from the box of oddments he'd brought with him, and rubbed it vigorously with a scrap of silk cloth. He put a feather on the comforter, and brought the bead close to it. The boy watched, his eyes bright with intense fascination, as the feather leapt to cling to the bead.

The boy reached out and pulled the feather away, then let it go, and watched it return to the bead.

"We think," Zorsha said, "that the force I generated in the amber and the force that holds us on the world are similar, though not the same. We call the first 'electricity' and the second 'gravity.' "

The boy's lips moved a little as he committed the words to his memory. "But—why don't you think they're the same if they both make things stick to other things?"

Zorsha chuckled, put the feather away and rubbed the amber again, briskly. "I'll show you—hold out your finger."

Yuchai did, and Zorsha brought the amber in close enough to the boy's fingertip that a spark leapt from the bead to the outstretched finger. The boy yelped in surprise and jerked his hand back.

"Now, since we don't keep getting stung by sparks all the time, we probably aren't being held to the world by electricity," Zorsha told him, putting the amber and silk away.

Yuchai cocked his head to one side and stared over Zorsha's shoulder, out the window at the mountains. The Hand had noticed that Yuchai always stared at the mountains when he was thinking. His brow was creased —but not in puzzlement. "That . . . spark . . . that was like a tiny piece of lightning," he said after a moment, making it a statement and not a question.

"Very like," Zorsha agreed.

"Is the spark you made the same stuff as lightning— only small?"

"We think so."

"There's always a lot of lightning in the mountains," Yuchai mused. "Could . . . lightning happen because— because clouds rub against the ground, the way you rubbed the silk on the amber?"

Zorsha felt his eyes widening in surprise. *I hadn't expected* that *jump of reasoning! Good for him!*

"That's one idea," he agreed. "There are lots of possible explanations, and that's one of them."

"But clouds are only air and water," Yuchai said, turning puzzled eyes on his teacher. "How could they rub against the ground when there's nothing there to rub with?"

"Are you sure that air is nothing?" Zorsha countered.

"Yes!—No." The boy looked back over the mountains. "No, it can't be nothing, not when I've been in winds so strong they knocked me over, and wind is just air moving the way the Wind Lords tell it to. And when the wind blows like that, in a *khemaseen* or a *syechali*, it can pick up enough sand to strip the flesh from your bones, which means that it's holding the sand up. So air *is* something. Is—is air like water, only very, very thin?"

"We don't know," Zorsha admitted. "We used to think that all things were made of four elements—air, water, earth, and fire. Now we know they aren't: we know that what we call 'earth' is made of a great many things. We call *those* things elements now, because they are 'elementary,' which means they can't be broken down into anything smaller. We think water is made of several elements, but we can't tell what they are. We don't know about fire. Or air. Or light, like from the sun. Those might be what we call 'energies,' or we might be able to break them down into other things some day—or they may be elements."

"There's a lot you don't know," Yuchai observed, fixing Zorsha with a stare that had mischief lurking at the bottom of it.

Gods above and below—if I should have a son one day, grant me one like this!

"Oh, yes," Zorsha admitted cheerfully, "there's a great deal we don't know. That just makes a great deal for someone to find out. Maybe you. Hm?"

The boy returned his gaze to the clouds moving above the mountains.

"It might be . . ." he whispered. "It might be me . . ."

The Khene's tent was very crowded. Of all his advisors, only the Shaman sat beside him to hear what the most senior riders of the Clan had to say about the wizards—and the truce. Jegrai wished with one half of his mind that he had the others with him.

But the more reasoning half of his mind told him that this must be dealt with—and he alone must deal with it. Else the Clan might begin to wonder who was Khene—Jegrai, or Jegrai's advisors.

So he kept his face impassive and listened with patience that was mostly feigned to the arguments and threats of his most argumentative people.

"I tell you, we have them at our mercy!" shouted a stocky, round-faced rider with a strong and authoritative voice, a voice that almost forced one to listen to it. This was the Clan Singer, Yuchai's father, Jegrai's uncle Gortan. "These fools leave their gates open to us by day or night—there are not so many of them that a war party could not steal in under the cover of the darkness and force them to *give* us the secret of the lightning!"

"Pah! The secret of the lightning!" spat Jegrai's half-brother Iridai, a man so like Gortan that they could have been brothers, save that Iridai did not have Gortan's power to ensorcel with his voice. "That is only too likely a secret the Wind Lords would curse us for having! If they did not curse us for taking it by force from these wizards! I would remind you all, these folk are too like the Holy Vedani for my comfort. I would be away from them, before we lose ourselves to them! Jegrai, we have the water-pledge, we have the truce—send back the envoys, take back our people and let us be away from here! Their land-folk are creeping out of hiding, and there can be none who could hold us less than honorable if we moved on to other pickings. The old ways are the best ways—"

"Iridai, my brother," Jegrai said softly, but with veiled menace, "the old ways would have let Yuchai die, or left him a cripple. The old ways would reduce us to *thieving* swords of steel instead of honorably forging our own. Is that what you want?"

Iridai gaped at him in surprise; Jegrai was quite well aware that his brother had claimed one of the first new swords with the glee of a child claiming a honeycomb.

"And uncle," he continued, turning to face Gortan

before he lost his advantage, his menace no longer
veiled, "would you have us break water-pledge? Would
you have us less in honor than the Talchai, cursed be
their name and Clan?"

Gortan shrank visibly.

"You are Clan Singer—would you record treachery
such as not even Khene Sen dared in the songs of
Vredai?"

"No." Gortan shook his head. "Khene, it maddens
me, this waiting at their table for crumbs—and their
choice of what we shall have, and what we shall not
have. They treat us as children, as fools."

Jegrai chose to keep silence upon that point, for it
sometimes galled him as well. *And it is well that Gortan
does not know this. My friend Teo knows—but can do
nothing. He is at the orders of his Khene, Master Felaras.
And Master Felaras does things for reasons only she
knows.*

Shaman Northwind spoke up at this point. "Gortan,"
he said pleasantly, "if you were to train a child to wield
a sword, would you place your brother's sharp new
steel blade in his hands?"

The Clan Singer snorted. "Of course not! I would
give him a weighted practice blade of wood suited to
his age, and . . . ah. I think I see where your words
take you, Northwind. You are saying that these wizards
teach us things that are like to a wooden practice blade."

"I am ," the old man said, his eyes twinkling. "And it
is a very humbling experience for a man of my years to
find himself less in knowledge than the youngest novice
in their Fortress. But a child must learn to walk ere he
can run—and even I, perforce, must learn with the
children before I can understand some of their mysteries." He sighed heavily. "Though it chafes at me, I have
not the tools of understanding to compass much of what
I have seen in their place of stone. I must wait to have

those tools before I can understand what they do, and not simply mimic it."

Gortan mumbled something, still plainly unhappy.

But the Shaman continued, and his voice held a power no less persuasive than the Singer's. "We must work with these wizards of the Order, Gortan. There are many, many things they wish to learn of us, as well. You all know that I have spoken with Master Felaras at great length. I think, although I do not know, that she has some distant plan, a plan that involves both our peoples—but as allies, Gortan, as equals. And equality implies that we will have the secret of the lightnings, and certainly have it before the passing of too many seasons. I advise patience; and I shall take care to follow my own advice, hard though it may be."

Grumbling, Gortan, Iridai, and the others gathered to speak with their Khene agreed—

Or seemed to.

The tent was pitched on the edge of the camp, and with the edges raised for ventilation there was no chance anyone could overhear Halun's conversation without being seen. Halun sighed, and spread his hands helplessly. "I feared that would be the way of things when you told me of this meeting," he told Gortan. "Your Khene is a young man, and the young are easily influenced by flattery and won by promises. Master Felaras can be most persuasive when she chooses."

Persuasive. Gods above and below, how she would howl to hear me describe her as "persuasive"! Bullying yes, and outright threatening, but persuasive? Ha. But this Gortan doesn't know that, and it's not likely he'll get close enough to her to find out.

"So you think that your Khene Felaras has no intention of giving us the secret of the lightning?" Gortan asked, his usually impassive face reflecting strong emotion of some kind, though Halun was unable to tell what.

"Why should she? While she holds it, you fear to leave, for you fear she may strike you with it on your leaving—and you think that she may yet give it to you if you are patient and good, like obedient children, so you wait to see if it is yet forthcoming. As for the Master, well! While she has you at the foot of her mountain, she can use your warriors as an unspoken threat, a blade at the throats of the dukes of Ancas and the princes of Yazkirn."

"Ha!" the Singer barked in obvious satisfaction. "I wondered what her purpose was!"

"And I wonder somewhat at yours, Clan Singer," Halun replied, bending closer with a wince for his tender knees. After several weeks down here, he still wasn't used to sitting cross-legged on the ground. "Why is it that you wish the lightning so very much?"

The Singer stared at him for a moment, broodingly. "It is no secret that we have enemies," he stated.

"Indeed," Halun agreed.

"We have something of a blood-debt to pay those enemies. A *great* blood-debt. I wish to live to see the lightning pay that debt in the space of a single battle. I wish to see the Clan of Talchai without a single warrior left whole."

Halun gazed into those cold yet passionate eyes, and shuddered. This man was not mad, or even half-mad. He was terribly, terribly sane. But so single of purpose that Halun would far rather flee to the ends of the earth than stand between him and his goal.

It would be safer.

"I cannot tell you if you will live to see that come to pass, Singer Gortan," Halun said truthfully. "But my experience of Felaras . . ."

Again, he spread his hands, thinking, *And the best lie is to tell the truth.*

The stocky nomad grunted. "So you have said. I thank you, scholar. By your leave, I must go to tend my duties."

Halun bowed slightly, and the Singer backed out of the tent, courteously.

When he was gone, Halun stretched himself out on his pallet with a sigh for his aching joints.

It's working, he thought with satisfaction. *They're unhappy, and the longer Felaras holds out on explosives, the unhappier they'll get. I venture to say that once the boy is healed and on his feet, Singer Gortan will make his move. And that move will be a direct assault on the Fortress by the dissidents.*

He contemplated the roof of the tent, slowly turning a soft rose color as the sun set.

An assault doomed to failure, of course. The Sword doesn't let anything larger than a mouse past them after dark. But . . . an attack will throw a good fright into all of them. Just maybe a good enough fright to send them running to the caves. Felaras will find herself voted out of office, and her two candidates are too young—that leaves me. That is, assuming Zetren doesn't get her first.

He laughed silently. *Oh, Felaras, Felaras, you're like a hare in a field full of traps! Whichever way you step, you're going to run into one! If only you knew who your opponent was—but I have no intention of giving you that weapon. And now that I think of it, I believe it is time to give poor Zetren another little prod.*

He closed his eyes, centered his will, and concentrated, and the tent, the camp-sounds, and all else faded into unimportance. There was only his will, and his *wish.*

I like this place. I like these people, Jegrai especially, Teo thought contentedly, as he and the Khene lounged together in Jegrai's tent, in unaccustomed idleness. *It's almost like . . . like he was one of the Trinity.* "You know, Jegrai, if I didn't know better, I'd swear Eriel is right," Teo chuckled, half sprawling over the saddle he was using as a prop.

"Oh? About what?"

Gods. He's got almost no accent anymore. He could walk into Targheiden in the right clothing and no one would look at him twice. "That you're one of us, reborn into a nomad body."

The Khene's brow wrinkled in perplexity. "Your pardon?"

Teo laughed outright. "That's Eriel's latest pet persuasion. That souls continue to be reborn into new bodies when the old ones die. She claims you're one of us, reborn into a nomad body, and she uses the speed at which you've picked up our tongue as proof."

"Tcha." The young man clicked his tongue disapprovingly. "But I have learned every tongue I have encountered with speed, even the Suno; and *that,* my friend, is a language only a nation of torturers could have devised. Which tells you all you need to know of the Suno. So, how would she explain that?"

"That you've been born into all of them at one time or another, I suppose," Teo replied, taking a hearty swig of *khmass.* Halun claimed even the smell of the fermented mares' milk made him want to vomit, but Teo rather liked it. He passed the skin back to the Khene, who squirted some down his own throat.

"She claims the reason I like your food and drink is that I'm a barbarian nomad reborn into a civilized hulk," Teo continued, still highly amused. "She was a little upset when I laughed at her."

"You? Who cannot even shoot from horseback?" Jegrai howled with laughter that was so infectious Teo joined him. "When even our maidens can *stand* upon the back of a galloping mare and hit the mark?"

"I didn't say it was logical," Teo protested, holding

his sides. "I just said that was what she has for her latest pet notion."

"And I am not so quick with your written word," Jegrai pointed out with rueful chagrin, once he managed to get control of himself. "And to your folk, the written word holds equal importance with the spoken. How could I have been one of you, and still be wrestling with your children's books and making little sense of them?"

"It'll come, brother, it'll come," Teo said soothingly. "When it comes, it'll likely come all at once."

"Tcha. Yuchai already outstrips me, the Shaman tells me he begins to—"

"Yuchai is also a deal younger than you, brother, and in matters of language, the younger, the better. Trust me. Besides, he has very little to do besides lie in bed and put his mind to work. You have all of a Clan to govern."

Jegrai sighed at that, and stared into the flame of the oil lamp hung on the centerpole above their heads. "I wish that I had not," he replied softly. "I wish—tcha, it is no good wishing. I am Khene; that is what I must be. But Yuchai—" His expression hardened. "—Yuchai shall have what I cannot. For all that he wishes to be my shadow, he hates fighting, he hates death—he is like my father. He is made for other things."

Jegrai's expression turned to one of near-anguish. "Teo—Teo, my brother, will your people give him those things? The learning he starves for?"

Teo was growing used to these confidences, and the way the Khene spoke freely to him. It was logical; he was an outsider, safe to confide in, not someone Jegrai had to command. But there was something more than logic behind it, and the confidences hadn't been one-sided. He'd told Jegrai about Kasha—how on the one hand he longed for something deeper than friendship, and feared the changes that would bring—and on the other shied away from the commitment implied. And Jegrai had listened with a sympathy he'd hoped for, but hadn't actually expected.

They weren't so dissimilar, his people and the Vredai.

Neither were he and Jegrai.

"Jegrai, I speak as the brother you have called me," Teo said carefully. "If this path should take him away from the Vredai, perhaps for all time, would you still wish him to follow it?"

Jegrai bowed his head and was silent for a very long time, staring now at the floor of his tent. Finally the words came; slowly, deeply thoughtful. "If he felt the calling—if *he* felt it was worth the sacrifice—how could I deny him?" The Khene raised his head and looked straight into Teo's eyes, and Teo could not help but see the pain there, and the longing.

If he could trade places with his cousin, he'd do it in an eyeblink. Gods. I can't give him everything he wants— but by all the gods—I'll give him what I can.

"Felaras pledged he'd be taught as one of our own, Jegrai. She meant it. Knowledge, learning—they're close to being sacred things for us. She doesn't make pledges like that lightly."

Jegrai let out the breath he'd been holding in a hiss, and nodded. His hand fell on the skin of *khmass*, and he looked at it as if he was surprised to find it there.

"You know, we have a saying. 'In drink, there is sometimes truth.' Do you feel up to more truth, Teo? Or shall we speak of the weather, or of horses?" He drank, then held out the skin, and his hand was steady.

Teo took it, took a long pull himself, and ignored the little chill that went down his neck. "Truth. If you really want to hear it." He passed the skin back.

"Northwind thinks that your Master has a plan that involves all of us—as allies. What do you say to that?"

"That your Shaman is a very wise man. And a very perceptive one."

"And my brother says as much by what he does not say as by the words he chooses," Jegrai replied sardonically, drinking and returning the *khmass*.

Teo shrugged, drank, and handed it back.

"So. And what if we, too, have plans—involving all of us as allies? Hm?" Jegrai demanded. "How would your Master reply to that?"

"It would depend, I think, on what the plans were, and in which direction those plans turned," Teo said as cautiously as he could, while Jegrai drank with one eye on him. "There are things we—the Order—had rather not do. And if that was your direction, well, there would be trouble. I should not tell you this, but . . . my brother, this is not to go beyond your ears. The Master does not rule unopposed. She can be replaced by another if it is the will of the majority of the Order. And Felaras is not altogether the most popular of Masters." He took back the *khmass*, feeling the need for it.

Jegrai's eyes went wide with surprise, then narrow with speculation. Finally he nodded as he accepted back the skin. "Let me say that Khenes have met with challenge also—and . . . 'accidents.' There are those who do not favor the path I have chosen for Vredai. And this is not to go beyond *your* ears. We walk a narrow bridge, I think, both of us. I shall have to think upon this." He shook the bag of *khmass*; it was as flat as a child's chest. "I think we have had enough of truth *and* drink for one night, hm?"

Teo stifled a yawn and nodded. "As it is, I'm going to wish to die in the morning. I am not entirely certain that I will remember my body finding my bed!"

But as he walked back to his tent in the cool night air, Teo knew he had spoken something less than the truth about being weary. Certainly his body longed for rest, and he was assuredly feeling the impact of the liquor, but his mind buzzed with unwelcome thoughts that kept him thinking even as he crawled into his bed.

Those uncomfortable speculations kept him staring up into the darkness long after he should have been asleep.

So. Jegrai has plans, too. That shouldn't have surprised me. And if those plans involve getting rid of whoever or whatever it was that chased him and his Clan west—I'm all for helping him. But what if that isn't the direction he's looking? What if he's figuring on cutting himself new territory? Like in Ancas? Or Yazkirn? What the hell should I do if I find that out? Should I tell Felaras? Do I tell her my suspicions now?

The night-sounds of the nomad camp soothed him, and reminded him of how little he had in common with those to the west and south of the Pass. And how little good the folk of those nations had done for the Order. And how much harm.

What's the rest of the world ever done besides give us grief, cast us out of our homes and livelihoods, even murder us in our beds?

The horses stirred restlessly on their picket, and a voice lifted in soft—but alien—song to soothe them.

These people—what did he really see of them past their surface? They had no written tradition at all; a reverence for learning, yes, but they had remained unchanged for hundreds of years, while the Order spawned change. *Gods. How can we side with illiterate barbarians with the intent of taking down civilized nations?*

Teo turned on his side; he could see the watchfire that flickered in front of the Khene's tent through the gauze of the insect-screen covering the entrance to his own. *Jegrai won't be illiterate for long—if he has his way, we'll be teaching every member of Vredai who wants to learn. He favors us the way nobody in those so-called civilized lands ever has. And he's a good man.*

But the Order had to look beyond the present.

What if the next Khene is a despot? Gods, where should my loyalties lie?

Halun lay unsleeping, staring at a single star, one that seemed to have been caught in the smoke-hole of his tent. There had been another meeting tonight, this one with not only Gortan, but the Khene's own brother, Iridai, and a handful of disgruntled nomads whom the Shaman had passed over in favor of the young man now calling himself Demonsbane. On a hunch, Halun had tested them, and found they had considerable raw, if untrained, power in the wizardry of ill-wishing.

That had not been the only surprise of the evening. Gortan had made him a proposition: a strange and very seductive proposition.

Help us, the nomad had urged. *Help us to raise discontent with Jegrai. You say you wish to teach us many things, but may be forbidden to teach them by your Khene. So; help us to be rid of Jegrai, then we will go from here, and you may come with us, you will be the right hand of the Khene, who will heed you in all things. You will teach us what you will, and we will honor you above even the Khene.*

He cradled the back of his head on his arms and tried to think things through logically. He had, by the gods, *not* expected that particular offer.

And in many ways it was a sweeter plum than the Master's seat. As Master, he would have to cajole, bully, and placate his fellows even as Felaras did now. He would be honored—when it suited them. He would be obeyed—if it suited them. He would rule only by consent.

But with the nomads he would be . . .

He would be a power in his own right. So, they were warriors by nature, well, that thought didn't cause him any misgivings. In fact there was a great deal he could accomplish, given a free hand with them. Granted, he knew nothing of warfare—but he knew weapons. He could make this loose aggregation of fighters into a terrible power.

With the tools they already have, we could make explosives, mortars, small cannon. Those are all portable enough to carry on horseback. Mortar-fire to demoralize and scatter the enemy—then the nomads charge with those wicked little bows of theirs. Most armies would think demons had hit them.

The star moved out of sight, but another was taking its place.

If Jegrai were to be deposed by his own folk, that would frighten the breeches off of most of my colleagues. Having the nomads turn up armed with explosives would drive them right underground. It wouldn't matter if Felaras was Master or not; she'd be overruled. That would put them right where they belong: in hiding. Safe, as this policy of Felaras' can never make them. And I—I would be—

A shiver ran over his skin. *I would be isolated from my own kind. Likely enough I'd never see them again.*

The star glittering down at him looked very, very lonely.

There was one candle burning at his bedside, but dimly. The view out the great window was as beautiful and alien as only the mountains could be to a boy used to the flat of the steppes. Yuchai stared at the cold jewels that were stars, suspended above the black bulk of the mountains, and tried not to cry. He was healing—quickly, according to both Boitan and Shenshu—but there were times when his injuries still gave him a lot of pain, and the pain was worse at night.

Worse than the pain, though, was the loneliness. Somewhere down there—and not even in the direction his window faced—were his people. His cousin, his father; his former playmates, those who weren't dead.

They might as well have been up in the sky with those stars for all that he could reach them.

What if something happens? he thought, for the hundredth time. *What if they leave me here? What if the Talchai come? They'd have to abandon me here, I can't even walk, much less ride.*

Kasha was wonderful, and Zorsha was nearly as high in Yuchai's regard as his cousin—but they weren't Clan. Their tongue was alien, and it either did not have words he longed to say, or he hadn't yet learned them. Their concerns, their way of life, the very food they ate was alien.

And Shenshu, Losha, Demonsbane—they're so excited, so involved in learning new things—they hardly ever have time to just talk. I'm just a child, anyway, to them. I'm not really very important, and I don't have much to talk about. They've got more things to worry about than me. More important things.

He sniffled, and scrubbed his sleeve across his eyes. The whole day had been like this; loneliness had made a lump in his throat that had made it hard to eat and drink, and the peculiar round-eyed faces of his new friends had given no comfort. The feeling would pass, it always did—but for now, he ached, he ached so. . . .

There was a tap at his door; someone had seen that he still had a candle lit, no doubt. He scrubbed at his face again, hastily, and whispered a "Come" that didn't quaver *too* noticeably.

"Still awake?" someone called softly. Then that someone eased around the edge of the door, and Yuchai saw that his visitor was Zorsha, carrying a pair of baskets.

"Thought you might be."

Before Yuchai could say anything, Zorsha came right over to the bed and sat down on the foot of it.

"I saw you had a candle, " he said softly, "and—you know, Yuchai, I wasn't born here, like most of the rest were. I'm from a good bit further west. I never knew my mother; lost my father when I was younger than you. One of the sister-houses took me in, decided I had a few wits, sent me on here. I loved it, I really did— but it wasn't home, you know? There were times when the food would just stick in my throat, it just didn't taste right. Seemed to me like you were having a little touch of that today yourself."

He cocked his head sideways, inquiringly, and his silky, strange gold hair fell over one shoulder and into his eye before he flicked it back with an impatient jerk of his head.

Yuchai nodded, unable to speak around the lump of unhappiness in his throat.

"Thought so; said as much to that Demonsbane lad. Did you know he's one damn fine cook?" Zorsha grinned. "Says it's because Shamans aren't supposed to have to depend on *anybody*. We—ah—went on down to the kitchen and did a little experimenting down there when the cooking crew cleared out. Losha had some of your spices in his kit. Anyway, Demonsbane says to try these."

Zorsha flicked the cloth off the top of the first basket, and Yuchai smelled home—the flat, tough bread that seemed to take days to chew, the savory, highly spiced, chopped mutton to fill it, and a chunk of raw honeycomb.

He started to stutter out his thanks, and found that he couldn't. Because Zorsha had snagged one of the rounds of bread, filled it with meat as neatly as if he were nomad-born, rolled it, and stuffed it into his mouth as soon as he opened it.

"Eat," he said, grinning. "You haven't done more than pick at your food for two days. And if you pine away on me, Boitan will *murder* me."

He ate, finding himself ravenous, devouring the food as shamelessly as a beggar at a feast. It wasn't until the last of the crumbs were gone, and he was sucking his fingers clean of the faintest hint of honey, that Zorsha replaced the first basket with the second.

"When I got half sick for home, it was old Ardun who brought me Ancas honeycakes and fried pies. And he brought me something else. 'You know,' he said, 'in Ancas they got gold hair like yours, the Yazkirn got noses you could split wood with, and us that were Sabirn are like little brown weeds—but no matter where I been, somehow a puppy is still a puppy, and boys and puppies seem to belong together.' "

With that, Zorsha upended the basket and tilted a warm, sleepy ball of soft golden-brown fur into Yuchai's lap. A round, fuzzy head, all floppy ears and eyes, lifted from enormous paws to yawn at him.

Yuchai froze, hardly able to believe his eyes. The Vredai *had* had dogs—just like they'd had flocks and herds. All were gone, lost in the flight west.

Yuchai had lost his own hound, Jumper, in the first flight. Jumper had been out minding Yuchai's little flock of sheep when the Talchai had attacked. Yuchai hoped he'd been driven off, and not killed, but he would never really know what happened to him. Jumper's loss would have broken his heart had there not been so much else to mourn.

Boy and puppy looked into each other's surprised eyes. It was the puppy who made the first move. He sniffed Yuchai's nose with great care, found him good, and sealed the decision with a wet, warm, pink tongue—which incidentally disposed of any remaining stickiness from the honey. Yuchai threw his arms around the puppy's neck, speechless with happiness.

"I'd have brought him sooner," Zorsha said apologetically, as Yuchai hugged, and the pup squirmed and licked, "but I was housebreaking him. If Boitan came in and stepped in a puppy-mess, he'd murder *both* of us! Well?"

Yuchai could only stare and try to get something out

as tears started to spill out of his eyes, and the pup cleaned them off his cheeks with proprietary pleasure.

Zorsha seemed to understand.

"You see if you can get some sleep, all right?" he said softly. "I'll come around in the morning and take him out for his walk. You can tell me what you're going to call him then."

He gathered up the baskets and left, giving Yuchai a last wink as he picked up the candle to take with him on his way out the door. The puppy took the extinguishing of the light as the signal to resume his interrupted dreams; he flopped down beside Yuchai with a weary, contented sigh. Yuchai gathered him close, and the pup snuggled into the circle of his arms, pressing his warm little body up against Yuchai's side. And like any young thing, he was asleep within a few breaths.

Yuchai stroked the silky little head and long, floppy ears, not knowing how Zorsha had known of his unhappiness, and unsure how to properly thank him for the curing of it. *I'd like to call you "Zorsha,"* he told the pup silently, *but then you'd get confused.* He almost laughed. *And Zorsha might not realize I mean it as thanks.*

He thought over the proper name for a long time. *How about "Lajas"—that's "Seeker."* He thought about it a moment longer, and nodded with satisfaction. *I think, yes. It's perfect. And Zorsha will know what I mean, won't he, Lajas?* He settled a little farther under the comforter, and the pup snuggled closer, laying his head just under Yuchai's chin. Yuchai continued to stroke the soft fur, and never quite noticed when he finally fell asleep.

Chapter Eight

I beg you to consider, my lords, what a friendly prince means to us here on the border. And what it could mean to have him consent to stay.

Felaras chewed the end of her stylus and considered the last phrase. Was there enough veiled threat in there? Too much? *Damn diplomatic jockeying around—*

Felaras raised her head from the palimpsest sharply as the triple-tap that identified Kasha as the knocker at her study door broke into her concentration.

Damn it, now what?

Kasha did not wait for an invitation to enter. The door was already half open anyway.

"Master Felaras, Jegrai and Northwind are here to see you," she said, opening the door completely and leaning through it. "They don't look happy. Ardun says there was some activity down in the Vredai camp earlier, and about twenty riders left and haven't come back. He says they had lots of spare horses with them, and what looked like all their gear."

"Lovely," Felaras muttered, rubbing her right eye. There was a headache starting there, springing into life the moment she'd heard what sounded like bad news.

166

It's all this tension. The gods must hate me, I guess. "I suppose that grumbling in the ranks Teo and Mai told me about has come to more than grumbling. And they want me to do something about it."

Kasha shrugged, and kept her face expressionless.

"What do I look like, anyway?" Felaras demanded in sudden irritation, wishing she could consign the last half-year to oblivion.

Damn Jegrai and all his crew!

"Do they think I'm Ruwan Dyr, the Goddess of Peace? It's not enough to be Master and juggle all the personalities of the quirkiest lot this side of Targheiden, but now I'm supposed to work miracles for a lot of nomads too?"

Her Second wisely kept her silence.

Felaras got herself calmed down, and warded off the headache with a relaxation exercise. *This isn't Jegrai's fault. He didn't ask to come here. If he had his druthers, they'd all be down on the steppes right now.* "All right, bring them up," she sighed, wishing she'd gotten more than a couple hours of sleep. "We'll see if it's what I think it is, and if we can actually do anything about it."

Kasha closed the door of the study only to reopen it a a few moments later for Khene Jegrai and Shaman Northwind. They entered and walked quietly forward to stand before Felaras' desk. Kasha stayed beside the door, but raised one eyebrow, asking Felaras in their own private code if she needed to stick around for this meeting. Felaras shook her head very slightly, and Kasha closed the door and took up her post as doorguard outside on the landing to make certain that there would be no unauthorized ears prying into the Master's affairs.

Although the Shaman was wearing his "inscrutable sage" mask, Felaras could see that Kasha was right. There was a tightness around his eyes and in the set of his shoulders that told her wordlessly that he was deeply worried. Jegrai was relatively easier to read than the Shaman, though she doubted that there were more than half a dozen folk in the Fortress who'd have been able to get past that deadpan "betting face" he had assumed. But she could see that the muscles of his neck and arms were tight enough to make him move a little stiffly, and that his eyes were narrowed in what, for him, was muted anger. Neither of them took the seats she offered them with a nod of her head.

Bad sign. They either are mad at us, or they think we're gong to be mad at them.

"Master Felaras," the Shaman began, not at all diffidently, but with a haughty, stone-faced air of *we're equals, and I'm telling you this only because I think you need to know.* "There has been some trouble with our people, which we fear may cause some difficulty—"

"Pardon, Northwind," Jegrai interrupted, his voice flat and expressionless. "But Master Felaras deserves plain speaking in this." He turned to Felaras, and folded his arms across his chest. "I will give you the whole of it. There has been a revolt among the Vredai, and some two hands of warriors have broken off and ridden out. They say they will not ride with Vredai while I am Khene—and that they will not ride with Vredai *at all* as long as Vredai subsists on the charity of outsiders. In other words, they expect the next Khene to break water-pledge with you, and violate our treaty."

"Charity?" Felaras said curiously. "Hladyr bless, what charity?"

"The food you granted us, the new herds, the very valley," Northwind replied, ticking the items off on his fingers. "And yes, I know that the valley is ours by the treaty, the food was part of what was granted to us to seal the water-pledge, and the herd-beasts payment for those who have begun riding patrol with your Watchers about the Vale. These who have ridden out, however, are all young hotheads who would, I fear, far rather take than earn."

Oh, so. The ones who've gotten a taste for raiding don't like giving it up. I guess I should be thankful there's only "two hands" worth of them.

"Earning takes too long," Felaras pointed out with dry humor. "And costs in terms of real work; boring, routine work. Not exciting stuff like fighting and raiding."

"Aye," Jegrai agreed, "and they have forgotten that while Vredai have always been warriors, we were warriors only to defend the herds. And the herds came first, before raids and counting coups. I heard much about the glory of war before they stormed out of my tent; enough to make me wish to take a stick to their thick heads, one and all. I should think they had seen enough of that kind of 'glory' to last a lifetime."

Northwind interrupted him. "Na, Khene, I did not once hear prating of the glory of facing the Talchai. The only 'glory' I heard of was the 'glory' of running down land-folk and taking the spoils."

Jegrai snorted a disgusted agreement. "Tending sheep brings no glory—and riding patrol offers no chance at fortune."

Felaras' already high estimation of Jegrai rose more. It wasn't often that a man as young as the Khene who came from a culture that had faced and adopted violence could see the benefits of peace.

"So they're going to go back to raiding my land-folk, just as we've got *them* settled back on their farms and at least tentatively convinced that you folk are going to guard them, not hurt them—"

"Exactly so," the Shaman agreed wearily. "And I could wish they had chosen some other time and place."

"How many of these dissidents have families of their own?"

"None," Jegrai replied positively.

"Huh. That has both good and bad points," Felaras

replied, propping both elbows on the desk and resting her chin in both hands. Jegrai frowned and shifted his weight a little, distracting her.

"Gentlemen, I am not going to pounce on you and turn you into frogs," she said impatiently. "You've proven yourselves my allies twice over by coming to me directly with this. Now, will you *please* sit down? We have some planning to do, and I'm tired of craning my neck up to look at you!"

Jegrai and Northwind exchanged looks—Jegrai's a bit startled, the Shaman's one of "I told you so" satisfaction— and they seated themselves across from her with a scraping of wood on the hardwood floor.

"All right; they don't have families, so we can't use blood-ties to lure them back. Or maybe I should ask first if you want them back."

"No," Jegrai said quickly. "Once traitor, what's to stop them from turning traitor again? Besides, to avoid the curse of having broken water-pledge, they have declared that they are no longer of Vredai. If they are not of us, why would we wish them back? And if we took them back, are they not oathbreakers? I should have to execute them. I had rather just eliminate them; either drive them back into the east or kill them in a raid-attempt."

"Good point. All right—are your people still using those red-and-black armbands we made up to identify them as allies of the Order?"

"Oh, yes," the Shaman replied with a tight smile. "Not the least because they are bright and handsome. The young riders are fond of ornament, and we lost most such things some time ago. And I think I see your next question—the rebels tore their armbands off and left them at Jegrai's feet ere they rode out, saying they had had enough of collars and leashes."

"Well, that means we won't have to change colors, at least," Felaras replied. "Seeing as your people like ornament, gentlemen, I'll see to it that the riders still with you get all they could desire. Headbands, scarves for their helms, ribbons for their lances, tassels for their bridles—anything you can think of, I'll have made up. Are you seeing where I'm heading?"

"Aye." Jegrai smiled a little. "Since your folk won't know one rider from another, you are intending that they should think my rebels have come from outside."

"That's it. Now . . ." she pulled a map of the Vale out of her desk and unfolded it on the desk top, clearing room for it by sweeping the papers she'd been working on to the side. "If you were whoever they'll pick to lead them, where would *you* go to hole up and make a base? And then, where would you start to raid?"

So. It's to be us.

Kasha's mare pricked her ears forward and brought her head up, and pawed the floor of the barn restlessly. Kasha put her hand over the mare's soft nose and forced it down before she could whicker a greeting to the horses she scented approaching and give them away.

Damn trouble with fighting a skirmish in spring, Kasha thought with annoyance. *Damn horses are in season, and damn nomads only geld about half their stallions. Hope they don't scent us. They shouldn't, we're downwind of them, but you never know.*

She was the only Sword among the nomad ambushers hiding in this barn, but she looked just as wild as any of them. Besides her normal dark clothing and armor, she was bedecked with a gypsy-motley of identifying ribbons. The rest of the nomads had even more; given choices of ornaments, most took everything. Red-and-black streamers and ribbons fluttered from the tips of lances and javelins and even from the pommels of swords. Red-and-black braided bands encircled upper arms and helms, and held hair off of nomad foreheads. Red-and-black tassels hung from reins and bridles, and some of the warriors sported several red-and-black scarves tied jauntily around their necks and around their legs just above the knee. The three young women in this party had even braided their hair with red-and-black cords before coiling it around their heads. They looked like they were decked out for a festival. But there would be no mistaking where the allegiance of this party lay.

There were a half-dozen of these ambush parties hiding at this end of the Vale, now that they knew where the dissidents had holed up. Between them, Felaras and Jegrai had identified that many likely targets—mostly flocks—among the Vale folk back on their lands near the rebel base. There had already been two raids by the rebels; one had succeeded, and one, by sheerest luck, had been foiled by a party returning from riding border-guard.

The rebels hadn't done much damage—yet. Mostly they'd ridden a destructive swath through a field of young oats, and stolen a handful of sheep. But both Felaras and Jegrai feared that was subject to change at any moment. The next raid could include fire, rapine, and murder—

Probably *would*, as they grew more sure of themselves.

And if that happened, no amount of red-and-black trimmings would convince the Vale folk that *any* nomad was trustworthy.

The lookout on the barn roof slithered down on the rope leading through the hatch to the second floor. Kasha tensed and turned to see what the leader of the party would signal. Though she had long since graduated to the rank of "serjant" in the Sword, this time *she* was not the leader of the party. That honor had fallen to one of Jegrai's older trackers, a hard-faced man called Abodai. Each ambush party had at least one Sword with it; and not one single Sword had been appointed as leader.

This was a calculated risk. The Watchers were going to prove themselves to Jegrai's folk—as fighters, but also as true allies, and not order-givers.

Abodai, watching through a crack in the door, jerked his fist, thumb up, in a silent order to mount. As neatly as if they had trained together, the ambushers swung into their saddles. Abodai did the same, then backed his horse a few paces.

Silence, except for the stamping of a hoof, the twittering of birds in the hayloft. Sunlight streaked through the cracks in the barn walls, the beams almost solid with dancing dust-motes. Hay-scent and dust-scent mingled with the salt smell of horse-sweat and the tang of the herbs the riders used to wash with. Kasha suppressed a sneeze.

Then—thunder of hooves in the distance, growing nearer by the moment. Abodai pulled one of his javelins from the quiver at his back; those with bows took that as a signal to nock arrows, those armed only with swords drew them.

Nearer—nearer—

War cries, and the splintering sound that meant somebody's mount had split the top rail of the fence.

Then, with a war cry of his own, Abodai spurred his horse forward, shouldering open the unbarred barn door. His horse was the only one clever enough and well-trained enough—and with enough innate trust in his rider—to do that little trick. Kasha spared half a second to envy him, and another to wonder if he'd let her put her mare to his beast when this was over—and then she was through, clattering past him in the boiling mass of flying ribbons and hooves and dust that slammed right into the path of the oncoming raiding party.

Horseshit! Torches—

They'd made this stand just in time. Given a free hand, the rebels would have burned this farm to the ground.

Even as she saw the four riders with torches, the distance-fighters cut them down; the torch-bearing rebel nearest Kasha fell out of his saddle with a javelin in his throat, to kick out his life in the dust as his horse galloped on. The black and red ribbons decorating the javelin fluttered with incongruous gaiety as he quivered and jerked.

But there was no time to stop and watch—the horses were crashing into the midst of the raiding party. The charge took them out of bow range, and it was hand-to-hand work. Kasha picked her target and spurred her mare at him; a man a little older than Jegrai, with an unkempt, straggly moustache. He saw her coming and snarled, pivoting his own horse to meet her.

Her blow bounced and slid off his shield, a smallish round-shield of brass-studded leather. She deflected his return with her own shield. Then cheated.

Felaras had warned Jegrai before this began that the Swords fought with any and all weapons, by any and all means. For a Watcher confronted by an enemy, there was no such things as "fair" or "foul;" there was only "win" or "lose." If they had not fought this way, there likely would have been no Order—but that was not yet for a stranger's ears.

And Jegrai had agreed to having the Swords along, knowing that they would resort to tactics his people would consider completely dishonorable.

Kasha deflected another of her man's strikes, ducked under a third—and swatted his horse with the flat of her blade as hard as she could.

Startled, it half-reared before he could control it, exposing the rebel's stomach as he threw his arms out and fought for balance. Her vicious backhand blow nearly cut him in half. She felt the soft shock up her arm, then ducked behind her shield; blood sprayed her as he toppled from his horse's back.

No time to think. She turned on the one behind him,

feeling the fighting-drunk she'd described to Yuchai take her and spread her mouth open in a savage grin of blood-lust.

He was already busy—*when did I get turned to face the barn?* She took this one from behind as he struggled with one of the Vredai women. The nomad had lost her helm, her sword had splintered, and she was desperately trying to protect her head behind the inadequate cover of her target-shield. Kasha was not about to thrust and have her own blade lodge in the corpse, though the fighter's unguarded back presented a tempting target. Instead she shouldered her mount into his as he beat down the woman's guard, and split his head just below the line of his helm. Cutting into bone this time—it was like hitting wood, and the impact quivered up her arm. The blade lodged for just an instant before she pulled it free.

She snatched his sword in her shield-hand as it fell from his fingers, urged her mare past the horse now standing puzzled and spent, and pressed the nomad's blade into the Vredai woman's hand.

Then instinct made her turn with shield up, and she was forced to defend herself from a furious attack.

He was taller than she, stronger, and just as well trained. All she could do was to use her shield to try to keep him off.

She didn't entirely succeed in that either; before too long her ears were ringing from one too many solid hits on her helm, her left arm going numb from wrist to shoulder, and her right arm burning from wrist to elbow with the pain of a long, shallow gash. He'd managed to cut the strap of her vambrace, which now was lying somewhere under the dust churned up by the hooves of the milling horses.

He was giving her no openings, and no chance to back out.

Never go head to head with a man your equal, she

could hear Ardun saying sardonically in the back of her mind. *Better reach and more muscle will kill you, girl.*

Time to cheat again.

There was one glaring weakness in the strategy of these nomads—they lived by their horses, so it was unthinkable to make a horse your target. Alive, it was a trophy, and a possession that was nearly part of your family. Dead, it was just so much meat. So the horse was off-limits.

Guess again. Sorry, horse.

She manuevered her mare in front of his, got in reach of its throat, and slashed open the great vein of her opponent's mount.

Its knees buckled as blood fountained over her and everyone else nearby, and it collapsed almost immediately.

The fighter screamed a curse at her as he kicked free of the falling horse. He staggered, caught his balance, and prepared to attack her with berserker fury glaring at her out of his bloodshot eyes.

Then fury was replaced by shock.

He fell with a javelin pinning him to his dead, twitching mount, a javelin rammed through his body at close range.

She looked up in surprise to meet Abodai's feral grin, white teeth gleaming in brown face, and then they each turned away to take on a new opponent.

They had begun this outnumbered almost three to one. Now the odds were even after a few moments of combat. They'd lost two: the rebels had lost at least a dozen, probably more. There was no way of telling for certain how many had fallen, not with the riderless horses dashing around in panic, adding to the confusion.

Only now were the remaining survivors realizing that this was a fight to the death, no holds barred.

Once again, this was something the strategists had counted on.

For Jegrai had finally told Felaras the bones of the

story of how Vredai had been driven into the West. And what that meant to the people who had suffered the physical and mental torments of that drive.

They may try to wound, rather than kill, unless they know they face strangers, Jegrai had said of the rebels, soberly. *There are so few of us compared to the Talchai, and of us all, only I had acquaintances in that Clan. We are more used to saving each other than killing— and only I of my Clan have faced those who were once my friends over the sword-edge.*

This reluctance to kill—won't that hold for your people, too? Felaras had asked him soberly.

Not after I finish speaking to them, had been the grim reply. *We have been betrayed twice now within my memory. We are not growing to like betrayal, let me tell you.*

Evidently Jegrai had been right.

Each of the surviving ambushers had a single opponent now, and the combat had turned from chaos into individual fights.

Sweat trickled down the back of Kasha's neck, and dust caked her lips. Her mouth was dry as the dust her mare's hooves threw into the air, and her right arm throbbed.

And none of this mattered. The intoxication of fighting had hold of her again, an exalted state where time stretched and she was focused in on herself and out on her foe. Nothing mattered but him, and she could see clearly every little detail of what he looked like and what he did, as if she was living a little bit faster than he was. This man was her size, her weight; a perfect opponent in every way.

His image branded itself in her memory. If she lived to be a hundred, she'd be able to describe this man so that an artist could paint him accurately; that was the effect of the battle-fever. He had dark skin, no facial hair; two braids that had probably been tucked up under his helm but which now were hanging free on either side of his head. Sweat was running into his eyes, and there were splashes of blood across one cheek. She wondered if it was his, but decided not. He had a gash across one leg, but like the one running up her arm, it looked to be shallow.

They circled their horses warily about each other, taking the measure of one another. She saw him frown uneasily, as her mouth was tugged again into that hideous grin by the rush of battle-lust.

It is lust. Gods, don't let Zorsha come near me until I get a chance to clean up and cool down. Or my good intentions will go right out the window with our clothing.

The man apparently decided that he didn't like the odds, and abruptly wheeled his horse in a tight little circle and spurred him at the fence.

Sorry, horse. Time to cheat again.

There was one lone difference between them, other than sex. Her mare topped his scrubby little gelding by three hands, and outweighed it proportionally. Over a long run that might have given him an advantage; all that weight could slow her horse down.

But out of the starting blocks the advantage was all hers—the more especially since her mare was a lot fresher than his beast. She spurred the mare after him; they had him in less time than it took to breathe. And she used the other advantage of her bigger horse: she rammed the gelding with her mare's shoulder; literally bowled him over and rode them both down.

As the gelding went over she heard bones snap, and heard it scream in agony—heard him scream too, as he went down trapped under the weight of his horse, and as her mare stepped on him at least once. And then he gurgled and wailed behind her as the gelding began to thrash in pain.

That was no way to leave even an enemy.

She wheeled the mare around, and saw the gelding

spasming wildly in the dust, saw the nomad clawing at
it in mindless agony with one arm flopping useless and
the leg he had free still lying over the horse's barrel like
a thing of wood. Two paces closer and she could smell
him—and knew his back was broken.

That was no way to leave *anyone*.

She dismounted, walked over, and dealt with it.

And when she looked around, after cleaning her knife
on the dead gelding's hide, she saw the others in the
ambush party staring at her with a mixture of approval
and fear, as if they were wondering if she was now
going to perform some kind of trophy-taking on the
body. And she saw that the only ones left standing were
wearing red and black.

It was over.

"You look like you took the first layer of skin off,"
Ardun observed, filling the mugs before him with wine—
Kasha's full, his half full. He pushed the mug across the
little table between them, then sat back in his chair,
cradling his own mug in both hands.

"I feel like I have," she said, taking her wine and
gulping down half of it. "I thought I'd never get the
smell of blood out of my nose."

He nodded; candles on the table between them soft-
ened his age-lines and made him look younger; about
her age. "Took me that way too. I'd come out of a fight
and scrub for an hour or more—then I'd go find Felaras
and she'd get me drunk and I'd bawl like a baby."

"Just like you do for me," Kasha observed.

Ardun shrugged, and a breeze from the open window
behind him made the candle-flames flicker. "When you
get battle-fever the way we do, you need somebody
steady around you after—somebody who gets drunk on
death like you do, who can tell you that you aren't an
animal for feeling that way." He gave her a long look

over the top of his mug. "And somebody who won't let you rape him."

She laughed shakily, and ran her fingers through her damp hair. "You got that right. First time it happened, if you hadn't been around, I'd have taken Teo right there in the courtyard. Poor Teo. He was only worried for me, and glad to see me back alive. He thought I was angry with him. He never knew how close he came to being raped in public. Gods, that makes me feel like some kind of savage. An animal; a brute beast."

Ardun shook his head at her. "You know what it is—your body figuring out you just escaped dying, and trying to force you into procreation before you go put it in harm's way again. Your body thinks your duty to the world is to leave a copy of yourself if you go out in glory. So do you listen to your body or your mind?"

"My mind, of course. That *is* why I'm here in your room and not in Zorsha's."

"And here I thought it was because you wanted my company."

Kasha laughed shakily.

"And I'll tell you again, because you need to hear it; no, you aren't an animal because you get drunk on killing, or because you're ready to jump anything male in sight when it's over. The fever is just your body again—trying to keep itself from getting killed, it makes you drunk so that you don't think, you just react. You're not an animal, because when it's all over, you agonize over your reactions. Zetren doesn't—he *is* an animal, a rabid one. And if it weren't that he's useful to the Order, I'd have contrived an accident for him a long time ago."

Kasha nodded soberly; Ardun was far more than the Sword Leader—he was a past master at every assassination technique the Order had ever encountered. Some he taught everyone. Some he taught privately. Kasha had gotten some of that private tutelage, as had others.

One of those others, and she had no idea who, would be Ardun's successor. That wouldn't be known until he died, and they opened his papers to see who he had left a certain little set of "tools" to. And whoever became his successor would secretly choose and train another.

So if tiny, wizened Ardun decided that Zetren needed disposing of—it would be done. And only Ardun would know that it had been no accident. Because if he ever did eliminate Zetren, it would be in a way that would leave nothing suspicious.

"You're not drinking," Ardun pointed out, breaking into her thoughts. "You're supposed to be getting drunk."

"I daren't get too drunk," she admitted. "Just enough to believe I'm all right. I've got guard on Felaras and the boy tonight, and I'm getting uneasy feelings. . . ."

She paused long enough to empty her mug and hold it out to him for refilling.

"Ill-wishing?" he asked.

"I think. But getting at the Master indirectly. There's just too damned much going on, and it's all muddled. Like there's a half-dozen plots going on that are not quite lurching into each other."

"Could be. It's like that last siege, when Kyle was Master. I remember the same feeling. Like there's something behind the door that hasn't made up its mind to try breaking in, but you can hear it breathing."

"Ardun—did the fever take you during siege-fighting too?" she asked, curious, and with the wine making her bolder than she might otherwise have been. The siege— the last in the history of the Order—had been long before her time. Felaras had been no more than one of Kyle's possible successors, and Ardun had only just been promoted to full Sword status.

He shook his head. "It wasn't that kind of fighting. Mostly I didn't even see the results of what I did. I was one of the ones chosen to sneak out the escape tunnels, infiltrate the army, and doctor the food supplies. What I did didn't even have any effect until the next afternoon."

"Aconite in the spiced meat?" she guessed.

He nodded, his face gone inward-looking as he called up past memories. "And ground glass in the salt, ergot in the flour, jimson weed in the fodder. Then Kyle up on the tower right after they'd eaten at noon, calling down death and madness on the besiegers. It was pretty damned impressive, let me tell you; he timed it to a hair. Between the ones dropping over dead and the ones taken by fits—and then even the *horses* going wild—your common soldier was pretty impressed with our direct line to heaven. Then we let loose with the mortars, which we hadn't used yet. We didn't hit much but the command tent; it was the only thing we could range on, but having the commander's quarters go under heavenly retribution was damned disheartening for them. That's why the Yazkirn, at least, don't condemn us as heretics, and haven't disturbed the sister-house we have down there. They figure we're under some kind of divine protection—by their theology, the powers of darkness can't strike at high noon."

Some of that Kasha had already known, but some was new. This was the first time she'd ever found Ardun willing to talk about it, and Felaras didn't even want to hear about the subject, much less talk about it. "Weren't you risking them getting those doctored supplies at morning meal?"

He shook his head. "No, that was what made it work so well. You can set a clock by the Yazkirn army cooks. Oat-and-barley porridge for breakfast, because they've cooked it the night before in big kettles. Stuffed rolls at noon, because they can be handed out to those on patrol. Two each, one spiced meat, one root-vegetable, and the men are known to trade, so some would have gotten a double-dose of aconite and some nothing but the ergot in the flour or the glass in the salt, and some nothing at all, depending on whether the barrels we doctored were close to being empty. We didn't doctor anything that wasn't already open."

Kasha nodded, stowing all that away for future reference. It was all written down in the chronicles, of course, but it was always useful to have certain things at hand, in memory.

"So to answer your question, no—the killing didn't give me the fever. The actual sally out to do the dirty work did. And I've gotten the same fever just sneaking out to look over a bandit camp, with no likelihood of combat. It's the going into danger that does it, girl, not the killing."

"Oh my head knows that," she admitted, pulling on her wine, and feeling a little "cleaner" than she had when she'd ridden in. "But you have to tell my gut every time."

"Ah, well, I know that." He gave her a crooked grin.

"So what do you think of Yuchai?" she asked him, feeling comforted enough to change the subject. "I was a little surprised to see you sparring with him."

"His moves are different enough that I didn't want to chance him getting hurt, especially with him only just out of bed," Ardun replied. "Put him with the novices and he *would* get hurt, sure's stars. I like the boy, Kasha, I like him a lot. If his people are anything like him—damn if we don't have more in common with them than any Ancas tightass. That boy is bright, he's quick—and in no way is he ever going to be in Sword. He gets in over my dead body."

She let out her breath in a long hiss. "You have no idea how happy I am to hear that. Why?"

"He thinks too much, and at the wrong time. You think too much, and so do I, but it's after everything is over and done with. *He* thinks about it when it's happening. So long as he's planning on going into one of the other two chapters, I'll tutor him all he wants—but you can tell him from me I don't want him thinking he's coming into Sword, because I won't permit it. If I have to hamstring him to convince him, I will. So help me."

"Good—you're going to make all of us happy, I think, right down to Jegrai. The boy's his heir until he breeds one, you know. Teo says he loves him like a younger brother. Maybe more, because there isn't a great deal of love between himself and his real brother."

"Aye, I can see where there wouldn't be," Ardun replied, looking a great deal happier about the situation. "If that's the way Jegrai feels about it, and you, and me, then we should be able to convince Yuchai. Unless he really wants it?"

"Thank the gods, no," she told him. "No, fighting makes him sick—combat, that is. He likes the physical exercise, so long as it's for points and touches, but I'd be willing to bet he likes dancing as much. Told me earlier that points and touches is the way fighting *used* to be between the Clans until some outsiders began stirring things up."

"Interesting. Accounts for their accepting Jegrai as Khene. So—what is it with Yuchai being so keen on fighting even though he hates it?"

"He's determined that he won't be the only able-bodied person in the Clan that can't defend himself. Given their past and their intra-Clan loyalty, I'm not surprised at that."

"Agreed. About the boy: do you have any idea how much of a thinker he really is? And how far ahead he plans things?"

Kasha shook her head. "My part's been mostly confined to teaching him Ancas and Sabirn and teaching him to read. Zorsha's been the one involved in lessons that didn't involve just memorization."

"Let me give you a notion." He put his mug down on the table with a soft thud, and leaned forward, half-resting on the table top. "You know that pup of his follows him everywhere, and I know that breed—golden gaze-hounds are protective bastards even as pups. I was going to lock the pup in the ward-room until his lesson was over, figuring it'd come for me the way Zorsha's did—" He chuckled reminiscently. "You know, I *still* have the tooth-scars on my ankle? There I was, dancing around on one leg with the pup holding on like grim death, my ankle bleeding like fury, and Zorsha screaming at me not to hurt his dog. I wasn't minded to repeat the experience. So I asked the boy to put the dog in the room and explained why—told him I'd rather listen to howls than have my ankle perforated."

"And he said what?" She waved the pitcher of wine away when he offered it; her head was buzzing enough, and she didn't need the guilt-numbing effect anymore.

"That he'd already thought of that. He gave the dog a command in his tongue, and told me to go ahead and start a drill. Well, I did, though let me tell you, I was not at my best, watching that pup out of the side of my eye."

"Nothing happened?"

"Not a damn thing, though the pup looked fit to burst every time I touched the boy. So then, when I laid him on his butt, he went over and made a fuss over the dog, then asked me to pair him for a minute with somebody I wasn't ever likely to again. Said he wanted to show me something. I set him up with Davy. They went at it for a couple passes, then he yelled something, and damn if that pup didn't come flying across the yard like an arrow—and before Davy or I can even blink, the pup's got his sword-hand wrist in his teeth, growling like he's going to chew it off."

"He didn't hurt Davy, did he?" Kasha asked in alarm.

"Not a bit, though I wouldn't have reckoned what would have happened if Davy'd tried to fight him. Pup just held on without even bruising the skin. So the boy gives the dog another command and it lets go, though it keeps a mighty suspicious eye on young Davy all the rest of that session. Turns out the boy had another dog when he started learning sword-work that pulled exactly the same stunt Zorsha's did. So he taught this one while he was laid up that everything was all right unless he yelled for help. See what I mean by thinking ahead?"

"Uh," Kasha grunted, nodding thoughtfully. "Uh-huh. So, what do you see him as? Book?"

"Not a chance; the boy's too inquisitive. Tower, I'd say, and Hand for preference. He's always asking questions, and they all run on *how* does this work, not *why*. Showed me why those swords of theirs are curved, and single-edged, and it makes damned good sense for horseback fighting. Going to have some made up for us and start training you good riders with them."

"So that the blade doesn't lodge and pull out of your hand?" Kasha hazarded.

He nodded.

She grinned. "Uh-huh, I wondered about that. Tell you what else would be nice; a bit of a lanyard on the pommel-nut. Lose your blade on the ground and you have a chance to get it back. Lose it on horseback, and you might as well forget it. But loop a lanyard around your wrist, and if it gets knocked out of your hand, you've still *got* it."

"Good thought. What do you think of their soft stirrups?"

"Not much," she said, "And some of the lot I rode with are modifying theirs to match mine. Too damned easy to get your foot caught in the thing, even if it does mean you need a heeled boot to use our kind. I don't fancy being dragged, and I can't see any advantage in the soft stirrups."

"Fine. Anything else?"

"We ought to show them our soft iron javelins. If they're really going to be with us, they won't have any problem with getting metal, and the way the soft javelins foul a shield is even more useful in a horseback fight than a ground battle. I mean, figure how much is your horse going to like getting his ears whacked with a stick every time you move your shield, hey? And I don't know how Abodai trained that stallion of his to do some of his tricks, but somebody ought to see if it's the horse or the training. You already know about those laminated bows—"

"Aye, with lust in my heart. We're working on it, but not just anybody can make a bow. That Losha up here can, but it's a long process. Seems it involves wood, horn, sinew of all damn things, all laminated into the bow, and somehow bone plaques get into it too. We've got one about half made, but with that much work I don't wonder that they won't sell or trade them. Might as well ask a farmer to sell his house. Or his wife!"

"Sounds like. But the range on those things—"

"Makes them worth every damn hour you put on them. Well, feeling more like a member of the human race again?"

"Feeling more like the human race won't reject me, anyway. And it's about time for me to take my watch."

She got up, did an internal assessment of the wine on her judgement and reflexes, and decided it wasn't too bad. But just as a check, she dropped her wrist-knife down into her hand, and pivoted on her heel to place it in the target she knew was behind her.

Ardun peered at it as she went to pull it out. "In the black?"

She shook her head. "No, a hair out."

"Don't aim for the eye then, until the wine wears off. Throat's a better target."

"Yes, father," she replied with mock humility. "Anything you say, father."

"Watch your tone, girl; I can still take you any time I want."

"Don't I just know it." She walked back over to his

side of the table and kissed his forehead. "Throat it is. And thanks for getting me out of my depression again."

He hugged her waist. "Any time, baby-girl. You do me proud, I hope you know that. I'd like to see you with the badge some day."

"Hm, well that'll depend on who happens to be Master—which is Zorsha at this point, which could be touchy."

"Seven hells, girl, I told you to think ahead, I *didn't* tell you to map out the future!"

"Yes, sir." She bowed. He made a fist and tapped her cheek. She covered the hand with her own for a moment. "I'll bet Yuchai will still be awake; your permission, I'll tell him what you said about him being in Sword—and that you think he belongs in Hand."

"Do that. It would make me feel better."

"Suspect it will make him feel better too. And me. And Zorsha. Thanks again, father."

He waved a hand at her. "Off with you. Or I'll dock your pay for being late."

She laughed and ducked out the door, heading for the Master's quarters with a lightened step.

Chapter Nine

Don't shout. Whatever you do, don't shout. Tent walls do not muffle voices. "Why didn't you stop them?" Halun demanded, on the verge of hissing with anger, standing nearly nose to nose with Jegrai's brother. He clenched his hands into tight fists in an attempt to keep his impotent rage under control. "Why didn't you do something?"

"How was I to stop them?" Iridai growled, teeth clenched, arms crossed tightly over his burly, leather-armored chest as if to keep his own anger pent. "I was the one who roused them up in the first place! What was I to do when they ceased listening to me—betray them to Jegrai? They declared themselves and rode out before I would ever have been able to do even *that!*"

Halun's anger passed as quickly as it had flared, and he forced himself to relax, closing his eyes as much from a wave of pure weariness as anything else. *Watch yourself; if you make an enemy of this man, you'll destroy everything. Damned barbarians. Say something to placate him, or you'll strangle your hopes with your own two hands.* "I'm sorry, Iridai; I shouldn't have said that. All of us misjudged this time, I think. It certainly wasn't your fault that those young hotheads were even more hotheaded than we thought. You couldn't have predicted that. Forgive me for accusing you. I had no right."

"Ai, that is something less than truth, wise one," Iridai admitted, his own anger quenched by Halun's capitulation and apology. "I knew how wild they were— and with my talk of honor and dishonor I drove them to their deaths as surely as though it were my hand that held the blade." This was Iridai's tent; it was as martial and spare of comfort as the nomad himself. There were none of the piles of cushions to sit on that could be found elsewhere; one sat on the bare carpet. Iridai went from standing to sitting in a single graceful motion that maddened Halun because of his inability to imitate it.

Halun folded himself slowly and carefully down onto what seemed to be a marginally softer spot. He longed briefly, but sharply, for his chairs, his restful bed, his long, comfortable robes. He couldn't even be easy in his clothing. These breeches and long tunics did not feel right, binding up in unexpected places. "You're being far too hard on yourself—"

"Am I?" Iridai snorted, tossing his braids over his shoulders with his right hand. "You heard all my lofty speeches to them about returning to the old ways—did you not see them, one and all, discarding those new swords at Jegrai's feet along with their armbands? And who was to blame for that?"

Halun saw signs that told him Iridai was about to fall into a melancholy from which it might take days to wake him. *Damned fool, this is no time to go into a brood!* "And who was to blame for them *staying* in the Vale?" he demanded harshly. "They could have gone away from here—there was no one stopping them. Jegrai made no moves to hunt them down until *they* started the trouble. East might be closed, but there is north, south—even west; they could have been over the pass and gone long before Jegrai alerted the Order that they were rebels. No one would have pursued them, not Jegrai, certainly not Felaras. But no—instead those lazy fools made their camp in the single most obvious place in the Vale, and proceeded to raid the very folk Jegrai had sworn to protect. They weren't just asking to be wiped out, they were opening their arms to destruction and embracing it!" *Just like the fool primitives they are, no matter how much they boast about valuing knowledge!*

Iridai raised his head at that, narrowed his eyes, and nodded his round head thoughtfully.

"We are, perhaps, well rid of them," Halun continued, deliberately choosing the most callous phrases he could. "Clearly they could not keep secrets; I think we may thank the gods that none of them were taken alive to betray us—although I must admit that Jegrai's ruthlessness took me somewhat by surprise. I did not expect him to be quite so thorough. I am sorry that Vredai has lost so many fine warriors—but it seems clear to me that they were warriors that were unable to think, or to plan. If Vredai is to prosper, its warriors must learn to use their wits as well as their hands."

"Truly spoken," Iridai agreed, though with some reluctance in his voice. "It is not a truth I care to hear, but it is nonetheless truth. As for Jegrai—once again I have underestimated him. I have mistaken his cleaving to the old ways for weakness. I shall not repeat that mistake."

At least you have that much sense, my uneasy ally. "Our concerns now are for the living, Iridai, and not the dead. How has this affected the others, those who are disaffected, but not yet rebellious?"

"I—I do not know," Iridai admitted. "I could guess, but . . ."

Halun shook his head. "Speculation is useless to us.

We must *know*, and know exactly. Else we act as fool-
ishly as those foolish boys."

"That is again truth. And a truth I will act on." Iridai
stood, his dark face now showing considerably more
resolution than he had demonstrated when he'd risen to
greet Halun.

"Good," Halun responded, getting slowly and painfully to his feet. *Oh, gods, will I ever see a chair again?
Is power worth my aching knees? Ah, stupid question.*
"Let us each go to those he knows best—you to the
warriors, myself to Gortan and those who have been
passed over when the Shaman made his yearly choices.
And we will see."

"Aye," Iridai replied, his eyes beginning to show
some life again. "We will see—and then, we will act."

"But if the world is a ball, and it is turning," Jegrai
objected, sorely perplexed, "why aren't we flung off of
it?"

Jegrai, clad resplendently in a new sleeveless tunic of
scarlet and breeches of soft black cotton—more of the
handiwork of the Order's looms and his mother's hands—
was theoretically holding court. What this actually meant
was that he was sprawled in the one chair that had
survived the Vredai flight into the west, under the
shade of the tree beside his tent. Teo, looking like a
servitor in his comfortably shabby brown clothing,
lounged in the grass beside him, doing his best to
explain Jegrai's questions about the book he was currently devouring. As Teo had predicted, the Khene was
beginning to fathom the mysteries of the written word,
and had graduated to the level of the beginning science
texts the novices read.

While Jegrai sat "in court," any of the Vredai with a
grievance, real or imagined, could approach him to
have it dealt with. In actuality, few of them did. The
Khene was scrupulously fair—and notoriously impar-

tial. So much so that those whose claims were a little shaky, or who might have some dealings they preferred to remain something less than public, had a very strong reason to settle their grievances in some court other than the Khene's.

So Jegrai had ample leisure to cross-examine Teo during these afternoon sessions, and took full advantage of the fact. He had little enough leisure at any other time. The Khene of Vredai was no less a worker than any of his people.

"Well?" he demanded.

Teo's brow was creased with thought. "I'm trying to come up with an example that makes sense, Jegrai," he began, when a stir at the edge of the camp caught the Khene's eye, and he motioned to his friend to hold his peace for a moment.

"Trouble?" Teo asked, sitting up straighter.

"Maybe. . . ." Jegrai squinted against the bright sunlight and the ever-present dust kicked up within the camp. The commotion resolved itself into three adults heading straight for him, followed by a horde of children, followed in turn by half the women of the camp. One of the adults was the young warrior Agroda, dressed in his finest—pale leather tunic and breeches, and so festooned with red-and-black bands and ribbons that he looked like a walking festival all by himself. But the other two—

One was a young woman of the Vale folk, with hair like a skein of spun sunlight; and the other, gold locks going to silver, looked to be her father.

Jegrai's heart sank to his boot-heels—

Until they came close enough for him to see their expressions. The young woman, dressed in a finely embroidered divided skirt, an equally elaborately embellished vest, and a delicately embroidered shirt that was so transparent it would have been obscene had the vest not been laced tightly over it, had the demure look of a cat that has just eaten the family dinner and knows the dog will get the blame. The older man, in a handsome set of riding leathers and an equally intricately embroidered shirt, was attempting to look sober, perhaps stern—and failing utterly. Every time he schooled his mouth to sobriety, he would glance at the girl or the Vredai, and a smile would begin to escape again. And Agroda was wearing the most fatuously foolish grin Jegrai had ever seen on a human face in his entire life.

The odd little party came to a halt the proper distance from Jegrai's chair. Agroda made one step forward, put right hand to left shoulder, and made the slight nod that was the formal salutation of Vredai to Khene.

"Speak," Jegrai responded, trying to keep his face still and impassive, but hoping wildly that this was what he thought it was.

"May we speak in Trade-tongue, oh Khene?" came the reply. "This good man of the Vale is also a warrior; he speaks but little of our tongue, and it were ill-courtesy to discuss what concerns him so closely in a language not his own."

I notice he doesn't mention the daughter, Jegrai thought, valiantly keeping his face straight. *Which means she probably knows our tongue as well as friend Teo. And I would not care to speculate on where or how she learned our speech.*

"Gladly," he replied. "It is only courtesy. And the warrior and his—daughter?—are welcome here. Is this a call for judgement, Agroda?"

"Of a kind," the young man replied, casting such a fond look on the young girl that Jegrai nearly choked on a laugh. "I would have my Khene to meet Venn Elkin, and his eldest daughter Briya. He was once a man of the sword in the service of the Princes of Yazkirn; now he and his daughter are both breeders and trainers of fine horses."

Oh-ho! Jegrai sat up a tiny bit straighter. *So there is more to this than a lovesick lad!*

The older man stepped forward and nodded; Jegrai returned the nod. The older man cleared his throat self-consciously. "I had occasion to meet your warrior, Khene Jegrai, under something less than ideal circumstances."

Elkin's command of Trade-tongue was excellent, as might have been expected in a horse-breeder, who probably dealt with traders on a regular basis. "Oh, so?" Jegrai replied blandly. "Was he trying to steal one of your stallions?"

The girl giggled, and the corners of her father's mouth twitched. "No, Khene—I fear he was trying to slip his mare into my breeding herd."

Jegrai gave Agroda a long look; the young man shrugged. "It was ordered that there be no stealing and no raiding," he said unrepentantly. "How else was one to get a tall-horse foal?"

"I was far less angry than in admiration, Khene," the horsebreeder hastened to say, laugh-wrinkles crinkling at the corners of his dark blue eyes. "And I will tell you that I had been looking to *your* beasts with a certain speculation. They are small, aye, and something less than beautiful, but they have a quickness and a stamina that are admirable qualities. I had thought of coming to some accommodation, but only idly, when your warrior forestalled me."

"And he kindly did not take his whip to my back!" Agroda laughed.

The horsebreeder coughed. "I—ah—detained him—"

"He ran me down into the corner of his field on his tall-horse stallion." Agroda hung his head mournfully. "I, mindful of my Khene's orders against raising hand or weapon against the Vale folk, I ran like a rabbit. But the horse was faster."

Elkin was doing his best to ignore the interruptions, but the laugh-wrinkles were growing deeper. "We spoke—"

Agroda raised his head, and sobered a little. "Fairly, Khene, he was in his rights to demand a judgement, but he wished to speak seriously of crossbreeding."

"When I finally got him to hold still long enough to *speak* to him!" Elkin chuckled richly. "Aye, and glad I was to know Trade-tongue. We left the mare to the attentions of my stallion; on his return to redeem her he sought me out and we spoke again."

"I thought, 'This is a most wise man.' I wished to have more speech of him."

"On this occasion, I spoke of a horse-colt I could not seem to gentle—"

"—and I offered to see what I could do if he would breed another of my mares to his stallion."

"Khene, if it were not that I have wizards in the mountains above me, I would have thought your warrior a wizard!" Elkin's face glowed with enthusiasm. "I had resigned myself to gelding this one, which would have been a sad loss—but in less time than I ever would have dreamed, he had it gentled and broken to saddle and halter!"

"Na, Venn." Agroda blushed. "It was only that the colt has too tender a mouth, I *told* you so. You frightened and hurt him with the bit—never meaning to—and he smelled pain on you thereafter. Me, I do not smell like you, I do not look nor sound like you, and I put on him a halter with nothing to hurt his silly mouth. He lost his fear very quickly—and quicker still when you gave him of sweet-root. Now when he smells you he thinks of long gallops and more sweet-root! So long as he neck-reins and answers to the knee, you need never subject him to a bit, and he will go gladly for you—"

"Your warrior is too modest," Elkin said mock sternly. "He saw at once what I never thought of."

"So this is where you have been spending your time, Agroda?" Jegrai asked. "With this good man? We missed you at practice and the hunt, but I think your time was better used than ours, now! But surely not all your days were spent in gentling one colt?"

"Ah . . . well . . ." Agroda blushed even redder.

"My daughter sought out his advice on my recommendation. She has charge of halter-breaking the young foals, and gentling some of the lighter horses to saddle," Elkin replied, that grin tugging at the corners of his mouth and trying to escape again. "I have no sons, you see. . . ."

"Ah," Jegrai nodded. "But a good daughter is worth any number of bad sons."

"In truth. I have never noted the lack of sons, except . . ." Venn contrived to look mournful. "A man knows, Khene—he would feel happier going to his rest, knowing that there was a strong fighter to protect his little filly foals, his sweet little mares—"

"*Father!*" the girl protested, blushing fit to match Agroda.

"I speak only of horses, do I not? But also—knowing that there will be others to carry on his work— grandchildren, Khene, a man would like to see his *grandchildren*—and the traders are not so like to try to cheat a man, a strong, tall man, a man with a sword at his side—eh?"

"Indeed, I have often seen it to be the case," Jegrai replied as neutrally as he could. "Although I must say that any trader who chose to bargain with my own mother Aravay would be lucky to come out with a whole skin."

The girl gave her father an "I told you so" glare.

"Well, the long and the short of it is, Khene, it seems that my daughter has halter-broke a stranger young colt than ever I had seen before—"

"*Father!*"

"—and your warrior and my girl here seem to have conceived a liking for each other."

They both blushed, and the grin escaped from Venn Elkin's control.

"I'm all for the match—but the young man says he must ask permission of his Khene."

"Well that he has. I'm sure you are aware that there will be problems," Jegrai replied. He leaned forward in his chair, and fixed the horsebreeder and his daughter with as serious a stare as he could manage. "Our gods are not yours, our way of life is not yours, nor our language."

"But I'll learn—" both Agroda and Briya burst out simultaneously.

Jegrai nodded. "That is what I wished to hear," he said, sitting back a little and crossing his legs. "Look, the both of you young ones—this will be no easy thing. You do not go to a wedding as you go to a light love. You must both be willing to change at least some things. Near every moment of your lives will be one of compromise. Yours, too, good sir," he said, looking over to Elkin, who also nodded. "You realize that by having one of my people in your household, you will be bringing change into *your* life, I trust?"

"I'd like to think I'm not too old to change, a bit," the horsebreeder said quietly. "Hladyr bless, if I can learn to train a colt to neck and knee, I expect I can learn to like meat spiced to burning and a son-in-law who spends half his nights sleeping out under stars! Aye, and a daughter out there with him!"

Jegrai exchanged a wry look with him—and was relieved by it. The man was under no illusions about what had been going on these warm starlit nights. And evidently hadn't been worried about it, so long as it wasn't rape. That took one burden off Jegrai's mind, assuming that all Vale folk were of the same customs as the horsebreeder. Clan women slept where they wished until they wed, though if one were bearing it were wise to have a name-father for the child. Teo had hinted that the Vale folk were something similarly minded, but Jegrai had wondered, and worried.

Even the Vredai had not always been so cavalier about beddings and bearings, despite the old teachings of "cherish the children." But they had changed. They *had* to change. Too many children had died for the Vredai to put overmuch stock in who fathered whom. Now a child was precious of itself, and welcome no matter its origins.

"One other thing," Jegrai said, still quite seriously. "Agroda's loyalties and duties lie chiefly with me and Vredai. If I call him to war, he must obey me. Can you abide this, Briya? I will have no broken hearts that I can prevent; I would incur no resentments because of prior vows. But we have had to fight in the past, and though I do not care to think of it at this moment, we are like to do so in the future. And we will need every hand that can raise a sword to do so."

"If I were a flatlander down in Ancas, my husband could be hauled off to some fool war whenever his duke felt like a bit of excitement," Briya said in a high, breathy voice, raising her chin proudly. "At least I know who my Agroda be fighting for, and what, and that you won't be doing it as a game, like. I can abide it. Tell you truth, Khene, m'Da taught me staff 'n bow. Need came to it, I might be right there with him."

"And your children—should they choose Clan life over life in walls, could you abide that as well? For you must pledge to offer them that choice."

"Agroda told me. I won't pledge to like it—but I've not tried it either." She smiled, and Jegrai saw why

Agroda looked ready to fall over his own feet whenever he gazed at her. She was utterly enchanting when she smiled, like a beam of sunlight given woman-form. "So by the time they come of age to choose, it may be me that's running about in tents, and them thinking their mam is a fool and a wild thing."

"Well spoken, lady." Jegrai gave her the bow of full respect he'd have given his mother. "I believe you have all thought this out, and I see no reason why this should not be the first of many matings between Clan and Vale." He looked out over the fertile little valley they were calling home—and realized, as he truly *saw* the "settled" look to the encampment, that the Vredai were, indeed, coming to think of it as their home, and not just another stopping-place. There were a full dozen of the great, anchored tents they called *eyerts* under construction, and they were not being anchored to wagons, but being given foundation-walls of stone from the river. Jegrai himself had never seen such a thing; only the Shaman had memories of such settlements.

They want to remain, to make a place of permanence. They'll fight for this place, he thought somberly. *They'll fight anyone and anything that tries to drive them from it. That was why the rebels didn't simply ride off. This place was home, and they didn't want to leave.*

"I do think," he said, half to himself, "I do truly think we are here to stay."

"Did you mean that?" Teo asked quietly, much later, after the evening meal, in the relative privacy of Jegrai's tent. "That you're here to stay?"

"If I had not meant it," Jegrai said, face very somber, "I would not have said it. This place has come to be home to us; I can see it every time I look about the camp. Indeed, it looks less like a 'camp' with each sunrise. You cannot tell me it has escaped your eyes, Teo."

Teo shrugged. It hadn't escaped his notice; the temporary jury-rigs of a people on the move were vanishing all over the camp. "Well, I thought things were getting to look awfully settled. Making that stone-lined pool for washing, for one; and there's talk of a steam-tent—and those big *eyerts*—and I overheard one of the old women talking about a kind of wooden *eyert*, and there were an awful lot of people listening to her with speculative looks in their eyes."

"Have you, in your tales of your gods, a place of afterlife, of reward?" Jegrai asked, an odd sort of longing in his eyes.

Teo nodded. "I think everyone does."

"I know not what your tales speak of—but ours speak of a place much like this valley you have given us. Much good grazing, sheltered from the storm yet open to the winds, shaded by trees, sweet water in abundance—how could anyone wish to leave paradise?" Jegrai sighed and rested his chin on his tucked-up knees, his arms wrapped about his legs. "And I ask myself: how long will we be allowed to keep this paradise?"

"But—" Teo protested, "Felaras won't—"

"It is not Felaras I fear, my friend, my very *good* friend. It is . . . what we left behind us." Jegrai's face took on a kind of grim determination. "Listen to me—some of this we have told your Master, but I wish you to hear all of it. I think it is time, and more than time, for all the truth to lie between us. I tell you: once the Vredai were twice, three times the number we are now—"

"But—"

Jegrai motioned him to silence with a wave of his hand, then changed his position to that of sitting cross-legged on his cushion, looking for all the world like Gortan about to relate a tale. "Hear me: farther than any of your breed has every been, off to the east so far that few even of my folk have ever seen it, there is a vast, bitter salt sea."

"We've heard of it," Teo agreed.

"So. On the shores of that sea there dwelt a people who called themselves the *Suno*. In their tongue—in their tongue that means 'Masters'; and not as your good Felaras means it. Their mastery is that of man over dog, for that is how they see all not born to their ranks. Indeed, their word for 'outlander' *means* 'dog.' "

"Not auspicious."

Jegrai nodded. "So. They became great, they spread themselves upon the land—and then they encountered the steppes and the *Vreja-a-traiden*. That is my people, the riders of the steppes—that is our name for ourselves, and it means *only* that. They could not endure us. Yet they could not conquer us, for we had no cities to destroy. They could not enslave us, for we killed our masters if we got weapon in hand, or killed ourselves rather than face enslavement. So instead they sought to destroy us from within, first by seducing some of us with pleasures, then by setting those they had seduced against other Clans. Always they spread the poison of praise among the sweetmeats, saying that this 'one or that one should be Khekhene by right, that all other should bow to him. Many were those who heard and many who heeded, save only my father, who heard, and saw the blade of the knife beneath the platter of sugared dainties. And who saw that the old ways of raiding and counter-raiding, of counting coup, were being replaced by blood shed in anger, and blood-feud called."

Teo raised one eyebrow. "Jegrai, my friend, my *good* friend, you see very clearly for one so young."

Jegrai grimaced, and shook his head. "I can see very clearly when the truth is shoved into my nose, my friend Teo. It was Northwind and my father who saw this—it was Northwind who foresaw this even before there was proof, and whether it was a vision from the Wind Lords or simply that he saw the Suno luring the eastern Clans to them, saw how rage was replacing reason among them, I do not know nor care."

"I take it that Northwind and your father tried to turn the tide that was running against them?"

"Aye. It was my father who tried to keep this from happening, with words of warning and water-pledges with as many Khenes as would give them. And all for nothing."

Jegrai's eyes went dark and brooding, and full of such sorrow that Teo felt his own throat close in sympathy.

"Vredai was the one game-piece, the single straw, the one support that kept the whole from falling into chaos. While the Khene of Vredai was pledged friend to all the other Khenes, the Suno plans came to nothing. But my father was the keypiece to Vredai's place as peacemaker. And with him gone—"

"Surely he saw his danger," Teo protested, "if he was as farseeing as you say."

"Oh, aye," Jegrai answered bitterly. "But the Khene must prove he is warrior from time to time; my father no less than any other. He led the warriors on a common, ordinary raid, a raid for cattle against the Suno—a bit of defiance, if you will. And in the old way—lightly armed and armored. But the Suno were warned and many and well armed, and my father died."

Jegrai's eyes closed for a moment, and to Teo's profound amazement, when he opened them again, Teo could see his lashes were wet. The sight killed the words he was going to speak on his tongue. He had never suspected Jegrai of that depth of emotion.

But Jegrai's voice showed no more emotion than before.

"My father had not been able to gain water-pledges Clan to Clan, as Master Felaras and I swore, the kind that would have bound all others against raising their hands to us. He could only get pledges Khene to Khene. And when he died, all such pledges died with him."

"And you?" Teo asked, finally able to speak. "Why didn't you lead the Vredai out of harm's way when he died?"

Jegrai shook his head, and looked down at his hands. "I was only sixteen summers, Teo—there was much dissension over whether I was fit to be Khene. By the time all were satisfied, Khene Sen and the Talchai were ready, backed by the Suno, who had told him that to be Khekhene he must destroy the voice of rebellion—the voice of Vredai. And I made the poor decision to speak out against Sen and his ambitions in the Khaltan, the great meeting of all the Clans. He—Sen—saw what I was, but also what I might become. The voice, not only of Vredai, but of the *Vreja-a-traiden.*"

His voice grew cold with anger as he looked back up and focused his eyes on some distant point beyond Teo's shoulder. "They fell upon us, not warband upon warband, but warband upon the encampment itself. That was where and when we lost the most of our folk—that one raid. It was a slaughter such as had never been in all the long history of Vredai. Once, in the dark time of long ago when men were little better than beasts, there were Clan-feuds of that kind, but sensible folk soon saw the folly of such things. But Khene Sen declared such a blood-feud on some trivial cause, and the other Khenes either upheld him or said nothing out of fear."

Jegrai's eyes closed in silent agony for a moment. "It was murder; there is no other word for it. With my own eyes I watched Sen trample children under the hooves of his horse. Oh, Wind Lords, my people . . . my people . . ."

Teo had never seen such emotional pain on anyone's face before, and finally had to look away.

Jegrai swallowed his grief, quieted his face, and continued. "I think the Suno counseled him in this. I think they reckoned that it would destroy the soul of my Clan, and leave me shattered and unable to lead."

"They should have known better," Teo said quietly. "That kind of atrocity only rouses people."

"Truth, it did no such thing as frighten us." Jegrai's face hardened. "Not the Vredai. We, who would not abide slavery under Suno hands, we who would not lick their feet and grovel as Sen did—how should *we* be made to fear? Never! Not though we perished to the last infant! I ordered the folk to pack what they could and scatter the herds. I ordered Northwind and Aravay to lead them into the West. Then I, and a handful of my best, young, and unwedded warriors went to work a delaying action on Talchai. We stole the Clan-altar, the shrine to the Wind Lords and the luck of the Clan—and when they pursued, we dropped it in their path, so that the hooves of their own horses shattered it and trampled their luck into the dust."

Jegrai's expression was at once proud and bleak. "We did not expect to survive that action, friend Teo. We expected to die at any point in that raid. Our aim was to buy time for what was left of Vredai with our blood. Yet—somehow—we lived."

He shook his head a little. "I still do not know why. But Sen and the Talchai could not—dared not—allow us to escape. Not after a handful of us effectively defeated them. This we knew. When we met with the rest of Vredai, we fled westwards, hoping to perhaps to outrun them, or to simply find some place to make a stand. We did not expect to find paradise—less did we expect to find friends."

He raised his head a little higher and stared soberly into Teo's eyes. "Have I miscalled you, Teo? Or have I called you aright? Are you of the Order desirous of real friendship, of brotherhood with us?"

Teo found it very hard to speak. "I—we—Jegrai, we

want to be your friends, truly we do—but what are you asking of your friends?"

A faded smile flickered at the corners of Jegrai's mouth. "I find I have lost the will to die, Teo. More than this, I find that I should like very much to—to be the strong warrior-lord your Order thought me when we first arrived. I come to this land of yours, and I find that, reduced as Vredai is, we are still an army compared to the armed strength here. If I stretched out my arm, and if I did not need to think about Talchai behind us, I could have such power, here."

Teo's breath caught in his throat; Jegrai looked at his paralyzed expression, and laughed dryly.

"Teo, Teo, I do not want to be anyone's master, Teo. I would very much like to be Khene of many people, of much land—but not at the cost of making war, and not out of conquest. I do not want slaves, victims—only friends, allies. I have a talent for leading; I wish to use it for more than just leading the Vredai. Is that foolishness, or vainglory?"

"N-no. I don't think so," Teo said doubtfully. "*I* wouldn't want a position like that, but . . . I'd rather you than the Yazkirn princes I've seen."

Jegrai nodded slowly. "That is rather what I had hoped. But—there are the Talchai. I do not think they will come this year, but come they will, and this time numbered enough to crush Vredai into the dust and destroy the very name of Running Horse for all time—"

Teo found it impossible to look away from his eyes. Like black fire . . .

"—unless I have the help of the Order. Your help in full, Teo. This means the sky-fire, and any other trick you have hidden away. Nothing less will serve. Because when the Talchai come, they shall come in the thousands, and they shall come with the intent of burning all before them. But they shall come at us in ignorance, expecting a handful of frightened, defeated, exhausted

refugees—and they shall come *knowing* they do not
have the Wind Lords with them, for their luck, their
Clan-soul, is gone. If they are met even once with your
lightning—it is *they* who shall crumble."

"Then what?" Teo whispered.

"Then . . . I should like to call what is left of the
Clans together. They would make me Khekhene; I think
there is no doubt of that. With my warriors and your
sky-fire, we could drive the Suno into their walls, and
make them fear to set foot beyond them ever again. It
might even be we could destroy them, but I do not
wish to waste lives—their own poisons will destroy
them."

"And?"

Jegrai lowered his voice. "And when they are no
more a threat, Teo, I pledge you now, on the life I gave
to the Wind Lords, that I will turn my attentions to the
enemies of *your* people. So that none will ever dare to
raise hands against one wearing the Order's badges
ever again."

Teo tried to get his mouth to work, but it was several
long moments before he could get any sound to come
out. "I—I can't speak for the Order, Jegrai. I can't even
speak for the Master. I can't guess what she'd say—but
you want me to ask her for you, don't you?"

Jegrai nodded. "I have assumed from the first that
you were her eyes and ears here. And I knew that she
knew. I think you are more than just her creature,
now—I think you have come to know us. I hope you
have come to appreciate us."

"I'd—prefer to think I'm your friend," Teo said softly.
"And yes, I do appreciate you. There's an awful lot
about your people I admire, Jegrai. Not the least of
which is your sense of honor. There's not a lot of that
around."

The young Khene smiled a little. "That is a good

thing to hear. Will you be *my* advocate, then, to your Master?"

"Yes," Teo heard himself saying. "Yes, my friend, I will."

Felaras had had the suspicion from the moment that Kasha brought word Teo was coming up the mountain that she was going to need something stronger to sustain her than chava.

One look at Teo's face convinced her.

"Teo, sit down before you fall down," she ordered, pushing him into the chair beside her desk. She turned to her Second. "Kasha," she said, rubbing the back of her neck and feeling the muscles already starting to go tense, "I know it isn't even noon yet, but—"

"Wine," Kasha replied. "I'll get it for you, I think you're going to need it. And I'll get Zorsha. I think you're going to need him, too."

The wine and Zorsha arrived at the same moment, and with every word Teo recited, Felaras felt more and more in need of both. Even the good news, the wedding of one of the Vale folk and the young Vredai warrior and Jegrai's wholehearted support of it, did little to leaven the feeling that she'd just had a mountain dropped on her shoulders.

"—I told him—no, I promised him—I'd be his advocate, Master Felaras," Teo said nervously. "I—I don't know, everything he told me seemed so reasonable last night, and I've never caught him in any kind of untruth. I want to believe him. But—supporting him militarily in a coup of his own, something that's not in our plan? I—I just don't know, I'm absolutely out of my depth."

Felaras sighed, and had a long sip of her wine. "Teo, you're the student of history. Are there any parallels?"

"Maybe," he replied, voice and face strained. "If you can believe Ancas folk-tales, oral tradition from peoples who hadn't a notion of literacy for the first couple hundred years of their ascendancy. The folk-tales say the leader of the Ancas was like Jegrai; charismatic, and with a long view. That was the one who supposedly overran the Sabirn Empire. But he didn't have the incredible hunger for learning that Jegrai has, nor the respect for those who have it."

"Kasha?"

"Mai says she'd follow him into hell," Kasha replied positively. "Hladyr bless, I've been down there and fought with his people, and I can tell you I'd do the same! All he needs is an edge, just the tiniest edge, and he'll *have* his enemies. We could give him that edge. And you know what he'll give us." She straightened and looked directly into Felaras' eyes. "I'll tell you what my father would tell you; the Swords like Jegrai. The Watchers would back him without a single second thought."

"Zorsha?"

"No such unity in Tower, Felaras," Zorsha said with regret. "But even though I may not be a student of history, I can tell you with Jegrai you're sitting on a dragon. You can ride it, and it will likely take you places you've never dreamed. But if you try to get off, it may crush you without even knowing it did so."

Out of the corner of her eye Felaras saw Teo bristle.

"Jegrai wouldn't—"

"Jegrai damned well would," Zorsha replied calmly. "His first, last, and holiest priority is his people. If he had to cut you down to save them, Teo, he'd do it. He'd give you the best funeral you ever saw, after, but he'd still do it."

"But—"

"You heard it out of his own mouth, Teo," Kasha agreed. "He was perfectly willing to sacrifice himself for them, and at what age? Seventeen, eighteen? At twenty his people have been in flight for years and he's suffered with every one of them; he'll buy them peace and safety with whatever coin it takes. His blood, yours, or mine."

"But the fact is, he won't roll over us unless we stand in his way—which, I trust, we're too wise to do," Zorsha continued, as Teo subsided into the chair, red-faced and abashed. "And what he's offering—Felaras, it's tempting. If I were in the Master's seat, I'd take it. We're not just one man anymore; we're not Duran. We're an ongoing organization, and we'll live beyond the span of any one man. We have the potential, not only to advise and aid a potentially very strong leader, *but all those who succeed him.* Have you thought what that could mean to the Order in particular—and the world in general? We could help to foster hundreds, maybe a thousand years of peace and learning, if we can stay uncorrupted by power. And I think that because of our organization we can."

Felaras nodded, slowly—and in her own mind eliminated Teo from the "competition" for the Master's seat altogether. Though Teo had had all night to consider what Jegrai had told him, his only thoughts had been personal, and confused. Zorsha had cut straight to the heart of the matter, and seen the long-view possibilities, positive and negative.

And being Felaras, she could not be less than honest with the three so close to her.

"Teo—what would you say if I told you I don't think you've got it in you to sit in my place?" she asked quietly.

Kasha and Zorsha went very quiet, and froze in their chairs.

Teo's face was suffused with only relief. "I'd thank the gods, Master. Honestly." Then he started a little, and his eyes widened. "Do you *mean* that? You're pulling me out?"

She nodded slowly.

He closed his eyes and sagged against the back of the

chair. "Oh, gods. Master Felaras, you will never know how happy you've made me. Every time I thought about having to make decisions—oh, gods, I just got so knotted up inside I wanted to puke." He opened his eyes again, and there was no shadow of falsehood in them. "Zorsha, you can have it all, with my blessing! Gods, I can just be me again. . . ."

Zorsha looked stunned.

"It had to come some time, and soon," Felaras told him. "There can only be one successor in the end. You're it, lad. I'm not sure whether to give you congratulations or condolences."

Zorsha shook himself a little, and managed to smile weakly at her. "From all I've seen, both. Well. Thank you . . . I think."

Felaras laughed. "Lad, just now you sounded so like me you could have been my echo! All right—Teo's brought us Jegrai's offer. You've all given your opinions and they match mine. We're in for a leg; we might just as well go in for the whole lamb."

Zorsha nodded. "What's first?"

"Those Talchai that Jegrai thinks are on his heels. Kasha, I want you to consult with your father about what it would take to truly crush an army of three or four thousand at the Teeth. That includes more fire-throwers than we currently have—both mortars and hand-cannon. Zorsha, I want figures on how long it would take to make those fire-throwers and the ammunition for them. Teo, get back down there and tell Jegrai he's got a bargain."

She looked about at her aides, her successor, and felt a kind of perverse thrill of excitement.

"All right, don't just stand there, people," she said, feeling an upwelling of energy. "Let's *move!*"

Chapter Ten

The workroom was swept clean, and there was only one source of flame: a tiny candle sheltered by a glass chimney. Zorsha took no chances when working with explosives; no Seeker would, nor would any of those of the Watchers whose duties included handling such things.

"*This* is what makes the lightnings?" Yuchai asked, regarding the little pile of black powder in the palm of his outstretched hand with doubt and puzzlement.

"Only that," Zorsha agreed. "Doesn't look like much, does it?"

"Not really." Yuchai poured it carefully back into the little leather sack Zorsha held open, and dusted his hands off on a bit of cloth. "It looks like dirt. Or ashes."

Zorsha grinned, a little tightly. "Trust me, it isn't dirt, and it's every bit as dangerous as real lightning. Listen, Yuchai, Felaras gave me open-ended permission to show you whatever you wanted to know in the meeting I had with her last night—and that 'everything' includes the fire-throwers. You told me a while ago that Jegrai wanted you to learn about them. Well, now Felaras figures he should know. But we're dealing with perilous stuff here—there've been Seekers and Watchers both blown to little bits just because some tiny thing went wrong. Still want to go on? It isn't just the explosives that are dangerous—even knowing about how they work could put your life in danger, outside these walls. There've been members of the Order tortured to death over this stuff."

He hefted the little bag of black powder. Yuchai bit his lip, but shook his head stubbornly. "I want to know. Even if Jegrai hadn't asked me to learn about it, I'd have wanted to know. You told me it wasn't magic. That meant it was something anybody could learn. If anybody could, I wanted to."

"I'm going to start by showing you a few things. First, I'm going to light a little bit of this stuff in the open." Zorsha poured a tiny pile of the explosive powder on a metal plate, set the plate on the workbench, and carefully uncovered the candle. With equal care he touched the candle to the pile. Yuchai watched in fascination as it sparked, and then went up in a *poof* of smoke, consumed in a bare instant of time.

"Now, this little paper tube has about the same amount of the powder packed into it." Zorsha took one of the tiny firecrackers used at festivals out of a metal-lined drawer in his workbench. "There's also a little bit of the powder wound into the paper fuse—that's the twist of paper sticking out of the end. Now watch."

He put the cracker on the plate, lit the fuse, and stood back. The fuse was a short one; he'd barely gotten out of the way when the cracker exploded. Yuchai jumped nearly a foot into the air.

"Now . . . logic, Yuchai. What was the difference between the firecracker and the pile of gunpowder?"

The boy's brows knitted for a moment.

"Think hard."

Yuchai shook his head, defeated.

"In the firecracker the force of burning was confined. It had nowhere to go, so it broke its container."

Yuchai's eyes lit. "Like putting a lid on a boiling pot?"

Zorsha chuckled with delight. "*Damn* good!" Impulsively he hugged Yuchai's thin shoulders, and the boy's whole face lit up. "Now watch this."

He took another firecracker and this time put a small metal measuring cup over it, leaving only the fuse sticking out. He lit the fuse.

This time Yuchai was prepared for the noise and didn't jump, but his mouth formed a soundless "oh" when the metal measure was thrown into the air and off the table.

"Now, what was the difference there?"

"The—force was more confined?"

"Partially. It was also confined so that it could only go in one direction. Obviously, the force was too small to move the table, so it could only move the cup."

"You use the—confined force—to throw things?" Yuchai hazarded. "Like a catapult, only farther and faster?"

"In part; look here." He rummaged through his document-drawer and pulled out a drawing of one of the hand-cannon. "Now, this is a drawing of a fire-thrower—a small one. You pack the explosive powder down in here, see? Then you add paper, you stuff it in so that it blocks all the cracks, so that the force can't escape around the edges of whatever you're going to use as shot. Then you put in the shot, then more paper. The shot is usually a round metal ball, very heavy."

Yuchai crowded up under his arm, studying the drawing with an intensity that allowed no distractions.

"Look here—here's the hole that the fuse goes in; you light that, and when the powder explodes, the ball is propelled out."

"But Jegrai said that the ground before him exploded—like lightning had struck there. No matter how hard a metal ball hit, it wouldn't do that."

"That's the fire-throwers we have on the walls—another kind." He pulled out a second drawing. "We call this one a mortar; it doesn't send things as far, because we don't use as heavy a charge, and we let a little more of the force escape by not using wadding. What it does fire is something like a very large firecracker, but one made of cast iron; which, as I showed you, is brittle enough to shatter if struck hard enough. When you light the fuse on the mortar, you also light the fuse on the canister, which is timed so that it goes off when it hits the ground. Mortars are a lot more dangerous to the handlers than the cannon, because the act of firing them can set off the charge in the shell."

"The fire gets through the shell?"

"No. It isn't just fire that can set off the gunpowder."

Zorsha put a firecracker unobtrusively on the bench, and pulled out a hammer.

"Impact can do it too."

He brought the hammer down squarely on the firecracker—and Yuchai jumped back, wide-eyed, at the crack of the explosion.

"You see? Hard enough impact sets it off."

The boy stared at the blackened place on the bench for a moment, while Zorsha rubbed his tingling fingers. It was an effective demonstration of how dangerous gunpowder could be—but a little hard on the hand.

"Zorsha, I am probably a fool—and I am not very learned," Yuchai said, shyly, but with those intense eyes focused on Zorsha's face. "But—I have a question. Two questions?"

"Go ahead."

"In battle, even *our* arrows often bounce off armor. The Suno laugh at arrow-fall when they are in full armoring; not even our bows can pierce metal. But— could—could a man not make an arrowhead, hollow, with the powder inside? And when it struck the armor or the shield, would it not explode?"

"Hladyr bless," Zorsha breathed. "I never thought of that. Even if it did very little damage it would certainly frighten whoever it hit white! And if it hit a rider—"

"The horse would bolt," Yuchai said simply. "No horse would abide that without being trained to it. A few archers could scatter an entire force of heavy cavalry, could they not?"

"They could—gods above and below, they certainly could. And your other question?"

"You told me of the Sabirn-fire, the fire that water only spreads? And you told me that you could not use it very often because it was so dangerous?"

"So dangerous we've seldom even used it with catapults. All it would take would be for the jars to break open a little, and the fire would be all over the catapult and crew."

"But cast iron is tougher than pottery, and still breaks. Why do you not put it in the hollow canisters of the mortars? You could throw it far beyond the lines of your allies. You could destroy the siege engines you told me of before they were even put into play. You would not even need to hit anything exactly, only near it, because the fire would splash and spread. You could take whole groups of fighters that way. Am I not right?"

"Yuchai—" Zorsha looked aghast at the boy. "Yuchai, that is a terrible thought."

The boy hugged his arms to his chest, as if to ward off a sudden chill, and his face took on a strange, masklike appearance. "If you made these shells, you could hurl such things at the Talchai when they came—you could burn them, burn them up. They couldn't stand against you, no matter how many warriors they had."

Zorsha took the boy's thin shoulders in his hands and shook him. "Yuchai, you can't mean that—you've never seen the fire; I have—it's a terrible thing, a weapon of absolute desperation."

"The *Talchai* are terrible!" the boy cried, his voice spiraling up and cracking. "The *Talchai* are—are—"

The boy's voice abruptly went flat and dead; his eyes stared at the stone wall of Zorsha's workroom, but plainly did not see it. His young face held more pain than Zorsha had ever imagined in his life.

The young Hand stared at what he had thought was just an extraordinarily bright boy. The "boy's" face was transformed, aged, and so bleak Zorsha would not have known him. He looked a hundred years old, and sick to death. And when he began to whisper in a harsh, strained voice, Zorsha thought, aghast, *No puppy is going to heal this.*

"If I saw them drowning, I would call for rain! If I saw them burning, I would throw oil upon them! I *hate* them, I *hate* them, and I want to see them die, terribly, horribly, I'd set demons on them if I could!"

He started to laugh, in that same suppressed way he'd spoken—but it was hopeless, hysterical laughter. It tore at the heart, and the boy began to tremble all over, then to shake.

Zorsha couldn't bear it. He seized the boy and held him close, face against his chest. For one moment there was nothing but silence.

Then the boy made a choking sound, and seized him with all the desperation of a drowning child.

Zorsha hugged him tighter, and Yuchai clung to him and began to speak again; slowly at first, brokenly—but then the words began pouring from him in a kind of deadly monotone, a flood of appalling words.

Words that blanched Zorsha and made him tremble; words telling of atrocities committed on the Vredai that exceeded Zorsha's wildest nightmares.

This was not imagined, or something the boy had embroidered with his own fantasy; no one could have imagined a massacre like the one Yuchai was describing, a hellish kind of festival of blood and death. Zorsha could hardly begin to take it in. Every incident the boy recited was worse than the one before—and Zorsha began to realize with soul-chilling horror that the boy had witnessed all this rapine and slaughter in *a single afternoon*.

For Yuchai was reciting the tale of the raid by the Talchai on the Vredai camp—a raid that had been staged when most of the weapon-bearers were out of camp on hunts or guarding the herds. There had only been the sick, women with young children, the elderly, and the children themselves. Of which Yuchai had been one. One small boy who escaped the fate of his playmates only because he had been hidden in a thicket of bushes as part of a game.

Gods, what was he? Ten? Eleven? Old enough to remember everything clearly—oh, gods, what can I do? What can I say?

It was the voice that was the worst—that dull, monotonous recitation of horrors. That, and the way the boy clutched at him, seeking a shelter from his own memories.

"Yuchai . . ." Zorsha couldn't think what to do to comfort him. *Could* there be comfort? "Yuchai—Yuchai, stop it! Listen to me!" Zorsha's own face was wet with tears as he shook the boy's shoulders and got him to look up at him. "Listen, Yuchai, listen to me—it won't happen again! Not ever! I pledge you on my life, *I* won't let it happen!"

The boy stared at him blankly for a moment—then burst into tears.

Zorsha just held him, rocking back and forth a little, weeping with him. It was all he *could* do.

Gods, gods—who made him hold all this inside? Who left this to fester? Or—gods, are they all like this? Every survivor down in that camp?

Appalling sobs shook the child, tearing themselves up out of his throat and racking his thin body.

In that moment Zorsha learned how to hate.

The study was very dark; very quiet. Felaras listened to Zorsha's tight-voiced recitation with growing nausea. She had no doubt that he was retelling the tale exactly as the boy had told it to him; he was white as salt, and just barely under control. She had never seen him so angry—she rather doubted anyone had. Zorsha the calm, the easy-going, the half-asleep—Zorsha had just been awakened to something he'd never anticipated.

When Zorsha finished, she steepled her fingers just below the level of her eyes and looked at him as searchingly as she had ever measured anyone.

His face was as tightly controlled as his voice had been—but just beneath that tight control there still was a terrible and implacable anger. Merely speaking had not purged him of it; if anything, it had intensified it. She was finding herself very glad that she was not the object of it.

"And your analysis?" she said, finally.

"I was trained to always demand both sides of a story, Felaras. Frankly, I don't care to hear the other side of this one. I really don't want to know what could bring men to act like that—like rabid beasts. All I want to do is destroy the beasts and the thing that made them that way. Which, to my analysis, is the Talchai and the Suno."

"That's not a rational way of looking at something—"

"I don't *want* to be rational!" he hissed. "You weren't with the boy down there; I was. You didn't look into that dead little face—into those hopeless eyes. This was a fourteen-year-old boy, Felaras! A child that age *couldn't* make something like this up!"

"I never suggested that he had," she said, overcome by a profound weariness for a moment. *Why me? Why is it me who must face this? Deal with this? Somehow rectify this?* "Is he all right?"

"I think so. As all right as he'll ever be. When he ran out of strength to cry, I carried him back to his room; Kasha got Boitan and Boitan gave him something that made him sleep. Boitan said he thinks this actually did the boy some good—'catharsis,' he called it." Zorsha shook his head, and only now did Felaras see that his eyes were red from weeping of his own. "I stayed with him until he was under. Kasha's with him now, and his dog." He clenched his hands on the arms of the chair; a white-knuckled grip that would have cracked weaker wood. "Felaras, the weapons the boy suggested are inhumane—and I want to construct them. I want to *use* them. I want to drive home the lesson that what the Talchai did will be paid for. I want them to think that every god above and every demon below has turned its hand against them. I want to make retribution so terrible that no one will ever contemplate atrocity like that against anyone again. And I want the Talchai, above all else, to know the reason why this is falling on them."

She parted her hands and looked at them with surprise; they were shaking. She'd thought her control was better than that—but the story had gotten past her defenses enough to make her tremble with the effort of holding in her own reaction. "Do me this favor, Zorsha. First, sleep on it. Second, speak with Jegrai and Northwind. *Then* decide. If you still want to construct these things—I'll back you. Reasonable?"

He nodded curtly.

"I'm going to ask a very personal question, and remember, it's because I've made you my successor and I have to know your strengths and your weaknesses. Why *this* boy? You haven't—" Her face flamed with embarrassment, and she looked away.

He read the embarrassment correctly, and snorted. "No, Felaras, I'm not a pederast. Gods help him, that would be the last thing Yuchai would need! No, set your mind at ease on that subject; I still want Kasha, quite healthily, let me tell you. It's because—I look at Yuchai, and I see myself all over again. He's enough like me inside to be my own son—more like me, probably, than a son would be. I've come to love him for his brave little soul and his bright mind as surely as if he'd been born my son." His face hardened. "And they hurt him. Hurt him in a way no physician can deal with. I think that no matter what Boitan says, the only thing that's going to truly let him heal and let him put his mind on something besides revenge is to *get* revenge. Or at least the promise of it."

Felaras nodded, slowly. "That makes a peculiar kind of sense." She cleared her throat a little. "I shouldn't admit this, but I agree with you. On everything. Just follow through on those promises, all right? Let's at least give this the appearance of rational thinking."

The chair legs scraped harshly on the floor as he pushed away from the desk and stood up. "I'd like to stay with him in case he has nightmares. Boitan thought he might."

"Fine, go ahead," she replied absently, still trying to make some kind of sense out of the catalog of horrors Zorsha had recited so tonelessly. "Send Kasha back here, would you?"

She stared at the flame of the single candle on her desk, letting it mesmerize her, trying to see some reason, any reason, behind what seemed so unreasonable. The things the Order, as a group and as individuals, had endured in the past—those things were actually understandable. Fear of the unknown, hatred for the foreign, greed, the desire for power—all normal human motivations. But this—

Even at third hand, it chilled her. Jegrai hadn't gone into the personal details of what had happened to his Clan. If he had, she might well have given him his bargain months before. But then again, she might have suspected an *adult* of fabricating at least part of the story—

Poor Yuchai. She couldn't begin to imagine what it had been like to live through it.

A shadow passed between her eyes and the candle flame, and she started.

Kasha was sitting on the edge of her desk, and had just waved her hand in front of Felaras' eyes to get her attention.

"I had a word with Shenshu and Demonsbane," she said quietly. "They've been figuring the boy for a breakdown for a while. Seems his father is one of those stone-faced, iron-willed types who finds any show of emotion something less than honorable. They're relieved, both that it came, and that Yuchai had an acceptable father-substitute with him to get him through the worst of it. They couldn't speak too highly of Zorsha, both for his handling of the situation and for his compassion. Right now, so far as Shenshu's concerned, Zorsha hung the moon."

Felaras shook her head. "That's not what's bothering me. It's *why*. How could human beings do that to other human beings?"

Kasha sighed. "I can only tell you what they told me. First, that this Khene Sen is just as charismatic and persuasive as Jegrai—and he's twelve years older. He had a lot of time to get his people brought around to his way of thinking. Second, that Sen's mother was Suno; an alliance marriage. Now think about what Teo told us: the Suno consider all other races to be inferior. Fit only to serve, to enslave."

Felaras nodded, seeing the pieces falling into place, seeing the pattern start to emerge.

"Put those two things together, add what the Suno have probably been telling Khene Sen, about how superior, how great a leader he is, and about how much they can give him—and then produce Jegrai. Charismatic, brilliant—and young. Young enough to beat Sen just by outliving him. And you get?"

Felaras sucked in a breath. "A very frightened man; a man who sees the possibility of being cornered staring him in the face. A man who sees the way to exterminate that threat now if he just acts quickly enough."

Kasha nodded. "That was basically what Demonsbane figured. 'Exterminate' is a good word-choice—remembering that Sen is half-Suno."

"Uh-huh; I can see that, especially if he's been doing his best to ignore the nomad half of his breeding. He wouldn't let his people see it as anything other than exterminating a dangerous predator—no worse than killing, oh, a plague of rats. But why not just use assassination?"

Kasha shrugged. "Damned if I know. Maybe because if Sen had pulled *that* little trick, he'd have lost everybody but his own Clan. The other Clans would have reckoned that if Sen would use a dishonorable tactic like assassination on Jegrai, he'd be perfectly willing to use it on anybody. Remember, even Sen pays at least lip-service to honor."

"So he makes it look honorable—at least to his own folk—to take Jegrai out by getting rid of the entire Clan?"

"Exactly. And by the time he got finished speaking to his fighters, they'd be ready to exterminate with enthusiasm. Remember, I've been there when Jegrai primed us to go hunting the rebels; I know what that kind of speaker can do. Frankly, we are just damned lucky Jegrai is rational, reasonable, and willing to listen to anybody's side."

"But why haven't we seen other children as emotionally scarred as Yuchai?" That was the last piece that wouldn't drop into place.

Kasha looked sick. "Felaras—we haven't seen any, because there *aren't* any. Haven't you noticed? Yuchai is the only young adolescent. Fourteen and over—now eighteen and over—were out with the herds. Younger than ten—some managed to hide and didn't see the actual slaughter. But all the rest, including Yuchai's peer group, were out in the open and cut down. That poor boy is the only child that saw what happened and was old enough to remember it clearly."

"Oh, gods—"

"Felaras, if anyone can purge him of this, it'll be his own people and ours working together. He's in the best possible hands." She smiled, a kind of rueful, self-deprecating smile. "I never knew Zorsha had this in him, frankly. One of the things that always annoyed me a bit was the way he seemed to drift through emotional encounters without ever getting pulled into the current. *Teo* has always cared passionately for things, and showed it. Zorsha always seemed . . . half asleep. I guess I was wrong about him."

"Looks like you might have been, a bit. But if you were, so was I." Felaras stretched out her fingers, and winced as the knuckles popped. "Kasha, you have just done me a world of good. I didn't know what to make of this story. It sounded like these Talchai were all mad, or drugged, or—or bespelled."

"Oh no doubt there was some of that last, too. Demonsbane thinks Sen has a whole stable of very powerful wizards. With enough folk luck-wishing him while he was speaking, he could likely get anybody to believe anything."

"That, I can deal with. That, I can defend against. Furthermore—" she paused as a thought struck her. "You know, it would do no harm to spread a couple of these stories of Yuchai's about the Order. Let our people get some notion of what's out there. We won't frighten the timid ones any more than they already are, and we might give the complacent ones some food for reflection. I think that most of them can add two and two—and realize that even if we'd had nothing to do with Jegrai, mad dogs like the Talchai seem to be would *still* tear our throats out in passing."

"Done," Kasha nodded. "I'll get Father and Boitan on it, and Kitri. Now, as your duly appointed watchdog, I say you should hie yourself off to bed before you fall over at your desk. You're beginning to sound a little drunk, and that's nothing more than fatigue."

Felaras stood up slowly, and wanted to groan—every joint ached. "Rain coming," she observed. "Before too long, by the way my knees feel."

As if to substantiate her observation, a very distant murmur of thunder mumbled at the open window, and there was a barely visible flicker of light that showed against the edge of the mountains beyond.

"Then you need to get to bed," Kasha said sternly.

"I need to make my rounds, first," she replied just as stubbornly. "Then I'd like to look in on the boy, I think. Have a word with one of the other nomads myself, first."

Kasha shrugged, and spread her hands in defeat. "All right, have it your way. You will anyway. I'll tell you what, I'll put everything to rights, and then catch up with you. I'm not exactly ready to embrace the god of slumber myself just yet. Too many things to think about."

"And most of them grim." Felaras moved around her desk, and paused in the door. "Thanks. . . ."

"Oh, get. You're so tired you'd make more of a mess than you'd clean up, putting things back in the wrong places," Kasha mocked. "And then tomorrow morning it would be 'Kasha, I can't find this, Kasha, have you seen that, Kasha, where did I put my stylus—' "

"Enough, enough!" Felaras ducked her head and winced. "I yield, I yield! I'll see you in a bit."

"*Don't* let anyone trap you into a night-long discussion."

Felaras let the door close on that last admonition, and headed stiffly down the corridor.

Gods. I'm getting old. I feel it more every time it rains. She sighed, and rubbed the knuckles of her writing hand. *I should complain—there's a child in the room next to mine with a soul in ragged little shreds. There's a young man down at the bottom of the mountain with the lives of his people literally in his hands. My successor has just learned the hard way how vile men can be. And I'm fretting because my bones ache when it rains.*

The Fortress could well have been deserted; the lamps along the corridor were turned to their lowest, and there was nothing to break the silence except her own footsteps. Being so high up on the Pass was a mixed blessing in summer—the air cooled down rapidly at night, but that same cold gave nearly everyone over the age of forty stiff joints overnight.

Still, the cool of the corridor was a blessed relief from the blazing sun that had baked its way even into Felaras' study. This was the time of year when the Master's Folly was not so foolish after all—if you were young enough not to have to worry about aching bones when there was dew on your bed come the dawn.

Selfish, selfish, thinking about myself, my aching bones. Or—is it? Maybe not. No, I'm not fretting because my bones ache—I'm fretting because that aching is the sign that my time is getting shorter. I'm getting old—my joints are going, but how long does my mind have? Or the rest of me? Will I have enough time to give Zorsha the training he needs? Did I wait too long before picking one of the lads? Gods, I wish you'd give me some notion of how much time I've got left.

As if answering her unspoken prayer, thunder boomed almost directly overhead, so close that she could feel the stone of the Fortress vibrating with it under her feet.

She sniffed, and took the turning that led to the old dead-ended corridor lined with workrooms on both sides.

Telling me that's hubris, gods? Or just warning me that however long I have, it's not going to seem like enough time?

This time there was a pause before the thunder pealed again, and she almost smiled at the realization that she had been on the verge of looking to the thunder to answer her.

The corridor was properly deserted at this hour—but it was part of the rounds. If there was anyone working here this late, Felaras wanted to be aware of the fact. *Gods, I'm as bad as Diermud. Next thing you know, I'll be talking to quartz crystals—and listening for answers. If fancies begin, can senility be far behind?*

Something impinged on, then disrupted her thoughts. A current of air, a shadow that didn't belong—whatever it was that alerted her allowed reflex to save her life.

She only knew that she sensed—*wrong*—and dropped to the floor and shoulder-rolled without a thought for aching joints and fragile bones.

And a stone came hissing past the place where her head had been to smack into the stone of the wall and clatter to the floor.

She was on her feet again with her back to the wall and her eyes scanning the corridor in two heartbeats. And cursing the carelessness that had left her belt-knife on her desk, where she'd used it to slit open some letters.

A blot of shadow separated from the rest and moved toward her, bulking huge against the wall. Blocky, looking like it should be clumsy—and moving like a hunting lion. Only one person within these walls looked and moved like that, or carried himself with his shoulders so high and tense.

"Zetren," she whispered.

He moved into the light. "Witch," he snarled, as thunder crashed again overhead. "Bitch-queen, think you're going to *be* a queen, don't you? Think this pretty-boy barbarian's going to set you up as Mother-Goddess and then conquer the world for you, do you? Reckon you can use the rest of us as a staircase to a throne—"

"Zetren," she said, honestly bewildered, feeling the wall behind her for support. "What in hell are you talking about?"

He ignored her—really, it didn't even seem as if he'd heard her. "Going to make us all your little fetch-and-carrys, like you did with those three lackeys of yours, aren't you? Figure you've got us all outsmarted—"

"Zetren—"

"I was too smart for you, bitch. I saw where you were going, even if nobody else believed me. I had you figured. And you can ill-wish me all you want, but this time it isn't going to stop me—"

He lunged for her, and she dodged and spun herself out of his way with real, cold fear closing around her throat. This corridor was deserted; there were no eager young Hands down here *this* night. Zetren was stronger than she was—faster; she couldn't possibly outrun him, even if she could get past him into the clear corridor.

She couldn't outlast him, either.

And she didn't dare take him on hand-to-hand; *he* hadn't been spending the last few years pushing papers around, he was in better shape than she was. He'd make pulp out of her.

"Zetren, what in hell do you think you're doing?" she gasped, sidestepping a deadly blow aimed at her neck, throwing herself away from him, and coming up against the stone wall with force that would leave her bruised. "You hurt me, and—"

"Not going to *hurt* you, bitch," he snarled, the red madness of the bear brought to bay in his eyes. "Going to *kill* you—"

He lashed out again; this time she managed to get in a quick side-kick of her own to his midsection and get out of grabbing distance, further down toward the dead end, before he could react. He *oofed* under the impact, but recovered quickly and pivoted into a counterattack faster than she would have believed possible.

"Going to *kill* you," he growled again, as thunder shook the walls, destroying her hope of anyone hearing a call for help. "Drop you down your own damn staircase. Senile old bitch trips and falls—no one'll think anything about it."

She didn't even waste a breath pointing out that bruises from blows and bruises from falling look a great deal different. Zetren wouldn't listen—and anyway, what would it matter to her at that point? She'd be dead, and beyond being concerned—

He kicked, and she squirmed aside, but his foot brushed her hip and made her spin into the wall. He followed up on the kick with unnatural speed, and she only avoided his clutching hands because he'd come in to strangle rather than to strike.

He's really going to kill me—oh, gods— For the first time in years she panicked—and though it was going to do no good at all, cried out her fear.

Thunder crashed again, drowning her voice, and Zetren grinned.

"How's it feel to be the helpless one, bitch?" he laughed. "How's it feel to—"

He was enjoying this too much, and not paying attention to her. She was too good a fighter to let *that* pass. This time *she* lunged for *his* throat, fingers stiffened—

And connected, but at the last minute her traitor knee gave way under her, and turned what would have been at the least a disabling blow into one that simply hurt. And she fell into a half-crouching position, unbalanced and terribly vulnerable.

He half roared, half choked, and reacted to the blow, kicking out at her with the power of a catapult.

This time he connected squarely with her ribs before she could scramble out of the way, and sent her crashing into the wall, her impact only partially under control. A tearing pain in her knee as she hit sent her dropping to the floor in agony, and she looked up a moment later to see him advancing slowly on her through a blur of tears of pain.

Oh, gods—not like—dammit, I'm not done yet!

Thunder, drowning everything; her desperate "No!" and his laugh; she could only see his mouth working, couldn't hear him at all. He reached for her—and before he could touch her, suddenly stiffened.

His eyes nearly popped out of his head, and his mouth worked again, but this time the shape was all wrong for a laugh—and as she shrank back against the stone, he collapsed like a deflated bladder, coming down in a heap with one hand brushing her foot.

She stared, unable to believe in her deliverance, while nearly constant thunder reverberated overhead.

It wasn't sound that alerted her again—it was movement, movement down at the open end of the corridor.

Kasha walked slowly through the light and shadow patterns made by the tiny lamps on the wall toward her, stalking the length of the corridor, something swinging from her hand.

A sling.

About then Felaras' nose told her that Zetren was no longer among the living.

For a moment more she sat in a kind of paralysis, both of mind and body, as the thunderstorm passed on and the nearly continuous shocks of the thunder faded into the distance.

Kasha prodded the body with her toe, then rolled it out of the way and wordlessly reached out her hand toward her superior. Felaras took it, climbing painfully to her feet. Her knee burned like somebody'd set it on fire.

"Found the sling back where he'd dropped it. How badly did he hurt you?" Kasha asked, tightly.

Felaras tried putting weight on the leg—it felt like bloody hell, but she could hobble on it. "Knee," she gasped, around tears of pain. "Sprained or torn muscle, I think. Still works, so it isn't broken. And I'm bruised some. That's all."

"You're just damned lucky.I was coming after you," her aide said angrily, then, "Oh, gods, Felaras, what am I saying? Why should you have to guard your back against your own people? We aren't assassins!"

"Kash—" she got out as she gritted her teeth against pain that was threatening to make her pass out. "—orders. Me to room. Boitan to me. Zorsha too. *Now.*"

It happened so quickly she was tempted to believe in a magic other than ill-wishings.

"All right," she said, as Boitan's pain medication began to make the room blur and slip sideways a little. "Have we all got our stories straight?"

Zorsha nodded. "Zetren fell off the wall during the storm. Nobody knows what he was doing up there; it wasn't his watch, and that part of the wall is bad when it's raining. You slipped on the stairs when the thunder startled you, and wrecked your knee. Right now we only know about you, we don't know about Zetren. Ardun is going to 'find' him a little bit after dawn."

"Good. Simple enough to be believed." She started to nod off, and caught herself with a jerk.

"Felaras, why the subterfuge?" Boitan asked.

"Kash—"

"Zetren said something to her about 'ill-wishing.' Boitan, this is to be dead-secret; Felaras and I are both wizards, and we've been detecting somebody trying to work against her since early spring."

Boitan sucked in his breath in surprise, bit his lip, and nodded.

"Now since that predates the Vredai, it has to be

somebody in the Vale or the Order."

"It seems likely," Zorsha interjected, "at least to me, that this 'enemy' found that his wishes weren't working—"

Felaras nodded tiredly. "Defense 'shield.' Have to train you in that, boy. Master has to have it."

Zorsha started, and she grinned weakly. "One of prime requisites for being candidate is wizard-power. Didn't know you had it, hm?"

"No—" he replied, looking stunned.

"Felaras thinks that when this wizard found himself blocked, he must have turned his attentions to someone with a known grudge against her, but with less protection. Zetren, basically."

"Had it too, not's good's I am, good enough to know someone stronger was on him, not good enough to deflect it," she explained, her words beginning to slur despite her efforts at control. " 'F he'd made it to Master, he'd've had t' get a Second like Kash t' handle that."

"So, unbalanced as we know he was, the ill-wishing took him right over the edge?" Boitan breathed. "And with Zetren, there's only one direction that would lead . . ."

"Got it," Felaras replied, catching herself again and forcing herself aware. "Good 'ssassination try. Couldn't know Kash's been playin' shadow since we felt ill-wishing start."

"But why the subterfuge?" Boitan asked.

"Rule one of the Watchers," Zorsha said. "Keep the enemy confused. As long as we stick to this story, he'll never know how close he came to his goal. That might drive him out of cover, where we can do something about him. But damn if I like the idea of there being a traitor in our ranks."

"Wait a minute—how do you know—"

"What else could it be?" Zorsha said simply. "Who else would have known to target *Zetren?* Who else would have known of the long-standing grudge he held?

To outsiders we've been very careful to present a united front."

" 'Xactly," Felaras said. "Kash I trust. Zorsh too. Nothin' for either of them t' gain. Ardun's fine, an' you, Boitan. Same logic. Could be *anyone* else. So . . . keep 'em confused an' see what . . . crawls . . . out."

She yawned, and fought her eyes open again, to see Boitan looking stern.

"Everybody out," he said. "Zorsha, you stay with the boy, and that will put you within shouting distance if there is trouble tonight. Kasha, you set up in the anteroom. There won't be anybody climbing in the window, not unless they're half-spider. And *you*—"

He glared at Felaras. She tried to glare back, without success.

"Stop fighting the drug and get some rest!"

"But . . . I . . ." she protested, and then made the fatal error of relaxing just a little. She slid into sleep, fighting it every inch of the way.

Chapter Eleven

Darkness came early to the Pass, and to the little valley the Vredai occupied below it. Although the sky to the west was still bright red, the valley was dark enough that Halun occasionally stumbled over rocks and animal-dug hummocks in the grass. He had been sorry to give up holding his meetings with the others within the camp itself, but after the defection of those young hotheads it had just become too much of a risk. The little cul-de-sac side canyon that Iridai had found was a perfect meeting place; no one could overhear or overlook them, and with one man standing guard at the entrance, no one could get near enough to the meeting to even see who was taking part in it.

Gortan and Iridai had learned from the mistakes of the youngsters; the guard they'd posted didn't look like he was guarding anything at all. He was sitting on a horse-blanket under the stone outcropping that half hid the entrance. He had a torch beside him, and was playing a solitare game of stones by the light of it. As Halun passed him, he looked up, grunted once, and went back to his game. And if Halun had not been someone known to him, there would have been no strongarm techniques—just a friendly skin of *khmass* and an invitation to make up a two-game. And since "stones" was a fairly boring game, it was unlikely that the intruder would stop for more than a drink or two.

There were dozens of folks scattered up and down the length of the valley this warm summer night. Some had minor hand-tasks that still needed work, and some weren't yet ready to sleep, and it was too hot to stay in the tents with any kind of flame going. Others were doing things that required a little more privacy than the closely crowded tents allowed, especially with their sides up. This guard wasn't doing anything out of the ordinary, to be out here alone.

The gathering itself had only a single source of light: a pocket-sized fire in the middle of the circle of nomads. As Halun approached, the dark faces looked up sharply, eyes flashing with reflected firelight. Then, silently, they made a place for him in the circle. He tossed the cushion he'd been carrying under one arm into the vacated spot, and eased himself down onto it, ignoring the stares. At least there didn't seem to be any derision there; while no one else had brought a cushion to sit on, his age and silver hair were at least giving him a reason to to do so himself.

Silence then, until the last of the group—Iridai— arrived. Halun found the silence somewhat unnerving. Crickets singing with all their might out in the grass beyond the firelight only punctuated the silence; they did not break it. Nor did the crackle of the fire. There was a tension tonight that there had not been during previous meetings. Halun fidgeted inside, but gave no outward sign of his restlessness. If they wanted to play this kind of stone-faced game, he would play it too, and outplay all of them.

Finally Iridai arrived, and dropped down into his place in the circle.

Gortan cleared his throat. "We are ready," he said simply.

Halun inhaled sharply, and got a lungful of resinous smoke; he suppressed his need to cough with an effort that left him struggling to breathe for a few moments.

"We, too, are ready," Iridai replied. "The tide of condemnation of the rebels has turned, and now folk wonder openly why Jegrai had them slain out of hand. There is restlessness among the young warriors, those who have not gone courting Vale-folk women, and they wonder how one can achieve wealth, fame and prowess when one cannot raid nor fight. The games and hunting begin to be not enough. My chosen ones are ready to lead them into opposing Jegrai and setting up a new Khene."

Gortan nodded, and all eyes turned to Halun. He felt them more than saw them, like the pressure of a warm breeze on his skin.

"We need to manufacture an incident," he said, laying out before them the plan he had made. "We need Jegrai to make some kind of very obvious mistake—yes, and Felaras, too."

Gortan nodded. "And then we use those mistakes to rouse anger?"

"Exactly. I had one such incident in the brewing, but I lost the man to a fall the night of the storm."

"That would be the man Zetren? The one who fell from the wall?" Iridai asked shrewdly, evidently hoping to impress Halun with his intelligence network.

Halun was not impressed, mostly because half of the Vredai spying on the Fortress were Halun's already, and the rest soon would be. "Exactly. I don't know what he was doing out there in the middle of a storm, but it appears to have been a genuine accident."

"Are you certain, wise one?" Gortan asked dubiously, leaning forward a little.

"Reasonably certain. Felaras has nothing at all to gain

by hiding the fact if he did make a failed attempt on her—Zetren was not well liked, and she would likely get a great deal of sympathy from it." Halun wasn't near as certain as he sounded, but he had to give these barbarians some assurances. "As I am certain you have learned, Felaras actually slipped and fell at the beginning of the storm—she was evidently in her bed and drugged against the pain of her injury when Zetren went out on the walls. I cannot see how she could have had anything to do with his death."

He shrugged then, dismissing the whole thing. "The man was half-crazed, and was quite devoted to the defense of the Order. My guess would be that he decided some of you were likely to try something under cover of the storm, and climbed up to watch for attackers. That section of the wall does face on the area from which an attack could be expected."

Gortan nodded his acceptance of the story. "Well then—how do we 'manufacture' this incident?"

"There are among you a handful who have been passed over when the Shaman, Northwind, made his selection of those he would train." Halun looked at the swarthy faces in the flickering firelight, and noted the expressions of discontent on several of them. "I have tested you, and found those of you with wizard-power. I have been instructing you in its use. Now we will use it; all together, and together we will be a force truly to be reckoned with. Half of us will concentrate on Felaras, and half on Jegrai. I have no doubt that we will meet with success."

Gortan nodded, his expression one of smug self-satisfaction. "And we will be waiting for the mistake that must come?"

"Indeed," Halun replied, "We will be waiting."

The Pass was cooler than the valley—and Felaras could just barely hobble from her bed to her study.

anyway. So Northwind and Jegrai were up here tonight, with detailed maps spread on the desk top, and
herself and Ardun standing for the Order on her side of
the desk.

She would have preferred Zorsha, but the lad was in
the throes of creation—and with this particular creation, she'd as soon have him finished with it in the
shortest possible time. It was something of a symbol to
him; a symbol of his promise to Yuchai. Nothing was
going to keep him from working on those canisters of
that vile fire-stuff until the project was complete and
ready to turn over to the munitions specialists for manufacture. He said he was on the verge of finding the
way to seal the stuff in without setting it afire in the
process, or making the canister so fragile it would break
open in the act of being fired. If he was close to a
breakthrough, best to let him be. Best to have that stuff
out of the Fortress workrooms and back into the munitions sheds. As it was, he wasn't using his own workroom, or even one of the bigger, common workrooms.
He had taken over an older workroom, the lower floor
of part of the oldest part of the Fortress; one of the
original stone towers in the north corner of the wall,
small and cramped and drafty, and not much used by
anyone for anything but storage these days. But Zorsha
had not liked the notion of working with the fire where
anyone else might be endangered, and Felaras had
agreed with him. So the rubbish that had been put
away there had been cleaned out, and Zorsha had moved
his own instruments and tools in.

"So, you think the Talchai will come in through this
way?" Ardun said, interrupting Felaras' thoughts. He
traced a line on the map with his index finger, a line
that did not follow the course of any of the roads across
Azgun, but rather moved along the line of a fairly
prominent ridge.

Kasha made a little movement and caught Felaras'

eye. She made a subtle hand-sign: *Somebody's ill-wishing again.*

Felaras lowered her barriers. *Strong. Damn. And this is not time for us to be distracted. Not only that, but we daren't take the time to do a proper deflection and send it back into their laps.*

She caught the Shaman's eye and repeated the sign Kasha had made. He tightened his mouth, closed his eyes for a moment, then opened them and gave a little nod in Jegrai's direction.

Wonderful. They're targeting the Khene, too.

She clasped her hands together; the Shaman considered, then nodded. In a heartbeat she could feel his shield meshing with hers—and his had the "feel" of more than one person.

Of course; he has Demonsbane, and whatever other shamans-in-training there are down at the camp, and probably all the Healer-women too—

Together they tightened a dome of protection over the Khene and Felaras herself that not even a sending that strong could breach. It would only bounce—and gods help whomever it hit.

Jegrai nodded, oblivious to the magic going on over his head. "I tell you my reasoning: first, there are many towns along this way, not too large, not too small, suitable for raiding. Like us, they will take what they need from those along their path. Second, they will be uncomfortable with the hills towering above them; we had some time to grow used to this, but Sen will be pushing them, they will be an army rather than a Clan with children, the old and the ill to slow them, so they likely will not learn to ignore the hills about them. So they will move to the highest point in the land, not thinking that this will make them very visible. Being visible has never been a factor in our kind of battle; on the steppes one can see for many day's travel in all directions—one can see the approaching army long before it reaches one."

Ardun considered the route. "You know, if we wanted to move into Azgun, we could ambush them at dozens of places along their path, and weaken them considerably at very little cost to ourselves."

Felaras shook her head. "No good; our diplomatic relationship with the lords has never been all that healthy, and bringing an army of our own will only make it worse. Especially an army of yet more nomads. No, much as I'd like to, sending in ambushers is out of the question. Now, working on their *minds*—that's something else altogether."

Northwind looked up at her, his sharp eyes catching hers across the map. "How so, their minds?"

"Oh, well, an elaboration of the 'great wizards' show we put on for you," she said wishing her knee wasn't aching so persistently. "Consider: you people don't fight at night, correct?"

"Correct," Jegrai replied, plainly wondering what she was getting at. They didn't fight at night because fighting on horseback when the horses couldn't see was worse than stupid, it was courting suicide.

But fighting wasn't what she had in mind. "So, figure the Talchai are all bedded down for the night—not asleep yet, but settled in. Suddenly the skies fill with thunder and fire, and weirdly colored lightning, and when it passes, their attention is directed to the ridge beneath where the lightnings were. Because up on the ridge directly above the camp there's a flash of light. When they can see again, there are half-a-dozen Vredai riders with the Running Horse banner—and they're all *glowing*. What would they think?"

"That ghosts had come to haunt them," Northwind replied positively.

"Then the skies open up again, and there's another flash of light, and the riders are gone. Say this gets repeated, at irregular intervals." She grinned. "Like overcast nights, or nights with no moon, but I'd bet they don't make the connection."

"Sen would probably be able to convince them that these were demons, which would make them certain that they were in the right, but that would not keep them from being terrified," Northwind observed shrewdly. "We have too many tales where the demons are the ones who win. You can do all this?"

She shrugged. *I need to take a pain-potion, and I need to stay awake. Gods, what a choice. Guess I'll stay awake.* "It's fairly easy, actually. We already have the fireworks, we use them at festivals. The phosphor is easy enough to get. Slimy stuff, but glows very nicely after dark. Getting the riders in place without being seen is not any kind of a problem—cover them with blankets and move them in while the sky is lighting up, reverse the process when you're ready. We could even supply some fairly weird noises, but I personally think that silence would be more effective."

Jegrai grinned ferally. "This will destroy their will," he said positively, "and Sen will be able to do nothing. So; where do we actually meet them?"

"Well, now, that depends on you, Khene," Felaras said slowly. "It depends on whether or not you want them to have the option of escape."

"How so?"

Felaras looked over to Ardun, who cleared his throat to get their attention. "Well, we can meet them either on the other side of the river, or just below the Teeth. If we hold them on the Azgun side, there's a good chance that once we get Sen—that is the plan, isn't it? Take out their Khene?"

"Yes," Jegrai replied. "Without him they will have no will to fight."

"All right, then; once we do that, they'll likely turn tail and run rather than surrender. After what they did to you folks, they aren't going to be expecting any kind of mercy out of you. But if we hold them at the Teeth, the river will be behind them and they won't have that option."

"Which means that they will fight like any cornered thing," Northwind observed. "This could be very bad for us, for we could sustain many losses. Yet—"

"Yet there is no small number of you who feel like Yuchai," Ardun replied dryly. "You want them destroyed, root and branch."

"Jegrai, I'm going to ask you to do something that would be hard even for one of my people, trained as they are in logical thinking," Felaras said wearily. "Certainly it's beyond Zorsha at the moment, and you and he are of an age—but I think you can do this. Look at the situation logically, and analyze it. Think of it as a problem in tactics, and not as if your heart were involved in it."

Jegrai did not look happy—but he did look thoughtful, which was a good sign.

"What is it you really want to do here?" Ardun asked. "Define your goals. Do you just want Vredai safe? Do you want Vredai safe and Talchai so demoralized they'll be out of the politics of the steppes for your lifetime? Do you want that, *and* to follow up on the gap they're going to leave behind? Or do you have another goal altogether?"

"If I were to have all my wishes?" Jegrai asked, face puzzled, and a little confused.

"Exactly; Khene Jegrai, assume that you know that the Wind Lords themselves have just luck-wished you. What do you plan to do with all that good fortune?"

He studied the map; if gazes had held power, he'd have burned holes in the paper.

"It is not the Talchai," he said slowly, each word falling like a stone into the silence. "It is not even Sen who is the root of our troubles. It is the Suno. They began it. Until they meddled, it was a rare thing for one of the people to spill so much as a drop of a brother's blood."

Northwind nodded, but said nothing.

"If Sen were gone—if we were to let loose upon the warriors your fire-throwers, or even that terrible Sabirn-fire of which you have spoken, the Talchai would run, if they could. If they ran, they would carry back to the steppes the word that Vredai has the powers of gods—or demons, it truly does not matter which. They would hide themselves, lick their wounds, I think—and I hope reflect on how none of this would have occurred had they not given ear to their Khene and his dishonorable plans to war against the helpless."

"Fine, to a point," Northwind said. "And Vredai is then safe. But there are those who would miss their half-breed warhound, eh?"

"The Suno." Jegrai took his eyes off the map and looked over at his advisor. "Which means—" He paused, and shook his head. "I do not know what it means. I cannot say what they will do."

"I can think of things they might," Northwind said, leaning his weight on his arms so that the desk creaked a little. "They might look to the Clans for another half-breed wardog, or even breed another themselves. They might try to simply corrupt another Khene. Certainly they will *not* act upon this themselves, sending an army out to find Vredai. But that does not mean they will leave the Clans in peace. They will do no such thing. We are too much of a threat to them."

"All wishes granted, Jegrai," Felaras prompted. "Think in the long term."

"I should like—to unite the Clans, as Sen tried," he said, eyes shining as he looked into his own dreams and picked out the best of what lay there. "But in honor, under true alliance and pledges to be trusted. And allowing those who would not come to go their own path. Then—I should like to take this war the Suno began upon us back to their own hearth."

"I think you've just answered the question about where we meet them," Ardun said, standing up with a sigh and stretching his back. They could all hear his back pop, so quiet was the study.

"Huh. Indeed. On the other side of the river, and let as many escape as we may, once Sen is no more." Jegrai looked across to Felaras, doubt shadowing his face. "Can we do this, Master? Even your folk and mine together?"

"We can try," she shrugged. "It's no more foolish a plan than Khene Sen's, and one with a great deal more concern for the well-being of everyone involved. My only question is, can you persuade your people to the first step?"

"Letting the Talchai go? I think so," he replied. "I must point out to them that to serve them as they served us is no less without honor—and to send them back with their tails tucked in will show every Clan on the steppes that Vredai will not be trifled with." He quirked one corner of his mouth in a half-smile. "Between maintaining honor, and being able to send the Talchai running in fear, I think I can persuade them to the task."

Felaras was considering what to say next, when the room shook with a roar that was not thunder.

"What in—" Ardun shouted, startled.

Felaras knew there was only one thing that could be—and given the ill-wishing going on and how close he was to *her*—

"Gods!" She threw her cane aside and ran, limping, for the door, urgency overriding pain. "Oh, *gods! Zorsha!*"

The calm of the warm night splintered.

Halun had just reached the side of his tent when the

roar of the explosion at the top of the mountain destroyed the peace of the night. He jumped a foot, and grabbed a rope tent-support for balance as his eyes went immediately to the crack between the peaks where the invisible Fortress sat beside the road through the Pass. A tower of yellow-gold flame rose from there, reaching upward like a demon's arm in the silence that followed the explosion for one breath—two—

Then it collapsed back down, leaving only an ugly red blotch reflecting against the rocks of the peak above the Fortress to show that the fire still burned.

Halun's heart lurched into his throat and stayed there, and he clutched the tent-rope so hard it cut into his palm.

Gods—did I do—oh, gods, I must have!

He turned and ran back the way he had come, only thinking *I have to get back up there!* He reached the stabling area and stumbled for the picketed line of horses, arriving in time to see Teo and Mai tearing off up the road to the Pass on their own beasts. One of the Vredai—*Thank the gods*—had already anticipated him; incredible as it seemed, his horse was saddled and bridled and waiting with a young herder-girl holding the reins. He scrambled into the saddle somehow—she handed him the reins—and then he, too, spurred off into the smoke-tainted dark, following the others.

"Not *water*, you fools," Felaras shouted at the top of her lungs, limping toward the scene of the disaster. "*Sand!* That's Sabirn-fire!"

The fire crews were black blots against the red and yellow of the flames; unidentifiable. Those carrying buckets of water literally dropped them. Someone, bless his or her quick mind, ran like a thin shadow up to where the sand barrels were kept on the top of the wall against siege fires, and began rolling them right off the edge of the walkway to crash and break open at the feet of the fire-fighters. The fire-crew stooped and scrambled after their dropped containers; the empty buckets were refilled with sand, and the fire-fighting continued with scarcely a pause.

Felaras clutched at Jegrai's shoulder, scarcely aware that she was doing so, and moaned. The little tower was wrecked; reduced to a heap of tumbled stones. The fire-fighters were getting the pockets of flame under control but—somewhere under that pile of rubble was Zorsha.

Or what—oh, gods—is left of him.

"Zorsha!" screamed a young voice behind them, and Yuchai darted out of the door in the wall and past them, heading straight for the wreckage.

Jegrai slid out from under Felaras' hand and sprinted like a champion foot-racer, reaching the boy before he even got close to the carnage, and tackling him.

They went down in a tangled heap of long limbs on the packed dirt of the courtyard; Yuchai tried to squirm away, but Jegrai kept a tight hold on him, shouting at him in their own tongue. All at once the boy capitulated, collapsing into Jegrai's arms and breaking into terrified sobbing.

The Khene got slowly to his feet and drew the boy up after him, holding him closely, then leading him back past Felaras.

"We can do nothing," he said as he passed her. "I will get the boy back to his bed; we will wait for word."

She nodded absently; the fire crew was doing a good job of smothering the blaze and even the thick smoke was being dispersed. Now most of the light in the back courtyard was coming from the torches and lanterns, not the fire itself.

Kasha came to take Jegrai's place as her support; her body was rigid beneath Felaras' hand, and she trembled. For that matter, Felaras herself was shaking from head to toe.

Oh gods, we should have thought of Zorsha—we should have thought *and brought him under the protection too. But I was sure I'd taught him enough to deflect properly—and surely he realized that he'd have to keep a shield up when working with the fire!*

Ardun strode past to take charge of the rescue crew—who were mostly Watchers, anyway. "Get those damned stones moved!" he was shouting. "No not those, *those!* No, no, you fool! Don't touch that support, you'll just start another fall of stone! Get the blocks *off* it first!"

There was nothing they could do but stand and watch—and hope.

Two horses galloped into the back court, followed by a third. The very first rider was Teo, easily identifiable because of his size; he flung himself out of the saddle, peeled off his tunic, and threw himself into the work crew all in one movement. His powerful young body made an immediate difference; he was able to get into places only big enough for a single man, and lift things from there that only a couple of the others would have been able to tackle. Tiny Mai was the second rider; had to be. The asexual shadow leapt from the horse and went straight to the bucket crew, taking the place of someone larger who was thus freed to join the rescuers.

Halun was the third rider, pulling his horse up beside Felaras and sliding off untidily.

"Who—" he panted.

"Zorsha," Felaras choked out. "He—he was working with Sabirn-fire."

Halun moaned and made as if to join one of the two crews. Kasha caught his sleeve and held him back.

"Not you, old man," she said in a dead, calm voice. "You're too old and out of shape. You'll only get in the way, or get yourself hurt."

As if to underscore her statement, Teo uncovered a pocket of the smoldering fire, which blazed up in his face. He jumped back in time to avoid more than a touch of the flames, and stood out of the way while a fire crew dealt with it.

When the flames were out he went right back in before the blocks of stone even had a chance to cool.

Boitan joined them, his arms and Shenshu's laden with supplies. "Is it only Zorsha?" he asked quietly.

"So far as I know," Felaras replied around her fear, ignoring Halun's groan. "He wouldn't let anyone else work with him; said it was too dangerous."

"What was he doing in there?" Halun demanded wildly; Felaras glanced over and saw that his face was contorted with fear, grief, and something she couldn't properly identify. "Felaras, what in hell did you set him to? What insanity possessed you to put him on Sabirn-fire?"

"Set him to?" Kasha choked. "Great good gods, Halun, she couldn't have stopped him if she'd tried! *You've* been living down with those folk, haven't you even heard *one* story about what happened to them when the Talchai took their camp?"

Halun shook his head dumbly.

Kasha stared at him in profoundest amazement. "Zorsha got it all in the face from young Yuchai—and since then, all he's been interested in is a way to decimate the Talchai as badly as they did Jegrai's folk. That's why the Sabirn-fire, he was trying to work out a way to seal it into mortar-canisters—"

She was interrupted by a hoarse shout from Teo. "Here! I found him! He's under here!"

They surged forward in a body. Of them all, only Felaras had seen victims of Sabirn-fire; that had been long, long ago, when she was a bare novice.

She was dreading what Teo was likely to uncover.

Teo tore huge blocks from the pile by himself, flinging them to the side with frenzied strength. His face was contorted, and tears made runnels through the crust of ashes on his cheeks; his chest was smeared with ash and shining with sweat, and he looked like something out of the lowest hells.

In moments he had the little coffin-shaped area in which Zorsha was lying cleared of rubble. Felaras only got the barest glimpse of something dark and twisted—and it was moaning.

"*Move*, dammit!" Boitan snarled, shoving his way between the rescuers; Shenshu and Kasha behind him, carrying a board from the wreckage. "Here—gently—roll him over onto this—"

The moans spiraled up into harsh screams, and Felaras looked away. Into Halun's eyes. And she recognized what she saw there.

Guilt. Terrible, soul-searing guilt. But why?

She had no time to wonder about that, for the rescuers had gotten Zorsha out of the tumble of stone and down onto the courtyard, laying him practically at her feet. She went to her knees beside him, as someone brought Boitan a lantern in response to a snarled demand for light.

It was as bad as she'd feared.

He'd taken the raw fire-blast right in his face; his eyes were—gone. Just a charred swath where they had been. From head to waist, he looked like nothing so much as badly charred meat; his tunic had burned right away, and bits of it flaked off every time he moved. His hands didn't bear thinking about. There was bone showing.

She looked at Boitan, who caught her eye, and shook his head slowly.

Oh, gods— Her throat closed; she couldn't breathe. All she wanted to do was howl in agony.

A harsh whisper caught her attention, forced her to look back down at the thing at her feet that had been the handsomest lad in the Order.

"—aras—" the lips whispered again.

"I'm here," she said, leaning down, but not touching him. "I'm here, lad. So's Halun."

"—alun? Ah—" What was left of his face spasmed in pain, as Halun joined her, kneeling beside her, looking as if he wanted to gather the boy to his breast.

The mouth moved again. Gasping half-words through pain that must have been unbearable. "—alun. —elp —elaras. Got to. Help—elaras. Boy. Jegrai. —redai. Swear!" The charred travesties of hands pawed at the front of Halun's tunic. "Swear! Swear!"

Halun was sobbing as Felaras had never seen him weep in her life. "I promise. Oh, gods, Zorsha, I swear it, I swear—"

The lips almost seemed to smile. "I—love—you—all," he said, clearly, and carefully. Then, just as clearly, but cracking with anguish, "Help—me—go."

Boitan caught her eyes again; his face was wet, but the hands holding the long, thin mercy-blade were steady.

She looked briefly down—and as if he had sensed her eyes on him, Zorsha whispered. One word. "Please."

She choked, and nodded. Boitan moved so quickly she almost didn't see it happen. Zorsha surely was in such pain he never felt the keen-edged blade slip between his ribs and find his heart.

He just sighed once—then—he was gone.

Halun flung himself across the body and broke into hysterical, punishing sobs of grief.

Felaras unashamedly did the same.

The potion Boitan had given her had numbed her physical pain, and had put some distance between her and her sorrow. But the grief was still there, a constant that filled her throat with tears and would not let her sleep. She gave up tossing on her bed after too many hours of staring at the ceiling, and lit a candle to stare at instead.

Now the candle was guttering out, and birds were hailing the dawn just outside the window. And the air still stank of ashes and burning.

Kasha and Teo . . . gods. She watched out her window at the bloody sunrise, not really seeing it. Boitan had kept pouring drugs into them until he'd knocked them out. They'd been out of their young minds with grief. Kasha had gone catatonic, and Teo had begun tearing out his own hair in clumps.

She wasn't sure which had been worse; Kasha's dead eyes, or Teo's near-madness.

Boitan said it was hysteria; that they'd be mourning more normally when they woke up. She damned well hoped so; she'd only lost one damned fine lad and her successor and . . . someone who had begun to be a treasured friend. *They'd* lost a third of themselves.

She remembered only too well how that felt.

She'd dreaded telling Yuchai, but Jegrai had broken the news to the boy—with a gentle lie. So far as Yuchai was concerned, Zorsha had been working on something for Felaras, not the Sabirn-fire. The child had enough to bear without that on his conscience.

The candle gave a last flare, and went out.

She wasn't sure what had happened to Halun; things had been very confused after Boitan had peeled her off the body.

The thought could have been a summons; someone tapped briefly at her door, and then opened it and slipped inside like a ghost.

Halun. He *looked* like a ghost.

"I thought you'd still be awake," he croaked, voice ruined from weeping. He'd cleaned himself up, but there were black circles all around his bloodshot eyes, and he was as pale as bleached parchment. "Felaras, I have to talk to you."

She pulled herself up into a sitting position and waved at the bedside chair, wearily. "So talk."

He did not take the offered seat, although he moved closer to the bed. "It was my fault—" he began.

She cut him off, angrily. "Dammit, Halun, do I have to hear that from *you*, too? I've heard it from everybody else—"

He interrupted. "Felaras, you don't understand!" he cried tightly, his face twisted with grief. "I caused what happened! I was the one ill-wishing you."

Not what she had expected to hear. She froze, her backbone turned to a column of ice. It took her a moment to recover enough to gasp out an answer. "*You?* But . . . why?"

"Ambition," he said, angrily, brokenly. "Stupid, selfish ambition. You had the chair. I wanted it. I convinced myself I only wanted it for the good of the Order, but I lied to myself, I wanted it because I wanted the power. I corrupted myself and persuaded myself I was doing the right thing—I was trying to undermine you at first, and then you and Jegrai. I was trying to get you to make the mistakes that would let us depose you both." He paused for breath, and twisted his hands together so hard the knuckles cracked. "You were protected; so I trained some with the power, and went after you tonight in concert with them. Only I added a little codicil. You probably don't understand—"

"Only too well, you bastard," she snarled. "I was the one protecting myself."

He goggled at her a moment. "I—I—" He got control of himself just enough to take up where he'd left off. "I set the wish so that if you were shielded and it bounced off you, it wouldn't go randomly—I set it to strike whoever was the one nearest you—"

"You damned fool!" She surged up out of bed and seized him by the throat. Her abused knee shot fire up her leg, pain that she ignored. "You gods-bedamned fool! What have you been doing down there? Sleeping?

I just made Zorsha my official successor! Who the hell *else* would it take?"

Halun paled down to near-transparent and shut his eyes, not struggling in her hands at all. "I didn't know . . ." he whispered. "I've been so busy with all those stupid little plots that I didn't know . . . I thought it would get Kasha, Teo—"

"I ought to break your damned neck with my own two hands!"

He opened his eyes again and looked directly into hers. His eyes were full of such pain that they nearly burned her soul. There was hell in those eyes, and self-condemnation that was worse than anything she could do to him. "I wish you would," he whispered miserably. "He was—my son in everything but the flesh."

She looked at her hands, clenched white-knuckled in the fabric of his robe, and back up into his face. It hadn't changed.

She shoved him away with such force that he staggered and came close to falling over backward. "What the hell am I going to do with you?" she asked, sagging back onto her bed, sick to the bones, and weary past all belief.

"I don't know," he replied, in profound desolation. "Just . . . I gave him my word to help you. Tell me how, and I will."

She considered him for a moment, as he stood there, waiting.

For what? Gods. Help me, he says. How in—

Then she knew, and rang the bell beside her bed for a novice. "Is there anyone else in the Order working with you?" she asked harshly, as she waited for the youngster to put in an appearance.

He shook his head. "No. Not even Zetren. All my co-conspirators are down in the valley."

The novice arrived, slipping in the still-open door; a

thin, dark girl-child of about fourteen. Memory put name to her; Daisa, another of Ardun's endless brood of daughters, and older than she looked, about to get full Sword status. Another Kasha-in-the-making, for which she was grateful. *It'll be a long time before I can see a blonde lad without crying. . . .*

"Get me Thaydore and Kitri," she said, "And Boitan, if he's still awake."

The child vanished. "Get me pen and paper out of that drawer over there," she said, pointing to the little writing-desk in the corner of her room.

Halun did so, as docile to her orders as the novice. She pulled the lap desk out from under the bed and set it up.

Then she glared at him; still in a rage, but no longer a white-hot one—and a rage that was fast being cooled by his very real guilt and sorrow.

"Sit down," she ordered. "You're going to be here a while."

He took the chair, obediently.

"Now," she said, pen poised. "Let's have all this from the beginning."

Chapter Twelve

Halun lit his lamp and hung it from the centerpole of his tent, and wished with all his heart that this farce was over.

The Khene's brother had come to Halun's tent as soon as he had returned from the Fortress; more than a week after he'd gone pounding wildly back up the road. Iridai brought word that the meeting they'd scheduled before all this happened was assembled and waiting for him.

Gods be thanked, this will be the last.

Behind him, Iridai put one hand lightly on Halun's shoulder. "I . . . my condolences, wise one," he said, awkward now that the message had been delivered. "I understand that the young man was once your pupil."

Halun shuddered, but did not remove the man's hand. *I have to act the same; thank the gods they all think it's just that I'm mourning Zorsha.* "Thank you," he said, stumbling over the simple words. *These men are acting out of belief that Jegrai is wrong. I acted out of lust for power. They aren't barbarians. I'm the savage.* "Yes, he was—something more than just a pupil, in

255

fact, he was an orphan when he came to us. I was something of a father to him. . . ."

He let his voice trail off, and felt the muscles of his throat tensing with the effort of holding back tears.

Not that tears would matter to these people—they would understand and give him room to weep. Except for Gortan, who was like a block of stone, they were mostly as open about expressing sorrow as they were about expressing joy. *Oh, Zorsha, I needed to be brought to my senses—but I would that I could have paid a less dear coin than your life.*

He still looked like something dragged through hell, and he knew it; too many sleepless nights, no few of them spent contemplating the amazing number of poisons in his workroom. But suicide would not have served to fulfill his promise to Zorsha. And he had a great deal to make up for.

Felaras had been amazingly decent about the whole thing; she could, so easily, have made every word, every hour painful for him, and yet she had done no such thing.

Not that she hadn't been tempted; she'd told him that herself, with that disconcerting frankness of hers, the day they'd buried the boy. But she'd also told him, "There's been too damned much pain already and damned if I'm going to add to it!"

A remarkable woman. And he'd been blinded to how remarkable she was by his own ambition. Now it was too late; too late for anything except a tentative alliance. Never a friendship. And never anything deeper.

What a fool I've been.

If it hadn't been for the boy . . .

For he'd finally met young Yuchai, who until then had been nothing more than a name and a huddled form under a blanket.

He'd been waiting outside Felaras' door for her summons, when he'd heard a strangled sob from the Mas-

ter's Folly. Thinking it might be Kasha or Teo, he'd
looked in, figuring on finding out which it was and
fetching the other. Mourning alone was a lot harder
than mourning with someone—as he now knew only
too well. And he couldn't think who else would have
been quartered next to Felaras besides those two.

But it hadn't been either of them; it had been a
young boy, crying painfully into the fur of a pale-gold
dog—

A golden gaze-hound like the one Zorsha had owned
as a novice . . .

Perhaps it was the sight of the dog that drew him,
but without knowing why, he found himself standing by
the boy's side. The boy had raised his tear-streaked
face, and he'd seen the shape, the bone structure of it,
so like Jegrai's; and knew then who it was, and why he
wept. So he'd held out his hand. "I'm Halun," he'd
said, swallowing down a lump in his throat. "I was his
friend too—"

And before he could blink, he had his arms full of
crying child, and then Halun found himself weeping
with him, and somehow when they both got under
control again, they were friends.

He'd picked up Yuchai's education where Zorsha had
left off, more out of a sense of duty than with any real
expectations. That was when he had discovered how
absolutely brilliant the boy was, and duty became
pleasure—the lone pleasure in all those bleak days.

*Gods willing, by tonight this whole messy business
will be dealt with, and I can go back to that pleasure.
Zorsha, I pledge you, that boy will have everything
you'd have given him!*

He looked at Iridai out of the corner of his eye, and
wondered how that stolid warrior was going to take the
shattering of his plans and his own disgrace before the
entire Clan.

No bloodshed, Jegrai had said. *There's been enough*

blood shed already. Felaras had agreed with him. Halun hoped this would work as well as they thought it would. . . .

"Where are we meeting?" Halun asked dully, half-turning, and watching the lamp flame over Iridai's shoulder instead of the man's face.

"Gortan's tent. It seems safe enough. If friends do *not* gather from time to time at the tents, it begins to look odd. And besides, Jegrai is up at the Wizard's Place."

Halun reached for the lamp again; he should have been feeling anticipation, but he felt nothing but weariness. "Now?"

Iridai nodded, and Halun put out the lamp, then ducked out the tent entrance, following him into the night. He glanced up at the sky; it was not overcast, but it was moonless.

It was going to be a perfect evening for Felaras' plan.

He followed along behind Iridai, stumbling now and again over a rock in the path. *Soon. It will all be over soon.*

His soundless litany might have been a conjuration: no sooner had they cleared all but the last circle of tents, where Gortan's tent had been pitched, then the sky above them opened up with an incredible display of—

Fireworks. Festival fireworks. But to the Vredai, it surely seemed like a visitation from the gods.

Every color possible bloomed up there, it seemed, accompanied by thunderous explosions that were close enough to hurt the ears. Not surprisingly, every person in the camp was out of his tent and gaping up at the sky within heartbeats—some with stark fear on their faces, some with less readable emotions, and the children with mingled surprise and innocent delight.

The guards at the entrance to the valley ran back to the tents, weapons at the ready, although from the despair on their faces Halun reckoned they'd already counted on those weapons as being impotent.

The stage was set.

The last of the fireworks bloomed and died, a spectacular burst of clusters of red that told Halun to ready himself.

There was a heartbeat of silence, then—

Horns blared from somewhere above them; horns like nothing the Vredai had ever heard, deep and menacing and incredibly loud. Not surprising; these were horns that had been sent to the Order by a wandering Seeker long ago, sent from some mountainous region to the north. They were as tall as a man, and used to warn of (or perhaps trigger, he'd said) avalanches of snow. Two of the most agile Watchers in the Fortress had scaled with ropes and crampons down the mountainside just after dusk with these things strapped to their backs, to set themselves up on the supposedly unclimbable cliffs above the valley.

There was a flash of fire and sulfurous smoke at the valley entrance—and a glowing figure rode through the smoke cloud, seeming to come *out* of the smoke cloud.

It was Felaras, but a transformed Felaras. The Vredai for the most part had never seen Felaras; those who had had certainly never seen her like this, with her hair streaming free beneath an ancient, dragon-crested Ancas helm, and her body encased from head to toe in burnished chain and plate. What was more, she burned with a bluish light of her own, as did the pale horse she rode—and the horse's hooves made no noise at all on the hard ground. It seemed to flow toward them, a ghost-horse ridden by a stern and angry spirit.

The Vredai behind Halun moaned with fear; Halun heard one or two mutters of "Wind-rider!" and "Lord's Messenger!"—and Iridai sank to his knees.

"Vredai, who were betrayed, you harbor traitors among you," Felaras boomed, using the voice that could be heard from one end of a noisy practice ground to another. And she wasn't speaking Trade-tongue, either; this speech had been carefully written out for her by Teo, transcribing Northwind's words into Ancas phonemes. "Treason is a disease; the Talchai touched you, and you are infected, you are sick with it. The Wind Lords brought you here to safe haven, but you brought a blight with you, in your hearts."

The Vredai muttered, the groaning of branches in the wind. Halun stifled a cough as a gust of wind carried spent smoke into his face. It burned on his tongue for a moment.

"And your sickness has its counterpart on the Wizards' Mountain," she continued, face as masklike as marble. "Vredai, will you hear the names of your traitors and deal with them?"

Far sooner than Halun would have expected, he heard a woman behind him shout "Aye!" Then there was a chorus of shouts of affirmation until Felaras raised her hand, and a heavy, anticipatory silence fell.

"Clan Singer Gortan," she began, each word having a sound of doom about it. "Iridai kan Luchen . . ."

She told off the entire roll of the conspirators, from greatest to least, all the names Halun had given them. Beside him, Iridai trembled and moaned. At the end of the list the hidden horns brayed again.

Felaras waited a moment while the list of names sunk in. "These would have betrayed your Khene, who brought you to this place under the guidance of the Wind Lords," she said, "even as he and you were betrayed by the Talchai. Now I ask you, in the name of the compassionate Wind Lords: what will you do with them, these traitors to Jegrai and to your safety?"

From the angry shouts behind them, executing the traitors seemed to be one of the more popular notions. Once again, Felaras raised her hand to gain utter silence.

"Has there not been enough Vredai blood shed?" she

asked, in a much quieter voice. "Treason is a sickness; it can be cured. Treason is a rot; rot can be mended. Take these men to you, people of Vredai. Watch them, but forgive them. To deal them death earns you nothing but more pain. Shed no blood of the Clans that you cannot avoid, people of Vredai. Rather, turn the fires of your anger upon the authors of the root treason. The spreaders of the sickness. The Suno. Consider how you should deal with them—and know that *they* merit none of your compassion."

Iridai was huddled in a knot on the ground, sobbing.

Felaras' voice strengthened again. "And there is another among you who is not of your blood, who merits none of your compassion, who fostered treason as a way to his own power and not because he felt that the Khene was faulty in judgment. Halun, Hand of the Seekers, of the chapter of the Tower, stand forth!"

Halun stepped forward until he was just within twenty paces of Felaras. He heard a slight rustle of the grass to his left as he took up his appointed position—and that was the only sign he noticed of Kasha getting into place and Mai passing him to plant her next surprise.

"See, people of Vredai—learn the reward given to those who betray for their own gain!"

Behind him, a flash of heat and light reflected off the metal surfaces of Felaras' armor and shining weirdly red off her eyes and the eyes of her horse told him that another flash-pot had been set off—and Kasha, so hellishly made up and garbed he would not have recognized her, leapt up out of the grass that concealed her and seized him with a howl of wild laughter. There were strange, moaning sounds coming from above, now; sounds he knew were being made by the toys they called "bull-roarers" being whirled around and around the heads of the concealed horn-blowers.

He put up a convincing show of struggle, as a third flash-pot went up at the entrance to the valley, and another glowing horse and rider—this time shining an evil green—galloped through it. They swooped down on Kasha and her "victim" and scooped both of them up.

Actually, Kasha leapt up behind Jegrai—who was about the only rider capable of pulling off this trick—while he hauled Halun up before him.

Jegrai's horse wheeled and headed back the way they had come, and Halun closed his eyes. Face-down across a saddle-bow was uncomfortable. Watching the grass whirl by while breathing powder-smoke was making him ill.

"Remember, Vredai!" Felaras called. "Remember!"

She made her horse rear and pivot on its hind legs, before following Jegrai and his poor overburdened mount back through the valley mouth as a fourth flash-pot went up behind them.

Once on the other side, all four of them dismounted as invisible hands took the reins of the horses. Invisible, because the owners were garbed head to foot in black, and their faces were smeared with soot. The glowing horses were swathed in blankets and the glowing riders in cloaks. And the entire contingent—except for Mai, who would be quietly collecting the spent flash-pots she'd set off—mounted up again and headed for the nearest farm with a well to wash off the phosphor.

Mai joined them in the lantern-lit barn before they were quite finished. "They're very impressed, Jegrai," she said quietly, dumping her four pots, still stinking of sulfur and brimstone, with the rest of the gear. "I don't think you'll be having any trouble with them for a while."

"Maybe," he said, pausing for a moment to look closely at the Master, with his hands full of towel and his hair dripping down his back. "But—Felaras, what of the time when we pull this same trick on the Talchai? They are bound to realize that they were deceived."

"Thought about that already, lad," she said, while Halun silently helped her out of her greaves. He unbuckled the straps and lifted them away, and she groaned and flexed her ankle. "Gods, I'd forgotten how damned heavy this crap was. Kasha, love, get the cloth off my horse's feet, will you? You won't be a part of that trickery, Jegrai—or at least your people won't. I'll have the Watchers do it, tricked out in Vredai gear. Some of your people will know, or guess, what we did, and some will learn how and why—but I'd rather it was the next generation down the line."

Jegrai nodded, and began toweling off his hair.

"I think you're likely to have more respect than you know what to do with when you ride in, Khene," Mai said with a hint of amusement. "They're convinced that Felaras is a Holy Messenger from the Wind Lords, and equally convinced that a pair of *kizhiin* carried Halun off to unending torture. Last I saw, Iridai and Gortan were in the process of giving away all their worldly goods, beating their breasts and praising the compassion of the Wind Lords for sparing them."

Jegrai snorted. "Give them a few days, and they'll be back to telling me I'm a fool to my face," he said, with just a hint of amusement in his voice. "But at least I don't think I need to be watching behind my back for plots for a while."

"I doubt you'll ever need to again, Jegrai," Felaras replied.

Halun nodded, and handed her a wet towel. "What they heard back there was the Messenger of the Wind Lords all but telling them that you are their special darling. There were no few of your people who'd have been willing to follow you through hell before this. Now all of them will be."

The surprised expression on Jegrai's face was rather funny. "Me?" he squawked. "God-touched?"

Halun nodded again. "Yes, Khene."

"Think about that, son," Felaras said urgently. "Think about that *hard*."

"Indeed," Halun said, with a sorrow too profound for release. "Think about that. I was told I was all but god-touched; you people have given scholars that cachet. I was listened to as if I knew all wisdom. I was offered power—and it turned my head—and because of my own ambition and pride and self-deception an innocent boy *died*, died horribly. Think very hard about that, and decide what you want to do about it."

Out of the corner of his eye he caught Felaras staring at him with a very thoughtful expression, and when he finished—

She put one hand on his shoulder.

Just that—but he knew then, without her saying a word, that out of some well of compassion of her own, those words of his had given her the strength to forgive him.

Even though he would never forgive himself.

"Khene," she said into the silence, "it's time you went back to your people, and me to mine. Our work is still only half finished."

"In truth," Jegrai agreed, and tossed his towel back to Mai, who caught it with a grin. He pulled on his tunic, and then turned to where his horse was standing—all the phosphor washed off him, now—and jumped into the saddle without bothering to use the stirrups.

"I expect a full report in the morning, lad," Felaras called.

He grinned over his shoulder at her; then, with a wave of his hand, sent his horse out the barn door at a brisk canter.

"Yes," Felaras said, looking disconcertingly into Halun's eyes, "our work is only half finished."

*   *   *

"All right, all *right*," Felaras shouted, her head beginning to ring from all the echoing voices around her. "Get settled, damn you!"

The din in the Hall died down, and complete silence took its place.

Felaras took a long, slow look around the Hall—this time she could see her audience; she'd need to, so she'd insisted that every one of them bring a candle or a lamp. Row after row of faces, each lit from below by a yellow flame—it was, in a strange way, beautiful. The Hall glowed with light, as it never had before—

And likely, as it never would again.

"You all know what's been happening," she said gruffly, taking her seat in the chair she'd had brought to replace the lectern. After all of this evening's work, her leg was aching like a demon was gnawing at the knee, and damned if she was going to stand! She settled herself carefully, but pain still stabbed up her leg and made her catch her breath for a moment. "You all know by now what Halun did."

There was a rising murmur—rather unpleasantly like a growl. Halun, seated on the lowest tier of benches and directly across from her, flinched.

"Shut *up!*" she snarled, surprising both herself and her audience, who subsided into silence. "Don't you think he's going to pay for that every day of his life? He *trained* Zorsha! Think about that!"

A moment more of silence, then a muted sigh as his fellow scholars took in the misery on Halun's face, and saw that she was right.

"Whether we like it or not, he forced something on us that we should have faced a long time ago," she continued, more quietly now. "And that's our future. We have no choice; we're out in the world, now. The temptation to use our knowledge for mundane power is a great one, and it isn't going to become less. Then there's the question—how can we really devote ourselves to truly seek knowledge for the sake of knowledge when we have an eager Khekhene peering over our shoulders."

A murmur of surprise at that.

"Oh, yes, the three Chapter Leaders and I decided that Halun—and Zorsha—were right. We'd be damned fools to let this opportunity pass. Jegrai is enlightened, eager to learn—we can serve at his right hand, guiding him. More than that, we can be the ones to train—and select—his successors."

Felaras smiled in wry satisfaction at the buzz that last statement provoked.

"You heard me correctly. Jegrai has agreed, as part of our bargain to help him against the Talchai, and ultimately the Suno, that it will be the Order who selects his heir—male, female, first, last or baseborn. And it will be the Order who has charge of educating all his children, in wedlock and bastard. There will be no discontented halflings if he has any say about it."

There were nods of approval and interest all about her. She smiled thinly, shifted her weight a little, and winced as her knee protested the move.

"*But*—" She held up an admonishing hand. "There lies temptation. There lies possible corruption, seduction by power, and ultimately, the end of what we know as the Order. Once again, Halun was right. We need to be in hiding in order to do our work freely and without either temptation or coercion. So now you're asking, 'how can we be both?' I'll tell you."

She took a deep breath, steeling herself. *Oh, gods, I don't want to do this—and I don't have a choice.*

"I'm splitting the Order."

She'd expected an uproar—and indeed there was one, but it died down within heartbeats. She looked about her with some surprise, then continued as she'd planned.

"About spring of last year some of the Watchers I sent out to keep track of Jegrai's Clan came back here with a report of another Fortress like this one, south and east of us, in Azgun. Roughly a week hard riding away. This one was smaller, maybe half the size of our Fortress. Thing is, it's no wonder we hadn't seen it before; it was so cleverly built into the side of the mountain that if Aned hadn't stumbled on it, he'd never have known it was there. I hadn't considered fleeing to it when the Vredai first showed up at the Teeth largely because to get to it we'd have had to get past them. The building is in good shape, the Watchers tell me—a little work, and it will be livable. Two years at most and it will be about as comfortable as this place. And nobody except Ardun, a handful of Watchers, and I know where it is. That's where some of you will be going."

"Which, Felaras?" asked a novice, in a high, un-steady voice. "Which of us are going?"

Good gods, she thought in wonder. *They've accepted it. They've accepted it without a fight. By the gods, Halun was right.*

"Let me first tell you what the plan is that we've worked out," she temporized, giving them a little more time to adjust to what she'd already laid in their laps. "There will be two Masters—the Outer Master, and the Inner. And the Master of the Inner Order will always have the power to overrule any decision of the Outer Master. The Chapter Leaders will all be of the Inner Order. Members of the Order will be allowed one— *one*— transfer in their lifetime; in either direction, but once the choice is made, children, you are stuck with it. Seekers, there will be very little, if any, research in the Outer Order, and most of the real breakthroughs will be the secrets of the Inner until they decide to dispense them. Archivists, there will be a very great demand for you; we have three duplicates of the Library in storage; one goes with the Inner Order, one stays at the Outer Fortress, and one goes with Jegrai. You will be the keepers of those volumes and the teachers of Jegrai's people. So . . . in the Outer Order there will be a great deal of temporal power, and very little chance for advancement or research. In the Inner, the opposite. And only the Watchers and the Master of the Outer Order will know where the Inner Fortress is located. Ever."

She scanned their faces, and saw thoughtfulness, anticipation—and no fear whatsoever.

"Watchers, yours will be the hardest job; to maintain communication between the two halves of the Order, to make certain that the Inner Fortress remains hidden— and, if need be, to make certain that no member *or Master* of the Outer Order *ever* betrays his or her trust."

She looked about her, and saw with pride the way the members of her own chapter took that.

Thank the gods. I made the right decision. They'll keep us safe.

"So, children, you've heard what I have to say. I want you to take a moment to think about which way you want to go. But first of all—Halun, come up here beside me."

Halun rose from his seat on the benches and walked, slowly and stiffly, toward her. His long silver hair was limp and neglected-looking, he had the appearance of someone only recently recovered from a long illness— and he acted at this moment like he was walking to his own execution.

And when I'm done here he might wish I'd had his damned head whacked off.

"Ladies and Gentlemen of the Order of the Sword of Knowledge—I make Halun the Master of the Inner Order."

Gasps and weak protests, which she overran with her practice-ground voice.

"Can any of you think of anyone less likely to abuse his power?" she asked harshly. "After what he's done? When all of you are going to be watching him like hawks for the least little misstep? Remember, the old rules will still hold—the Convocation can unseat any Master with a two-thirds vote. If he turns out to be untrustworthy, take him down."

She cast a look over to Halun, who looked utterly stunned.

"As I'm certain you have deduced, I will be the first Master of the Outer Order. And again, the old rules still hold. My successor will have to be one *not* of my chapter. So now, while the rest of you think about who you want to serve under, and whether you're fit for a long trek and an uncomfortable couple of years, I am going to ask those of you who knew what I was going to do what their choices will be."

She looked over at Teo, who still wore his grief like a cloak. "Teokane, Outer or Inner?"

He looked up at her. "Outer, Felaras," he said simply—and a little sadly. "Jegrai needs me. And you do, too."

"Then I make Teokane my chosen successor," she said. "Not the least because the things he has faced have made him a different person from the Teo we knew. Teokane, step to my right. Halun, to my left."

Obedient to her will, they did so.

"Yuchai . . ." The boy looked up at her in astonishment, surprise replacing mourning. "I've had words with your Khene, lad, and he's released you to this choice. And he said—may I quote—you'd be a damned fool to swing a sword when you can send your mind out to the stars. Outer or Inner?"

"I—Inner, Master Felaras," the boy said, hesitating

only for a moment. "Jegrai has all the strength you can give him now, he doesn't need me. And Zorsha—" a catch in his throat, then his voice strengthened. "Zorsha wanted me to stay."

"Kasha, Outer or Inner?"

The girl took a long breath, and looked her squarely in the eyes. "Forgive me, Felaras—Inner. Yuchai needs me, and I need him. Any of my sisters could be trained as your Second."

Kasha turned and looked up behind her at the tiers of seats. "Take Daisa, she's ready for her full status, she's as good or better than I was, at everything. And she's as disrespectful as I am. . . ."

Felaras nodded; after the way Yuchai and Kasha had been huddled together this past week, she'd more than half expected that decision.

"Ardun? Do you back Kasha's suggestion?"

"I agree, Felaras. What's more, I'll make her full Watcher, as of this instant."

"Daisa?"

"I'd—" The girl gulped, and seemed unable to reply— but got up and took her stand at Felaras' right, letting her actions speak for her.

Felaras nodded again.

But what she didn't expect was Halun's reaction.

"Then I name Kasha *my* successor," he said, as soon as Daisa had taken her place. "All of you to witness. It is only because she was of the same chapter as Felaras that she was passed over before. She is fully worthy to sit the Master's seat."

Kasha stared at him for a long, long moment, then seemed to come to a decision of her own. "It isn't usual," she said, "but it isn't unheard of for the successor to name *her* successor. I name Yuchai as mine. I can't think of anyone else more likely to live up to—" She choked, and brought her hand over her eyes to hide her tears "—his teachers—"

"So witnessed," Felaras said, softly but clearly, swallowing down tears of her own. *Not now, old girl. Later. Not now.*

Kasha and Yuchai took their places beside Halun, who put his arms around them both, so that they supported each other.

"Ardun?"

"Inner, please, Felaras," he said, looking at her pleadingly.

"Inner it is. And I'm glad of it. You're the best Sword Leader we've had in decades. Kitri?"

"Outer! This is the chance I've prayed for all my life!" The—now former—Book Leader's face was alight with a fierce joy.

"Name your replacement."

"Jesen."

"Jesen, do you agree to go Inner?"

Jesen, a tolerably young man, but one who lived and breathed books, nodded. He moved across the row of benches to Felaras' left, and Kitri to her right.

"Thaydore."

"Inner, Felaras."

"Boitan?"

"Outer."

"Mai?"

"Outer, Felaras."

So it went on, name after name, from the Leaders to the youngest novice, each of them making his choice and moving to the right or left of the Master's seat.

Finally it was over. Felaras looked over her people, and sighed. It had gone as she had not dared dream. Most of the Tower would be Inner—*none* of the Flame had chosen the Outer Order, and only about half of the Hand, mostly those who were far more technically oriented than investigative. *Bridge constructors,* she thought with hope. *Healers, and toolmakers. Surveyors and teachers. Those who will build the future I can't even imagine.* More than two thirds of the Book had chosen Outer, along with their former Leader, and all of them had that same glow of anticipation in their eyes. Jegrai's people would have good teachers. And the Sword had split roughly in half—

She looked to her right, to Teo. *Poor lad—he's lost one best friend, and now he's losing the other. He's lost all chance of real advancement—Kasha will be able to overrule* any *decision he makes—*

Teo seemed to feel her regard, and turned to look into her eyes. To her astonishment, he reached out for her hand, and squeezed it briefly. "It's fine, Felaras," he said softly, though his voice shook a little. "I'm going where I'm needed. Really *needed.* Isn't that the important thing?"

She glanced at her other side; Halun, Kasha, and Yuchai. They looked nothing alike—Halun tall, and Ancas to the cheekbones, Kasha tiny and pure Sabirn, lanky, exotic, Yuchai. But they stood like three generations of a *family.* Supporting each other. And she somehow had the feeling that this was no passing thing— that this was a bond that would continue through all their lives.

No worry there.

She looked out over the last Full Convocation this Hall would ever see—and still saw no fear. Only determination, and an impatience, now that the decisions had been made, to get on with it.

My children. By the gods, how proud I am of you!

Then, wryly, *And so much for a peaceful old age! Starting all over again. Training a new Second. Well—at least I got to keep the Fortress that* doesn't *need repairing. I don't envy Halun those winter and spring storms.*

"All right, people," she said into the waiting silence. "I'll want you on the road five days from now. Take whatever you think you'll need, we'll replace it somehow. Make your farewells—if you can't stand it, change your minds, but I don't think many of you will. May the gods go with you all."

She filled her eyes with them, one last time.

"The Convocation is dismissed."

An excerpt from MAN-KZIN WARS II, created by *Larry Niven*:

The Children's Hour

Chuut-Riit always enjoyed visiting the quarters of his male offspring.

"What will it be this time?" he wondered, as he passed the outer guards.

The household troopers drew claws before their eyes in salute, faceless in impact-armor and goggled helmets, the beam-rifles ready in their hands. He paced past the surveillance cameras, the detector pods, the death-casters and the mines; then past the inner guards at their consoles, humans raised in the household under the supervision of his personal retainers.

The retainers were males grown old in the Riit family's service. There had always been those willing to exchange the uncertain rewards of competition for a secure place, maintenance, and the odd female. Ordinary kzin were not to be trusted in so sensitive a position, of course, but these were families which had served the Riit clan for generation after generation. There was a natural culling effect; those too ambitious left for the Patriarchy's military and the slim chance of advancement, those too timid were not given opportunity to breed.

Perhaps a pity that such cannot be used outside the household, Chuut-Riit thought. Competition for rank was far too intense and personal for that, of course.

He walked past the modern sections, and into an area that was pure Old Kzin; maze-walls of reddish sandstone with twisted spines of wrought-iron on their tops, the tips glistening razor-edged. Fortress-architecture from a world older than this, more massive, colder and drier; from a planet harsh enough that a plains carnivore had changed its ways, put to different use an upright posture designed to place its head above savanna grass, grasping paws evolved to climb rock. Here the modern features were reclusive, hidden in wall and buttress. The door was a hammered slab graven with the faces of night-hunting beasts, between towers five times the height of a kzin. The air smelled of wet rock and the raked sand of the gardens.

Chuut-Riit put his hand on the black metal of the outer portal, stopped. His ears pivoted, and he blinked; out of the corner of his eye he saw a pair of tufted eyebrows glancing through the thick twisted metal on the rim of the ten-meter battlement. *Why, the little sthondats,* he thought affectionately. *They managed to put it together out of reach of the holo pickups.*

The adult put his hand to the door again, keying the locking sequence, then bounded backward four times his own length from a standing start. Even under the lighter gravity of Wunderland, it was a creditable feat. And necessary, for the massive panels rang and toppled as the rope-swung boulder slammed forward. The children had hung two cables from either tower, with the rock at the point of the V and a third rope to draw it back. As the doors bounced wide he saw the blade they had driven into the apex of the egg-shaped granite rock, long and barbed and polished to a wicked point.

Kittens, he thought. *Always going for the dramatic.* If that thing had struck him, or the doors under its impetus had, there would have been no need of a blade. *Watching too many historical adventure holos.* "Errorowwww!" he shrieked in mock-rage, bounding through the shattered portal and into the interior court, halting atop the kzin-high boulder. A round dozen of his older sons were grouped behind the rock, standing in a defensive clump and glaring at him; the crackly scent of their excitement and fear made the fur bristle along his spine. He glared until they dropped their eyes, continued it until they went down on their stomachs, rubbed their chins along the ground and then rolled over for a symbolic exposure of the stomach.

"Congratulations," he said. "That was the closest you've gotten. Who was in charge?"

More guilty sidelong glances among the adolescent males crouching among their discarded pull-rope, and then a lanky youngster with platter-sized feet and hands came squatting-erect. His fur was in the proper flat posture, but the naked pink of his tail still twitched stiffly.

"I was," he said, keeping his eyes formally down. "Honored Sire Chuut-Riit," he added, at the adult's warning rumble.

"Now, youngling, what did you learn from your first attempt?"

"That no one among us is your match, Honored Sire Chuut-Riit," the kitten said. Uneasy ripples went over the black-striped orange of his pelt.

"And what have you learned from this attempt?"

"That all of us together are no match for you, Honored Sire Chuut-Riit," the striped youth said.

"That we didn't locate all of the cameras," another muttered. "You idiot, Spotty." That to one of his siblings; they snarled at each other from their crouches, hissing past barred fangs and making striking motions with unsheathed claws.

"No, you did locate them all, cubs," Chuut-Riit said. "I presume you stole the ropes and tools from the workshop, prepared the boulder in the ravine in the next courtyard, then rushed to set it all up between the time I cleared the last gatehouse and my arrival?"

Uneasy nods. He held his ears and tail stiffly, letting his whiskers quiver slightly and holding in the rush of love and pride he felt, more delicious than milk heated with bourbon. *Look at them!* he thought. At the age when most young kzin were helpless prisoners of instinct and hormone, wasting their strength ripping each other up or making fruitless direct attacks on their sires, or demanding to be allowed to join the Patriarchy's service *at once* to win a Name and house hold of their own . . . *His* get had learned to *cooperate* and use their minds!

"Ah, Honored Sire Chuut-Riit, we set the ropes up beforehand, but made it look as if we were using them for tumbling practice," the one the others called Spotty said. Some of them glared at him, and the adult raised his hand again.

"No, no, I am *moderately* pleased." A pause. "You did not hope to take over my official position if you had disposed of me?"

"No, Honored Sire Chuut-Riit," the tall leader said. There had been a time when any kzin's holdings were the prize of the victor in a duel, and the dueling rules were interpreted more leniently for a young subadult. Everyone had a sentimental streak for a successful youngster; every male kzin remembered the intolerable stress of being physically mature but remaining under dominance as a child.

Still, these days affairs were handled in a more civilized manner. Only the Patriarchy could award military and political office. And this mass assassination attempt was ... unorthodox, to say the least. Outside the rules more because of its rarity than because of formal disapproval....

A vigorous toss of the head. "Oh, no, Honored Sire Chuut-Riit. We had an agreement to divide the private possessions. The lands and the, ah, females." Passing their own mothers to half-siblings, of course. "Then we wouldn't each have so much we'd get too many challenges, and we'd agreed to help each other against outsiders," the leader of the plot finished virtuously.

"Fatuous young scoundrels," Chuut-Riit said. His eyes narrowed dangerously. "You haven't been communicating outside the household, have you?" he snarled.

"Oh, *no*, Honored Sire Chuut-Riit!"

"Word of honor! May we die nameless if we should do such a thing!"

The adult nodded, satisfied that good family feeling had prevailed. "Well, as I said, I am somewhat pleased. If you have been keeping up with your lessons. Is there anything you wish?"

"Fresh meat, Honored Sire Chuut-Riit," the spotted one said. The adult could have told him by the scent, of course, a kzin never forgot another's personal odor, that was one reason why names were less necessary among their species. "The reconstituted stuff from the dispensers is always ... so ... *quiet.*"

Chuut-Riit hid his amusement. Young Heroes-to-be were always kept on an inadequate diet, to increase their aggressiveness. A matter for careful gauging, since too much hunger would drive them into mindless cannibalistic frenzy.

"And couldn't we have the human servants back? They were nice." Vigorous gestures of assent. Another added: "They told good stories. I miss my Clothilda-human."

"Silence!" Chuut-Riit roared. The youngsters flattened stomach and chin to the ground again. "Not until you can be trusted not to injure them; how many times do I have to tell you, it's dishonorable to attack household servants! Until you learn self-control, you will have to make do with machines."

This time all of them turned and glared at a mottled youngster in the rear of their group; there were half-healed scars over his head and shoulders. "It bared its *teeth* at me," he said sulkily. "All I did was swipe at it, how was I supposed to know it would die?" A chorus of rumbles, and this time several of the covert kicks and clawstrikes landed.

"Enough," Chuut-Riit said after a moment. *Good, they have even learned how to discipline each other as a unit.* "I will consider it, when all of you can pass a test on the interpretation of human expressions and body-language." He drew himself up. "In the meantime, within the next two eight-days, there will be a formal hunt and meeting in the Patriarch's Preserve; kzinti homeworld game, the best Earth animals, and even some feral-human outlaws, perhaps!"

He could smell their excitement increase, a mane-crinkling musky odor not unmixed with the sour whiff of fear. Such a hunt was not without danger for adolescents, being a good opportunity for hostile adults to cull a few of a hated rival's offspring with no possibility of blame. *They will be in less danger than most,* Chuut-Riit thought judiciously. *In fact, they may run across a few of my subordinates' get and mob them. Good.*

"And if we do well, afterwards a feast and a visit to the Sterile Ones." That had them all quiveringly alert, their tails held rigid and tongues lolling; nonbearing females were kept as a rare privilege for Heroes whose accomplishments were not *quite* deserving of a mate of their own. Very rare for kits still in the household to be granted such, but Chuut-Riit thought it past time to admit that modern society demanded a prolonged adolescence. The day when a male kit could be given a spear, a knife, a rope and a bag of salt and kicked out the front gate at puberty were long gone. Those were the wild, wandering years in the old days, when survival challenges used up the superabundant energies. Now they must be spent learning history, technology, xenology, none of which burned off the gland-juices saturating flesh and brain.

He jumped down amid his sons, and they pressed around him, purring throatily with adoration and fear and respect;

his presence and the failure of their plot had reestablished his personal dominance unambiguously, and there was no danger from them for now. Chuut-Riit basked in their worship, feeling the rough caress of their tongues on his fur and scratching behind his ears. *Together*, he thought. *Together we will do wonders.*

From "The Children's Hour" by Jerry Pournelle & S.M. Stirling

THE MAN-KZIN WARS
65411-X • 304 pages • $3.95   ___

MAN-KZIN WARS II
69833-8 • 320 pages • $3.95   ___

These bestsellers are available at your local book-store, or just send this coupon, your name and address, and the cover price(s) to: Baen Books, Dept. BA, 260 Fifth Ave., New York, NY 10001.

Paksenarrion, a simple sheepfarmer's daughter, yearns for a life of adventure and glory, such as the heroes in songs and story. At age seventeen she runs away from home to join a mercenary company, and begins her epic life . . .

ELIZABETH MOON

THE DEED OF PAKSENARRION

"This is the first work of high heroic fantasy I've seen, that has taken the work of Tolkien, assimilated it totally and deeply and absolutely, and produced something altogether new and yet incontestably based on the master. . . . This is the real thing. Worldbuilding in the grand tradition, background thought out to the last detail, by someone who knows absolutely whereof she speaks. . . . Her military knowledge is impressive, her picture of life in a mercenary company most convincing."—**Judith Tarr**

About the author: Elizabeth Moon joined the U.S. Marine Corps in 1968 and completed both Officers Candidate School and Basic School, reaching the rank of 1st Lieutenant during active duty. Her background in military training and discipline imbue The Deed of Paksenarrion with a gritty realism that is all too rare in most current fantasy.

"I thoroughly enjoyed *Deed of Paksenarrion*. A most engrossing, highly readable work."
—**Anne McCaffrey**

"For once the promises are borne out. *Sheepfarmer's Daughter* is an advance in realism. . . . I can only say that I eagerly await whatever Elizabeth Moon chooses to write next."
—Taras Wolansky, *Lan's Lantern*

*   *   *   ,   *   *

Volume One: Sheepfarmer's Daughter—Paks is trained as a mercenary, blooded, and introduced to the life of a soldier . . . and to the followers of Gird, the soldier's god.

Volume Two: Divided Allegiance—Paks leaves the Duke's company to follow the path of Gird alone—and on her lonely quests encounters the other sentient races of her world.

Volume Three: Oath of Gold—Paks the warrior must learn to live with Paks the human. She undertakes a holy quest for a lost eleven prince that brings the gods' wrath down on her and tests her very limits.

*   *   *   *   * .

These books are available at your local bookstore, or you can fill out the coupon and return it to Baen Books, at the address below.

All three books of The Deed of Paksenarrion ____
SHEEPFARMER'S
  DAUGHTER   65416-0 • 506 pages • $3.95 ____
DIVIDED
  ALLEGIANCE   69786-2 • 528 pages • $3.95 ____
OATH OF GOLD 69798-6 • 528 pages • $3.95 ____

Please send the cover price to: Baen Books, Dept. B, 260 Fifth Avenue, New York, NY 10001.
Name_____
Address_____
City_____ State_____ Zip_____